TENTACLES

AND

TEETH

LAND OF SZORNYEK: BOOK 1

BY ARIELE SIELING

Watch out for monsters!

This book is dedicated to:

MOM,

*for teaching me how to survive
with impossible odds.*

CONTENTS

Chapter 1: The Nagy 7

Chapter 2: The Rarohan 26

Chapter 3: The Gamba... 60

Chapter 4: The Pok... 82

Chapter 5: The Kover 101

Chapter 6: The Hulla.. 140

Chapter 7: The Fulek 160

Chapter 8: The Gyiks... 191

Chapter 9: The Barlang....................................... 221

Chapter 10: The Elnok... 248

Chapter 11: The Minket 266

CHAPTER 1: THE NAGY

THE NAGY TOWERED over her, beady little eyes sunken into its round eggplant-colored head. Askari stared for a moment at the rows and rows of yellowish teeth spiraling around the gaping black hole that functioned as a mouth. Then she gagged at the putrid smell blasting her face and ducked as an enormous tentacle crashed into the brush to her left. Being eaten by a nagy—it was an interesting way to die, but not preferred.

As the monster roared, Askari dove to the right and landed on her elbows, a long, slimy tentacle whipping past her left ear. She rolled under a bush and then dragged herself upright. She needed to find Shujaa, and fast. Alone, there was no way she could kill it. She would have to run, and hope she was faster than it was—fast enough that it would lose her scent. Or else find help. Or else die.

Another tentacle crashed into the ground beside her. Bracing herself with one arm, she reached out her other hand, grasping her knife, and sliced as deeply into the nagy's flesh as she could. Black blood gushed from the wound and the nagy let out a loud shriek, pulling the tentacle back abruptly, away from Askari.

She launched herself forward and took off through the forest, ducking under tree branches, leaping over bushes, feet pounding against the earth. Her heart thundered in her chest. A bow and quiver bounced on her back, useless against such thick skin. The nagy would never stop following her, she knew that. Its sense of smell was too good, and while nagy might be stupid, they were also stubborn—it wouldn't let up on what it thought was easy prey. She had to confuse it or kill it, or she'd never escape.

Branches whipped across her face, leaving scratches. Pricker bushes ripped and tore at her clothes, and sticks cracked under her feet. Deciduous forests were always the worst—heavy with underbrush and hidden surprises—like the nagy, that could silently slither through the trees or rise up on its tentacles, like legs, and smash anything in its path. Glancing briefly over her shoulder, she grimaced. She couldn't see it—that was a bad sign. It had decided on stealth, which meant she had to rely entirely on speed.

Ahead of her she could see the top of the Tuske, a towering tooth-shaped mountain that rose up from a largely flat landscape. It was covered with old pines and rock faces, and at this time of the summer, tiny white and yellow flowers ran down in streaks as if someone had dumped cans of paint at the top. If she could make it there, maybe she could outclimb or outwit the garg, the stupid monster, the relentless nagy. Another advantage to the Tuske was that it was in the opposite direction of her community. If she led the nagy toward them, it could kill everyone, as opposed to just one stupid warrior wandering around the countryside on her own.

She ran faster. Her thighs and calves burned; sweat dripped down her cheeks. Her hair was tied in a tight braid, but she had snagged it on so many branches, it had started to escape from its bindings in a thick black frizz with a mind of its own. To her right, a flock of bright orange mandarak birds burst from the trees in a cacophony of chattering and chirping. Too bad the nagy didn't prefer fowl to human flesh for dinner.

Light filtered down through the trees ahead, slightly to the left. A clearing? She burst out into the sunshine and skidded to a halt. No—a cliff. Steeply angled rocks rose up in front of her, twenty, thirty feet, with tufts of trees and plants growing out of them in very few places. A tuske-goat scurried across the top, no doubt heading for safety in the face of the monster due to arrive any minute.

Askari turned left. If she couldn't go up, she would have to go around.

The nagy let out a roar that shook the trees. Stones rattled down the cliff face as Askari ducked under low-hanging vines. Then she heard a sharp, piercing whistle. She looked up. A short figure stood at the top of the cliff, waving both arms back and forth, pointing in the general direction Askari was running. There must be a trail, partially hidden under the brush.

She scanned the ground, looking for any telltale signs of the trailhead, moving as quickly as she could. Then, she heard a shout. Looking back up, she saw the figure pointing in the other direction. She must have missed it. Turning, she elbowed her way through the brush until she stumbled on a narrow, overgrown trail. The nagy roared again and reared up over top of the trees, knocking one over with its massive arms; the tree crashed to the ground.

Askari climbed up the Tuske. And up and up and up. This was much harder than running through the forest. Her legs didn't just burn, they slow-roasted over coals and then were doused in gasoline and set ablaze. Rocks slid underneath her shoes, making it difficult to keep her balance. She slipped more than once, bloodying the palms of her hands when she caught herself.

"Hey!" a voice called.

She paused her ascent and looked up. Shujaa stood a few yards ahead, holding a basket in one hand and a knife in the other. Askari collapsed to her knees and tried to breathe.

"What are you doing here?" Shujaa asked, a small frown on her face.

"I've been looking for you," Askari gasped. Her lungs had also apparently caught fire, and now her mind swam as the oxygen tried to catch up to her. She panted for a moment longer and then coughed.

"I was fine on my own," Shujaa said, shaking her head. She reached out to help Askari stand. "We have to keep going though."

"Fine, fine." Askari took deep breaths to help slow her heartrate. "Where's the garg?"

"It's at the bottom of the cliff," Shujaa said.

Askari nodded once, and then followed Shujaa up the mountain, more slowly this time.

They ran and walked intermittently for a while. The trail wound back and forth up the side of the mountain, which Askari found frustrating—given its size, the nagy could skip past all of the winding and weaving if it chose to follow them, but the brush was so thick up here that there was no way they could avoid it. Not to mention, the trees were high enough that she couldn't see over them to keep an eye on what the nagy was doing. She would have to rely on listening to the crashes and roars of the creature. Finally, Shujaa hollered for Askari to stop. She had halted a few yards back and was pointing over the edge of a ridge.

"Look!" she exclaimed.

Askari made her way over to the edge and looked down. The nagy still sat at the bottom of the cliff, staring up at them. It probably couldn't see them, but could likely smell them.

"It's not following," Askari said, plopping down on a rock and wiping sweat from her upper lip. She stretched her legs and her arms as she tried to catch her breath. "Think we can sneak down the back of the mountain and head to camp? Maybe it's lost interest."

"I don't think that's the smartest idea," Shujaa said, frowning. Her hair was pulled back into a tight knot on top of her head, and her dark skin glistened with sweat. "Nagy are too stubborn. They don't give up on prey that easily. More likely it'll wait at the bottom of the mountain for a while to see if we come down. When we don't, it'll circle the mountain until it finds our scent, and then it will follow us—track us until we lead it right back home. Then it will kill all of us, at least if we don't kill it first."

"Couldn't we confuse it, like walking in circles around the mountain for a while?"

"If there were a river handy," Shujaa said, "we might be able to throw it off our scent. But I think our best bet is to kill it."

"And how are we supposed to do that with only two of us?" Askari scowled and crossed her arms. With one person, it was impossible. With two? Also impossible. "The garg is the size of a barn! It's got impenetrable skin, slime that'll paralyze you if you touch it, and teeth that can slice through a cow. We'd be better off letting ourselves get eaten than leading it back to the community."

"Well," Shujaa replied, shrugging, "if we're going to let ourselves get eaten, we should at least have a go at killing it, right? Give it our best shot."

"And how do you propose we do that?"

Shujaa smiled a little. "I guess we'll have to get creative." She began to walk up the mountain again.

Askari sighed and stood up, stretching her stiff and tired muscles, and followed.

"What were you doing out here, anyway?" Askari asked as Shujaa leaned over and sliced through the stem of a plant with her blade, stabbed it, and put it in her basket.

"Collecting juneberries."

"You know you're not supposed to go off alone."

"I know, but I'm still underage—for two more days at least. I can't get in that much trouble. Plus, I was planning to sneak out and sneak back in again—no one would ever have known I was gone if you hadn't come looking for me. You, on the other hand, are expected to follow the rules. Like not wandering off alone. Which you did. Who knows what punishment they'll give you when we get back?"

"I was just doing them a favor—finding you!" Askari shook her head. Sometimes, the Baratok community rules were stupid. What they needed were guidelines, not hard and fast rules. They needed principles, not laws. "You didn't show for breakfast and hadn't been to dinner the night before. I was afraid you were lost."

"Why didn't you go to the elders, then?" Shujaa asked, glancing over her shoulder with raised eyebrows.

"They were busy," Askari said, frowning. "Fia was having her baby. I didn't want to bother them—it's not like I couldn't find you eventually. There was no need to worry everyone. Plus, it was a great opportunity to practice my tracking skills."

Shujaa let out a short laugh. "Guess you need some more practice."

"I found you, didn't I?"

"If you say so." Shujaa grinned at Askari and bent down to pick another plant from the ground, this time wrapping a rag around it before pulling it up by the roots. "But it kinda seems like I'm the one that found you." She raised her eyebrows at Askari. "Anyway, we should probably talk strategy." She gestured toward the sun, which had begun its descent. Night would be upon them in only a few hours. "Tell me everything you remember about nagy."

"Well, they're big, for starters," Askari said. Her teachers had beaten more than a few facts about nagy—and plenty of other species of garg—into her head. "They have twelve tentacles with suction cups that can stick to anything from a rock to a rabbit to a human to another garg. They have sharp teeth that can gnaw through nearly anything—including wood and metal if they need to get to their prey. They can't see well, but their sense of smell is insanely good. They hate pain, even the mildest, like when I cut it earlier. And their skin is rubbery. It's very difficult to get an arrow to lodge—they bounce off."

"Don't forget the slimy, mildly paralytic agent that covers their entire body," Shujaa said. "It makes them moist and prevents prey from getting away."

"Yes, that." Askari shivered. She had almost touched the monster multiple times, and not only when she had sliced it open with her knife. She looked at her hand—no weird bumps or bruises and it wasn't numb, so she was probably fine.

"So, what do you think?" Shujaa asked. "We could lure in another monster and get them to fight while we run."

"Ha," Askari said. "Then we'd have two gargs after us. Great idea. We could also pray to the universe to strike it dead with a bolt of lightning."

"There aren't any clouds out," Shujaa replied, a smile on her lips.

Askari thought it almost looked like she was having fun, despite their impending death.

"We could try waiting it out. Maybe it'll go away overnight." Shujaa picked a couple more plants, then clambered over a pile of rocks.

"Why?" Askari asked.

"Well, you don't normally see nagy this far north. They like it where it's warm and humid. Maybe it'll get cold and go away."

Askari raised her eyebrows. "That's not really a plan. It's more of a 'if we get lucky' type of scenario."

"Yeah, wishful thinking."

"I was going to run. And keep running." Askari shrugged. "But I'd need to sleep eventually, and then I'd die anyway."

Shujaa pursed her lips. "I might have another idea, but it's a long shot. Worth a try, though, or at least a discussion. Do you have arrows left?"

"Yes," Askari replied, shifting the quiver that hung across her back. "You think I should shoot it? Because their skin is practically tougher than metal. Even if I could shoot at this distance, hit it, and have the arrow pierce the skin, it would probably annoy it, not kill it."

"Yeah, that's true," Shujaa said, bending down to pick another plant from the ground. She pursed her lips, thinking.

"If shooting at the garg is going to be part of the plan, I'll need a better spot," Askari added. "Somewhere without too many trees, where we can see it."

"If we follow the trail a little further," Shujaa said, "I think it comes out on top of the cliffs."

They climbed higher. The bushes grew thinner as the soil became rockier. When she looked out behind them, Askari felt like she could see all the way to the edge of the earth—though she knew that was probably not true, because legend had it the world was round.

The trail eventually curved back around and dropped them on a flat ridge overlooking the cliff face. They could see the nagy below, its tentacles waving in the air, reaching, stretching upward like it was debating whether or not to climb.

"Could you shoot it from here?" Shujaa asked.

"Yes, but I doubt I could pierce its hide up close, let alone at this distance."

"What about in the eye?"

Askari shook her head. "Maybe, but its eyes are so small, it would be a tough shot."

"How about the mouth?" Shujaa asked. "Maybe if we can make it roar...?"

"Hm," Askari said. That was an interesting idea. It might at least injure it, if not kill it. "How would we make it roar?"

"I'm not sure yet."

"Maybe if we drop rocks on it," Askari suggested. "Or we could set a plant on fire and burn it."

"I need fire anyway," Shujaa said, "so we might even be able to make hot rocks."

"What do you need fire for?"

"I want to dip the tips of your arrows in poison from the plants I've been gathering," Shujaa said. "I'm going to mix them together, heat it up, and hopefully it will have more effect than plain old arrows."

"Wow." Askari raised her eyebrows. "Good idea."

Shujaa grinned at Askari and pointed at some of the plants in her basket. "I grabbed some wild foxglove and some nightshade. This green spiky-leafed plant is jimsonweed, and the dark shiny one is poison ivy. Had to be careful grabbing those. No one has found any one poison that works on nagy, but I'm hoping that if I mix enough different ones together, I can cook up something really nasty that will bring down even a garg as big as it is."

"I'm willing to give it a try," Askari said. "It's not like I've thought of anything better. What do you need?"

"Well, fire for starters," Shujaa said. "And a rock to mix the plants on. You do the fire—I have a better idea of what I need the rock to look like."

"Works for me."

They split up, each going about their respective chores. Shujaa went hunting for stones, while Askari headed into the bushes and began to snap off dead wood and old branches for fire starters and kindling. There weren't many large branches this high up, but what she could find she dragged out onto the ridge.

After a while, flames licked into the sky, spitting sparkling specks of burning plant matter into the darkening deep blue of night. A few stars twinkled in the darkness, and the full moon glowed. That was good—they would have enough light to navigate back to camp if they managed to kill or incapacitate the nagy.

Shujaa waited for the flames to turn to coals, and then set her concave rock on top of them. She had also found an oval rock, and began to pound and mash the various poisonous plants into a noxious solution that steamed, hissed, and smelled awful.

"Don't breathe any of the steam," she said. "It might kill you."

"Seems like sound advice." Askari hastily stepped back away from the fire.

"If you're going to be shooting all of your arrows into the nagy's mouth," Shujaa said, "maybe you should go make us some spears, so we have something to protect ourselves with on the way home. But leave your arrows here—I'll coat them with the poison."

"Good call." Askari turned and made her way a short distance down the mountain, picking her way carefully by the light of the moon. She located some slightly taller trees a bit farther down the mountain and scavenged some more dead branches, these ones bigger and more difficult to break. She looked for live branches too, but found most of them too willowy, bending at the slightest pressure.

The shadows cast by the moon wavered as a breeze caused the trees to sway. The wind this high up was chilly, chapping Askari's skin. She shivered, but focused on her objective: spears. After choosing the four best branches, she began to make her way back to the fire. Then she heard a branch crack.

She froze, squinting into the trees around her, hoping she could see whatever had made the sound, but nothing moved in the darkness. She slid her knife out of her belt and stilled her movements, treading as quietly as she could. Askari wished she had a way to warn Shujaa without shouting, but since she didn't know what was out there, it seemed that moving as quickly and as silently as possible would be a better option.

Another rustle came from the trees, this time from the other side. Askari froze. Were there two things out there? Or was she being paranoid? She began to move more swiftly, less focused on silence and more on speed. The bright round moon overhead cast fewer shadows as she moved out into the open, and Askari squinted as far as she could around her, trying to discern if there was something hiding there. The moon was round and bright. It would be full in just a couple of days, and the elders always said the gargs did crazy things on a full moon. She hoped that was an old wives' tale.

Then she heard a scream.

Askari broke into a run, bursting out onto the ridge a few moments later. Shujaa was on her feet, waving a flaming stick in the air and clutching a shallow wound in her side.

"What happened?"

"Gyiks!" Shujaa exclaimed. "Nasty little gargs. I chased off two, but they travel in packs. There could be dozens!"

"Well, I can make the spears if you can hold them off for a minute." Askari ran forward and sat down beside Shujaa. She pulled out her knife and began to whittle the ends of the branches into sharp points as quickly as possible. They didn't have to be pretty—just solid and sharp.

With a crash, a reptile-like creature the size of a dog with a long, spiked tail burst out of the trees. It had greyish-greenish scales covering the body, sharp talons on its front and back legs, and razor-like teeth. Big, bulging eyes looked out in two different directions, and right above those, two antennae stuck out of its forehead. Its long legs propelled it forward as it aimed its claws for Shujaa's face. Shujaa yelled at the top of her lungs and brandished the flaming branch. The gyik squealed and disappeared back into the trees.

"Here!" Askari called, tossing the first partially finished spear to Shujaa. Shujaa began to shave the end into a sharper point as Askari turned her attention to the second one. She finished and had just set it down when another gyik leaped into the clearing.

"Watch out!" Askari yelled, launching herself to her feet and shoving Shujaa out of the way. She threw her knife; it spun through the air, glittering in the light of the fire, and landed squarely in the gyik's chest. The gyik fell over, dead, and Askari ran forward to retrieve her knife.

"Thanks," Shujaa muttered, dragging herself to her feet. She checked to make sure the spear hadn't broken in the fall, then took a defensive stance facing the direction the gyik had come from, spear in one hand, flaming branch in the other.

"We have to move!" Askari hissed.

"But the nagy!"

"I know." Askari scanned the edges of the darkness for any signs of more gyiks. "That's what I mean! We have to kill it now."

Shujaa nodded. "The arrows are by the fire. Already poisoned."

A gyik leaped out of the woods, spitting and hissing. Shujaa jabbed it with the spear, catching it in the eye. It howled in pain and fled back into the woods.

"Those were probably scouts," Askari guessed. "The rest of the pack will be here in a minute." She pulled an arrow out of her quiver and fitted it into her bow. "Next problem—how do we get the nagy to open its mouth?" She peered over the edge of the cliff, trusting Shujaa to either protect her or warn her when the rest of the gyiks made their attack. She could see the shiny head of the nagy reflecting the light of the moon below, but she wasn't sure where its mouth was.

"Another one is coming!" Shujaa exclaimed. "Two! Three! Four!"

Askari spun around, loosing an arrow at a gyik. As soon as the arrow pierced its skin, the garg fell over and began to convulse. She reached down and grabbed the extra spear, shifting her body weight forward to avoid falling off the cliff. She jabbed at the next gyik that attacked. Her weapon slid right through the gyik's abdomen, and it fell, tripping the one behind it. Askari yanked her spear out and threw it at the other gyik as hard as she could, piercing its skull. When she looked up, Shujaa had killed the last one and once again stood in a defensive stance, watching the darkness and the trees.

"We need to get the nagy to open its mouth." Askari looked down again at where the nagy lay in wait. They had rocks and dead gyiks. Throwing things at it seemed like the easiest thing to try.

She bent down and grabbed a spear stuck through one of the nearby gyiks. It slid right out, so she bent down and grabbed the garg with her hands. "Ow," she muttered as its sharp spines sliced through her skin. She ignored the pain, dragged the lizard's body to the edge of the cliff, and shoved it over. It was dark, making it impossible to see where it fell. But the next moment, the nagy let out a roar, and she knew it had hit her mark.

"More gyiks incoming!" Shujaa yelled.

Askari spun around to see Shujaa trying to fight off two gyiks at once with a third one coming in close behind them. Askari ran forward and speared the third gyik, then stabbed a second one through the heart at the same time as Shujaa did.

"I'm going to start shooting," Askari said, yanking her spear back out of the dead lizard garg. "You okay?"

"I'll do my best to hold them off," Shujaa said. "But hurry."

Askari dragged three more bodies of dead gyiks to the edge of the cliff and placed them in a row. Taking a deep breath, she notched an arrow and aimed it toward the nagy. Then she kicked the first gyik. It rolled over the edge and crashed against the rockface. The nagy let out a roar.

"Keep doing that!" Shujaa stabbed a gyik that had slunk out of the darkness, and then turned to face the two that rushed in behind it. "It's making them nervous!"

Askari kicked another gyik over the edge, and let an arrow fly as she did so. The nagy howled again, this time louder. The third gyik tumbled off in a slightly different direction, but the nagy let out another roar, and Askari shot another arrow. This time, the arrow itself made the nagy screech so loudly Askari ducked and covered one ear with her hand. She had made it angry—actually hurt it.

"I have three more arrows," she said.

"Keep trying!" Shujaa gasped for breath as she drop-kicked a gyik to the ground. She waved the flaming branch in the air and a few gyiks leaped backward into the brush. The gyiks chattered, and a couple of them jumped forward, but Shujaa was ready for them. She dropped the branch on the ground and sliced one across the face with her knife, then drove her spear through the other's gut. Askari darted forward and dragged their corpses back to the edge of the cliff.

She peered over the edge. The nagy was still there, but it looked bigger. She frowned. Bigger? Her jaw dropped as she realized it had started to climb. One tentacle slapped against the edge of the cliff, creating a suction with the paralyzing liquid covering its body. Another tentacle followed the first, as it slowly moved up toward them.

"It's climbing," she whispered, standing frozen for a moment. Then Shujaa stepped close and kicked a dead gyik over the edge. The nagy roared and something yellowish flashed in the darkness. Its teeth! Askari could see its face!

"Do it again!" she yelled.

Shujaa kicked another one over the edge, and Askari took careful aim and loosed the arrow. It flew straight and true into the nagy's mouth.

"Got it!" Askari exclaimed. "Two more times!"

"Again!" Shujaa said, and kicked the gyik over the edge. The nagy roared; Askari let an arrow fly, again right into the mouth. This time, its roar was so loud the ground shook; the sound echoed across the valley. It started low in pitch, but rose slowly until it was a piercing, unending scream that made Askari feel like her brain was melting slowly into a viscous liquid that would start dripping out of her ears at any moment. The gyiks screeched in return and then fled, running as fast as their spiny, bony legs could carry them. Shujaa fell to her knees, holding her hands over her ears with an expression of pain.

But the nagy kept climbing. The tentacles slapped the rock face, pulling the monster higher, one now over the edge of the cliff. In no time, it would be on top of them. Askari had no trouble finding its face now. She could see every nasty tooth, the back of its throat, its beady little eyes.

Askari gritted her teeth and aimed again, not for its mouth this time, but for its eye. "I hope it hurts," she muttered. The arrow flew straight and true through the pupil and lodged in its skull.

The piercing scream ceased abruptly, and with hardly a twitch, the nagy let go of the cliff and tumbled, end over end, to the base of the Tuske. It landed with a crash and an eruption of dirt and leaves.

Askari stared after it. Shujaa leaned forward and peered over the edge as well.

It didn't move.

"Did it work?" Shujaa whispered.

"I think so," Askari replied. "It's not moving."

They stared into the darkness at the bottom of the cliff for a few moments longer.

"We should go," Shujaa said abruptly, breaking the silence. She gathered up her spear, flaming branch, and basket, and began the trek back down the mountain. Askari slung her bow across her back and grabbed the other spear.

The nagy was dead, and they had lived. At least for tonight.

CHAPTER 2: THE RAROHAN

THE SUN HAD JUST begun to nose up over the horizon, painting the low-hanging clouds shades of pink and gold, as Askari and Shujaa stumbled out of the woods into the Baratok camp. Elder Kira was waiting, arms crossed and bags under her eyes. A scowl pursed across her lips as she watched them limp past.

They slipped into the medic's tent where Leka was patching up Adelbert, a younger warrior with a nasty gash on his arm.

"You take care of that," she said, "and come see me in a couple days."

"You got it," Adelbert replied, brushing past Shujaa and Askari as they entered.

Leka gave them a knowing look. "Sit down," she said, "and let me have a look at you."

A few moments later, she was stitching their wounds and checking to make sure they hadn't sustained any serious injuries. She wasn't particularly gentle on either of them, but

Askari felt they probably deserved it. They had both broken community rules, after all.

"I'm all set," Askari said, pulling her hand away from Leka when she had finished stitching.

"No, you're not!" Leka said. "You need extra bandages so you can keep it clean, and your leg needs—"

Her thought was cut off as Elder Kira burst into the tent. "You two are on latrine duty for a year!" She loomed over them, her scowl so deep that Askari thought it would permanently engrave creases into her already weary skin. "Well, not you, Askari. You should know better—your punishment will be more severe."

"I'm sorry, Elder." Askari bowed her head. She knew it was best to at least pretend she was sorry—if she didn't apologize, she would never get off latrine duty. Ever. She winced a little, trying to imagine what could be worse than a year's worth of latrine duty, but her imagination came up short. She glanced at Shujaa who was crying a little. She really was sorry—or at least afraid of Elder Kira.

"Me too," Shujaa whispered, swallowing back her tears.

"I believe you, Shujaa," Elder Kira said. "Not you, Askari. What were you two thinking?"

"I wanted to pick some juneberries as a surprise," Shujaa said quietly. "I wandered too far."

"I went to find her is all," Askari said, meeting Elder Kira's eyes defiantly. "Everyone else was busy with the baby."

"Yes, the baby," Elder Kira said. "Well, you'll be happy to know both Fia and the child survived, no thanks to you two.

And they will continue to survive unless one of you does something stupid that puts the whole community in jeopardy. Like leading a nagy back to camp. Yes, we heard it screaming. It kept everyone up all night. Once you're done here, Shujaa, you go get some rest. Askari, you are coming with me. Myself and the others want a report on exactly what happened."

Askari looked over at Shujaa, jealous of the sleep she would be getting. No doubt Askari was in for a full team scolding, since she was of age and Shujaa wasn't—though that would only be the case for a few more days. It wasn't fair— they were only two years apart, and Shujaa was more than competent as a warrior. The rules here didn't make any sense. At the same time though, she was glad Shujaa wasn't going to get in too much trouble.

Elder Kira ducked out of the tent as Leka bent down to examine the scratches on Askari's leg. She cleaned them and then turned her attention back to Shujaa.

"Thank you for coming to find me, Askari," Shujaa said. "I never would've survived that nagy on my own. I hope the elders aren't too awful to you on account of me."

"It's my own fault," Askari said. "I decided to come after you alone. I should have stayed with the camp or gotten some others to go with me—at least gotten permission. I figured I could handle it on my own."

Leka ripped off the end of the clean rag she had used to tie up Askari's wound once the stitches were securely in place. "Shujaa, I want you to sleep here so I can keep an eye on you. Askari, don't rip out those stitches, and tell Kira I require at least two days of healing before you start in on whatever punishment they have planned."

"Okay," Askari replied, standing. "Thank you, Leka."

"You can go now," Leka ordered.

Askari sighed and pulled back the flap of the tent, staring at the busy encampment. Everyone had been up since the crack of dawn. The Baratok had been in this spot for two weeks because of the baby, but now that he was born, they would have to pack up and move. It was dangerous to be in one spot for too long. Once one garg learned where you were, all the others would eventually figure it out too, and hunt you down for dinner. At least, that's what the elders said.

"Out!" Leka called.

Askari sighed again and stepped out into the center of camp. A few people gave her glares as she walked through the rows and rows of tents set up inside the large clearing. A team had cut down several trees around the edges to make room for everyone when they had first arrived, and even so, some of the tents were under the cover of the canopy. The tents were made from the skins of several varieties of monsters salvaged from previous attacks. The Baratok community didn't hunt monsters, but when they were attacked, they fought back, and then made as much use of the remains as possible. If they didn't have to leave so soon, the elders would probably have sent a team to collect bits and pieces from the dead nagy.

"Chin up, Askari!" Janko called, waving at her from the other side of the fire that blazed in the center of camp. "Sun's up, smiles out!" She gave him a small smile. Janko was probably the most cheerful person she'd ever met, and it was hard not to smile when he took time to say hello, even when she was heading toward her doom.

Kira's tent, which was where the elders met, was set up directly opposite the medic tent, on the other side of the massive fire that was always burning. Askari walked as slowly as she dared, her feet scuffing the dusty ground, hands clenched into fists at her side.

"Askari!" a voice called. She turned to see Harcos jogging toward her, his fluffy head of curls bouncing. He wore a leather vest over his bare chest and ripped-off pants they had found during a ghost village raid. It was rare that the Baratok ventured near these empty towns—usually they were afraid of what gargs might be lurking. But in the most recent raid, both Harcos and Askari were old enough to patrol the border, and Harcos had sneaked into a house and found this pair of pants. He was proud of them.

Harcos and Askari had been fast friends since she had rescued him from an older warrior's "remedial" quarterstaff trainings, which consisted of him beating the then eight-year-old Harcos to the ground before walking off laughing. Harcos was not particularly athletic, but he was one of the few next generation community members who had learned to read. He was also good at math, strategy, and thinking in general, and only fought when absolutely necessary.

"Hey," she said, bracing herself for the lecture she knew was incoming.

"What were you thinking?" He skidded to a halt next to her. "Why didn't you ask me to go with you? You could have died! And now you're up for disciplinary action, and who knows what they'll do! Idiot." Then he made an overdramatic sad face. "Plus, I thought we were friends."

"We are friends," Askari said. "I figured it wouldn't be a big deal."

"It was a big deal!" Harcos said. "You could have died!"

"I'm sorry, okay?" She crossed her arms and frowned at him. "It's too late now."

"Is Shujaa alright?" he asked.

"She's with Leka," Askari gestured over her shoulder, "getting fixed up. She also gets to sleep. I do not get to sleep. Because I'm of age."

"Yeah, no kidding." Harcos rolled his eyes. "You should've known better. I'm going to check on her."

Askari watched him jog off before strolling the remaining distance to the Elder Kira's tent. She stopped outside and tried to listen to what they were saying, but the noises of the camp made it impossible.

"Come in!" a voice boomed from inside the tent.

Askari took a deep breath, then slowly pulled back the tent flap, ducking to step inside. The elders sat on cushions on the ground in a circle. Elder Kira was directly across from the entrance, with Elders Faro and Timo to her left, and Elders Sheo and Dano to her right. They were an intimidating bunch, all together like this. Kira's hair hung in long braids over her shoulders, and her face was stern. Elder Faro kept his hair cut short, and it was starting to grey. He had a nice face, Askari had always thought, a wide nose and square jaw, and his wrinkles were mostly smile lines. Sheo was tall, and even sitting she looked imposing, especially as her hair poufed out around her head, making her seem even taller. Dano was slim and narrow-boned, the quietest of the elders, who listened more than she spoke. There were only two elders missing: Elol, who was responsible for strategy and training the warriors, and Vica, who took care of things like food prep, scavenging, and fresh water.

The tent was largely empty of things. A trunk sat in one corner, likely with Kira's clothes and possessions, and a bedroll had been folded up and left on top of the trunk. Beside it was a backpack, stuffed full, and Kira's preferred weapons—an axe and several knives.

"Sit," Elder Kira ordered. She was the oldest of the elders and had put in a great deal of effort into building the community to become so large and successful. She had a lot of clout, which was not good given that she and Askari had been at odds for as long as Askari could remember.

Askari lowered herself gently to the floor across from Elder Kira and tried not to slouch. It was hard. All she wanted to do was go run and hide. Plus, her hand hurt and her head was throbbing, and she really, really needed a nap.

"First," Elder Kira ordered, "tell us how you killed the nagy." All the elders' eyes were on her. This was new for Askari; she had never been disciplined by all of them at once before. It was usually just Kira and Faro. Her stomach was in knots.

"It was Shujaa's idea," Askari said. "We ran up the mountain and the nagy didn't follow us—it was waiting for us to come down, we think. She made a poison from a mixture of different plants she picked on our way up the mountain. She dipped my arrows in it, then when the nagy screamed, I shot it in the mouth."

"How did you know it would scream?" Elder Kira asked, crossing her arms and gazing at Askari with a frown.

"We didn't," Askari said. "We dropped dead gyiks on it, hoping that would make it mad. I'm not even sure the poison killed it, because it was climbing a cliff face, and I shot a poisoned arrow through its eye. It let go and crashed to the ground."

"You also fought gyiks?" Elder Faro interjected. He was leaning forward, eyes intent on Askari. He seemed more curious than angry, she thought.

"Yes, sir," Askari said. Even though Kira was older, Askari respected Faro more. He was kinder, and more prone to forgiveness than Kira.

"How many?" he asked.

"I'm not sure," Askari replied. "There was at least a full pack of them, but I think we only killed about ten or so. We dropped most of them over the cliff on the nagy, and when it started screaming, they ran away."

"Interesting," Faro mused, leaning back. He began to rub his chin with one finger almost unconsciously, as if he were deep in thought.

"Thank you," Elder Kira replied. "We will also be asking Shujaa to write out a more detailed account, so we can have that information for our records. If we need any other information about the incident from you, we will be sure to follow up."

Askari looked around at the elders. They all wore their traditional necklaces, filled with the teeth and claws of monsters they had killed. Kira had six strands, and the others had at least three or four. Askari didn't have a necklace yet. Technically, she had killed a couple of gargs, but the tradition was that someone else had to give you your first tooth to get the necklace started. It was a symbol of maturity. No one had taken it upon themselves to give Askari one yet. The elders each had dozens of teeth, and it was rather intimidating to think of how many creatures they must have killed, especially combined.

"Askari," Elder Faro said gently, interrupting her thoughts. "It's time for us to discuss your recent behavior."

Askari swallowed and nodded. She had a feeling that the word "recent" meant they were going to be discussing a lot more than her jaunt away from camp yesterday.

"Two moons ago," Faro continued, "you were out with a group collecting tubers."

Aww, garg's blood, Askari thought. They were bringing this up. Hadn't she already apologized? What more did they want from her?

"You saw a trail, presumably made by some kind of monster. What did you do?"

"I left the group and followed it," Askari said. "But they still had three other warriors—"

"That doesn't matter," Faro interrupted, cutting her off with a wave of his hand. "You left them vulnerable. Baratok law states that had they been attacked and killed, you would be to blame for their deaths."

Askari nodded and looked down at her hands. They were clenched so tightly, the skin on the back was stretched completely smooth.

"Then one moon ago, you were on sentry duty."

Askari sighed. She had already been disciplined for this one too.

"You left your post."

"I heard a noise," Askari replied. "I wanted to make sure it wasn't anything."

"You left your post. You should have stayed and called for someone to investigate. We have these rules for a reason, and I know you don't agree with all of them, but you still have to follow, just like everyone else here."

"I know." She hadn't wanted to cry wolf, but that wasn't a good enough excuse. It was so frustrating to not even be allowed a little bit freedom, to not be allowed to make any decisions for herself. But it was about the community, not about her—at least that was what they always said. "I'm sorry. I completed the terms of my punishment, though."

"Then, last week," Faro continued, "you were again supposed to be on sentry duty, but switched your shift out with Zaj."

Askari felt a twinge of guilt. She shouldn't have dragged Zaj into it—she should have waited until she had the night off.

"Now, Zaj shouldn't have agreed to it, of course, but your reason wasn't because you were sick or because you hadn't slept the night before. No. Your reasoning was that you needed a night off, and where did you go on this night off? To practice your tracking skills. Alone. In the dark."

"I know," Askari said. This hadn't been her best choice, she knew that. But they only ever practiced tracking during the day, and doing it once hadn't seemed like a big deal at the time. How was she supposed to improve without practice? She had enjoyed herself a great deal, but had paid heavily with several days of solo latrine duty. "I'm sorry."

"And then yesterday, you went off in search of Shujaa, alone. Do you know what the consequences of that could have been?"

Askari dropped her eyes toward the ground. She wasn't ashamed of her decision. Shujaa could have died, and because they were together, both had lived. But she couldn't face the piercing stares of all the elders at once.

"You could have led that nagy back to camp," Faro said, "risking not only the community, but the life of a brand-new child. You know how difficult it is for us to have children in the world we live in, and yet you let your impulsiveness drive your decision making."

Elder Kira raised a hand. "We have put your punishment to a vote. Some felt that forcing you to leave the community was too harsh."

Askari jerked her head up, eyes wide. Had Elder Kira just said the words, "leave the community"?

"Others of us felt that your behavior was far too rash, and given your..." she cleared her throat, "...heritage, there is too much chance that eventually your impulsive decisions would destroy the Baratok, resulting in many deaths." She smoothed the fabric of her pants, and then braided her fingers together. "We have decided on a compromise."

Destroy the Baratok? That was a bit overdramatic, Askari thought.

"To atone for your behavior, you will be sent on a mission," Faro said, clasping his hands in front of him. "You will venture out, alone, to a village a short distance from here. While there, you will find an item which has been left for us, and then return. We will be moving on from here, so you will have to find us, but we'll show you the general direction we are headed. It shouldn't be too hard, but it will be dangerous."

Askari could hardly breathe. This was the worst punishment she had ever heard of. Being forced to leave the community, by herself, even if for a short time, was just short of a death sentence. If she ran into even one garg, what were the chances of her survival? One garg happened upon her while she was asleep? Dead. Step in one batch of paralytic slime? Dead. Accidentally wander into the territory of any carnivorous garg? Dead. Maybe the elders wanted her dead. Maybe this was their version of execution—temporary exile and may the best one win.

"Find the item, return it to us," Faro finished, "and you will be welcomed back into the Baratok community. We expect that you will use this time alone for some contemplation, and to gain a new awareness of the reasons for and value of the structure we have created here."

"But... but..." Askari's hands became tightly clenched fists, her nails biting into her palm. "This... this... how... what am I... how... this is—" she stuttered, unsure of how to phrase her shock and horror. "How am I supposed to survive? I... I'm a warrior. My job is to fight, hunt, track. But I'll die if I go out there alone!"

"I think you'll be surprised at how possible it is to survive," Faro said. "Difficult, yes, but we survived, those many years ago when the monsters first appeared. And if we could survive back then, when everything was chaos, you can survive now that it has calmed down."

"What if I refuse to go?" Askari pressed. "I could pretend to leave and follow the community at a short distance." She probably shouldn't be saying these things out loud. She might need this strategy.

Elder Kira held up her hand. "Askari, you have no say in this. And if you try anything like that and we catch you, we will tie you up and leave you to get eaten."

"Leka says I have to rest for two days," she tried.

"We'll send rags and antiseptic so you can keep your wound clean."

"But... but..." Askari sputtered. "Am I not even allowed an opportunity to defend myself?"

"No," Kira said. "The decision has already been made."

Faro held up his hand. "I think it's only fair we give her the chance to speak in her own defense." He nodded at Askari.

"Fine." Elder Kira crossed her arms and leaned back, a scowl settling into her wrinkles.

"Please," Faro said, nodding at Askari. "Speak."

"Shujaa could have died!" Askari said. "If I hadn't gone and found her, either the nagy or the gyiks would have done her in. That should at least count for something. Together, we were able to beat the garg!"

"Perhaps," Elder Faro replied. "But Shujaa knew the risks of going out alone. And she shouldn't have. And from your story, it was her quick thinking that ultimately saved you, not the other way around."

"It doesn't matter how it happened," Elder Kira said bluntly. "You broke the rules of the community. You also knew the risks. And because you keep disobeying the rules, you are increasing the chance that one of your foolhardy risks will end badly. For all of us."

"Why aren't you threatening to exile Shujaa then?" Askari asked, although she knew she was just being spiteful at this point.

"Shujaa is not yet of age," Elder Kira replied, "and she does not have a history of repeat rule-breaking like you do. At any rate, her punishment is none of your business."

"And this isn't exile," Faro said. "We are sending you on a mission. You are going to accomplish something for the community and prove your value, and then we will welcome your return."

Askari's heart began to race and her face flushed. Anger burned in her chest as she thought about the punishment. Part of her railed that she wasn't even sure she wanted to stay if they were going to treat their own community members like this, but on the other hand, she was one of the most skilled warriors in the community. They needed her! They couldn't send her away! But it didn't look like they even took that into consideration.

Faro was about to speak, but Askari broke in with one final attempt to defend herself. "I'm one of the most skilled warriors," she said. "What if you get attacked and need help?"

"We have hundreds of warriors," Faro said gently. "It is because you are a skilled warrior that we think you can handle this mission. Now, I would like to give you the map, if you don't mind."

Askari's mind raced. How would she survive on her own? She knew the basics about survival, but what if she encountered a monster she couldn't handle? What if she injured herself? What if she encountered another community, a violent one? What if she got captured by slavers? What if she couldn't find food, and starved? She would likely not even last a moon.

But there was nothing else she could do. She had to go. They wouldn't let her stay, and as Kira said, if she pretended to leave and followed at a distance, they would inevitably catch her and tie her up to get eaten by the next lucky garg. Her best bet was to collect as much food as she could, along with her bedroll, extra clothes, rope, cooking utensils, and anything else she might need; make sure she had a solid blade in addition to her bow; and listen to everything Faro said, because one single detail might save her life.

Faro pulled out an old wrinkled piece of paper and spread it out before Askari. It was a map, with roads and a river drawn in black ink. There were words, but she couldn't read, so she had no idea what they said. He pointed to an X drawn in blue ink.

"We are here," he said. Then he pointed to an X in red ink. "You must go here."

Askari bent down and examined the drawing a little more closely.

"This is a small village on the other side of the river. In it, you will find a square building with a painting of an eagle on the side."

Askari shook her head. "What's an eagle?"

"Um…" Faro paused, "it looks like the head of a bird. It's blue and it's got a beak and some feathers."

"Okay," Askari said, listening closely.

"Enter the building and turn right. You will see a grey door in front of you. Inside that door to the left will be a large basket with a book in it. Get the book."

Askari nodded and then repeated the instructions back to Faro. "Find the building with the head of a bird. Inside the door, turn right. Walk through the grey door. The basket to the left of the door will have a book." Askari pictured the actions as she said them aloud to Faro. She had to remember them, so she promised herself that she would repeat the instructions over and over all the way there if necessary.

"That's correct," Faro said.

"What if I find more than one book, or none?" Askari asked.

"Then bring them all or come back," Faro said. "But there will be a book, I have confidence."

"But there's a chance it won't be there?" Askari pressed. Maybe this was an opportunity to get out of the mission or to get them to assign another warrior to go with her.

"Of course," Kira cut in impatiently. "It's not like we can pick up the phone and ask if it's done, now can we?"

"Phone?" Askari frowned. She had heard the word before. Some kind of communication thing, she thought, but didn't know how it worked.

"Never mind," Faro said. "Just go. Cross the river, head north, find the village, and get the book. If you can't find the book, bring us back something else to let us know you tried."

"And don't die," Askari said, almost to herself.

"Yes," Faro replied, giving her a soft smile. "And don't die."

"When do I leave?" Askari asked.

"You need to collect your things," Elder Kira said brusquely, "and leave before sundown."

At that moment, Zaj, a tall, thin warrior who was in charge of training the younger warriors, stumbled through the tent flap and collapsed to his hands and knees, breathing so hard he could hardly speak.

"Rarohan," he gasped. "Pack. Twelve. Coming this way full pace." He coughed and spat on the dirt. "Sentries mobilizing."

The elders leaped to their feet as one.

"Askari," Faro ordered. "Go rouse the sleeping warriors. Tell Elol to brief them and make a plan for attack." He turned to Dano. "You go to Fia. Sheo, go find Leka and prepare her for casualties. Kira, find Vica and get the community ready to move." Faro stepped forward and offered Zaj some water from his flask. No one argued—they moved.

Askari didn't wait to hear any more. This was her chance. Maybe if she proved her worthiness to the elders, they would let her stay. She ran through camp, calling for Elol. He appeared from behind some tents.

"Rarohan!" she yelled. "Incoming! I'll wake the sleepers!"

The community hadn't been attacked in months, and never by rarohan. The gargs were rare, but they roamed in packs, making them especially dangerous. They ate whatever meat they could catch, including humans. They were as big as horses with huge heads and skeletal bodies. Their two front fangs were a foot long, and their tails had spikes. Their fur—what little they had of it—and mane were varying shades of blues, greens, and greys that let them blend into tall grasses. One rarohan could rip a full-grown man to shreds in seconds. Not to mention, they were extremely difficult to kill. You had to sever the head from the body—they didn't feel pain, and a mere arrow would do nothing to stop it, unless you hit it squarely in the eye.

"Wake up! Wake up!" Askari yelled, running through the quiet end of camp, where last night's sentries slept. "Rarohan! On the way!"

Sleepy warriors began to pop their heads out of their tents, asking for details and instructions on where to go. "Weapons, then find Elol!" Askari said, rattling tents of those still sleeping and making as much noise she could.

The biggest problem with rarohan was that every single one had to die. A pack of them would hunt the Baratok endlessly, particularly since a community like this offered so much food. Even if you killed them off slowly, one by one, the remaining ones would continue to hunt the community until the food supply ran out.

Askari rushed to the armory wagon. No one was managing it—they were all preparing for the fight. She had her bow, but this time she needed a blade for head severing. There were three machetes left, so she grabbed one, and then jogged to the cluster of warriors in the middle of camp. Elol, the elder in charge of all warriors and warrior training, stood in the middle, shouting and waving his hands.

"Senior Warriors," he yelled, "you're the last line of defense. Protect and defend the camp. Do not let a single rarohan close enough to even see our children." The Senior Warriors broke away from the main group. They were the oldest warriors and a much smaller group. Many had retired from fighting and now served as teachers, cooks, and other less physically demanding roles in the community. But they still knew how and were willing to fight.

"Third Rank Warriors, you're in the woods. Groups of four patrol the outskirts of camp. Support the sentries. Everyone must be on high alert. Call for help from other groups if you need to." This group turned, broke off into practiced teams, and headed for the woods. These were the younger warriors, many of whom had not come of age yet. Shujaa would normally be in that group, but she was probably still with the medic.

"First and Second Rank Warriors," he continued. These were strong, healthy, resilient warriors who were all of age, in their peak of skill and health, and who had passed the lower-level warrior trainings. "Break out into your groups. Leaders, here."

Askari was a Second Rank Warrior, and her team leader was named Agi, a First Rank Warrior. Agi was the tallest woman in the tribe, and extremely skilled with a blade. Askari still found her intimidating, even after years of working and training with her. Harcos was also on Askari's team, but he was easily the least skilled member of the team. He was often called on for strategy recommendations, though, and had a good head for planning.

"Team Ot!" Agi called. "West!"

Askari fell into line behind Lyront and in front of Sasa, and they began to jog toward the west, through the camp, and into the forest. As soon as they hit the trees, Agi called out, "Fan!" and the platoon spread out, still all jogging at the same speed. They moved through the forest silently, keeping their eyes open for any sign of the rarohan.

They jogged for nearly two miles before Agi called for them to stop. They drew around her in a circle, still focused on the landscape around them, searching for any movement, any indication that they were about to be attacked.

"Half a mile ahead is the edge of the Plains of Tork." Agi stood in the center of the group, shoulders back and chin up, projecting strength and confidence. "The rarohan will be hard to see in the grass. If you do see one, shout. They can likely smell us already, so don't worry about alerting them to your whereabouts. Remember, there are only two ways to kill one—an arrow through the eye or cutting off the head. Focus on cutting off heads. Watch out for their claws."

"And their venom!" Lyront called out.

Everyone laughed. Rarohan had a poisonous liquid they secreted from their teeth, but while it paralyzed other monster forms, it only caused a mild rash on humans. Everyone laughed about it to ease the tension, even though nothing else about the rarohan was a laughing matter.

"Big bad tiger going to give me rash," Sasa added.

Everyone laughed again.

"Groups of three," Agi said. "Let's go."

Askari looked around for her team of three. She was usually paired up with Lyront and Zaj, both of whom were excellent archers. They could do a lot of damage all shooting together.

Zaj was already a good distance into the trees. Askari began to jog after him. The trees in this area had trunks that Askari couldn't even wrap her arms around. They stretched high into the sky, creating a thick canopy that only let flickers of daylight through. There were plenty of small animals living here too, and the community had managed to catch a multitude of meat dinners during their stay. Askari's favorite were little fuzzy tree climbers with big ears and bony tails called portos. They got fat around this time of year, and their meat was sweet and rich when smoked. Askari was good at shooting them, plus she found they made for great target practice.

Askari burst out into the open. The Plains of Tork stretched out for miles away from the forest, and the community would head in this direction next. The sun burned down on them, and if she hadn't been sweating already, she would have started now. The tall dried grasses were nearing the end of their season, but waved gently as a soft breeze wafted through the open field.

To her right, Askari saw a sentry sprinting toward the forest. Zaj paused in front of her and held up his fist to acknowledge the sentry's presence.

"They're coming!" the sentry yelled, waving a red piece of cloth in the air. The cloth signaled danger.

Askari could see other warriors running out of the forest and into the clearing.

"Ahead!" Agi yelled, and Askari fell in line between Zaj and Lyront, her bow at the ready.

"We're gonna try to shoot while they're still a ways out," Zaj said, "even though it's pretty much impossible to see their eyes when they're crouched down in the grass. If we could land just one, it would still make our jobs easier. When they get close, aim for their heads."

Askari nodded, her body tense. She was exhausted, but adrenaline ran through her, making her feel much more alert than she should be. This, she reminded herself, was the only chance she would have to avoid exile. If she could make a difference in this fight, they might consider letting her back into the community. She had to try.

Then, all at once, there they were, their bony backs visible above the grass. They kept their heads low, and she couldn't for the life of her guess where to aim, but she guessed anyway, and let arrows fly.

She had seen drawings of the rarohan, but they didn't do the creatures justice. They were as big as horses, with skeletal bodies covered in a thin casing of translucent grey-blue skin. Their rib cages were visible through a hard covering, and their tails ended in a spiked ball of bone that could take off a human's head. The tail itself probably weighed a hundred pounds. Their heads, on the other hand, were covered in green and brown fur that made it impossible to tell where the grass ended and the rarohan began. Dozens of sharp, spiked teeth filled their mouths, and their tiny eyes were almost invisible beneath their manes. They each had four paws covered with talons that could rip open prey with one swipe—and Askari knew that if they couldn't kill these things now, everyone would be dead in a matter of weeks.

Arrows flew through the air. She had a limited number, so she tried to focus on only shooting if she knew she would hit, but the monsters were moving, jumping, roaring, and it was hard enough to predict where they would be three seconds in the future, let alone be sure that it would hit them in the eye. She was a good shot, but this was nearly impossible.

Then, one went down.

"Nice shot, Zaj!" Lyront yelled. He had given up on shooting and slung his bow across his back. He ran forward and sliced the head off of the rarohan that lay unmoving on the ground.

That was smart, Askari thought. Guarantee its death, in case it was only wounded or unconscious. She also slung her bow across her back and ran forward, coming face to face with a rarohan with a huge scar across its nose. This garg had seen battle. It towered over her, and she stepped back, ducking as it swiped the air with one of its enormous paws. It missed her by a fraction of an inch.

"What're you gonna do, big cat?" she yelled. "Purr me to death?" She leaped forward, machete in hand and smacked it across the face. The rarohan stepped back once and let out a roar. Then Zaj came up from the side and brought his machete down forcefully on the creature's neck. The head popped off and rolled across the ground, and bluish-red blood sprayed color across the brown and green grasses.

Around Askari, dozens of rarohan roared and charged at the nearest warriors. Their teeth glistened in the morning sun. The warriors around her yelled and attacked, some acting as bait while their team members took the heads off of the rarohan, others advancing full force and trying to avoid the power of their talons and teeth.

Another rarohan leaped out of the grass toward Zaj. Askari gasped. She hadn't seen it there, which was clearly the point of their camouflage colors. It slammed into Zaj, knocking him into the ground.

"Oh no you don't!" Askari yelled. She ran forward and leaped up onto its back. It reared, throwing her onto the ground. Zaj rolled out from underneath it as its claws hit the dirt once more.

"Here kitty!" Lyront called from the opposite direction. The garg growled and began to prowl forward. Askari took her opportunity and sprinted toward it as fast as she could, holding her machete over her head. She brought it down on its neck, and its hot blue blood sprayed all over her. She only managed to sever the neck halfway through, though, and the rarohan reared again, roaring. Lyront rushed forward on the other side and brought his machete down through the remaining tissue. Askari gave a huge sigh of relief as it sank to the ground in a heap of blood and bones.

Almost immediately, another rarohan appeared in front of them. Askari ducked as it lunged forward with the intention of getting her head between its teeth. Zaj had gotten to his feet. He pulled an arrow from his quiver and took aim, and a moment later the rarohan collapsed, the arrow sticking out of its eye. Lyront ran forward again and sliced off its head.

"Help!" they heard from a few yards away. Sasa was waving her arms frantically. "Erzci is down! He's bleeding! Help!"

Askari, Zaj, and Lyront began to sprint toward them. The biggest of all the rarohan reared up out of the grass. It towered over all the others, and its fangs were two feet or more in length, dripping with Erzci's blood. Askari felt her stomach turn over as she saw Sasa raise her sword in the air and begin to whack at its ribcage as hard as she could. Askari's feet pounded against the ground.

"Run!" Zaj yelled. "Sasa! Run!"

Sasa dove out of the way just as the creature's front claws landed on the ground where she had been. She rolled and jumped back on her feet, turning to face the monster. Zaj was shooting. He had managed to pull his bow back over his head and aimed one arrow after another at the monster, but they all bounced off. The rarohan roared and shook its head, annoyed at the onslaught. Then Harcos appeared behind the monster, yelling as loudly as he could. He ran forward, machete in one hand, and leaped onto the back of the garg.

"Die!" Harcos yelled. Askari almost laughed. She knew everyone shouted stupid things when they were in the heat of battle, but Harcos, well, he almost always shouted "die" repeatedly. He began to hack at the back of the rarohan's head. It reared up on its hind legs with surprising force, and Harcos went flying through the air, landing in the grass.

"No!" Askari shouted, and then sprinted forward, machete aimed for the rarohan's neck. It landed, buried all the way up to the hilt. The rarohan reared again, and Askari hung on, trying to wiggle the machete so it would slice all the way through the neck. Instead, it slid out and she landed on the ground in a crouch, staring right up into the gaping mouth filled with bloody teeth. She could see all the way into the back of its slimy, bony throat.

Askari rolled to one side, and Zaj sliced through the neck of the pack leader. It fell to the ground in the same spot Askari had just vacated.

A howl went up from one of the nearby rarohan. All the ones that remained took up the cry, and abruptly turned and slipped away, making themselves invisible once more in the tall grasses.

"Erzsci!" Sasa called, running toward him.

"Harcos!" Askari sprinted in the direction Harcos had flown from the rarohan's back. She searched frantically through the grass, looking for any sign of him. Then she noticed a line of grass that had been knocked down in a semi-straight line. She squinted in the bright sunlight and saw the glint of light on metal. "Harcos!" she yelled again, and began to jog down the narrow trail.

Then she saw it: another rarohan, slowly dragging Harcos away from the fray.

"Oh no you don't," Askari growled under her breath. She ran forward; the rarohan looked up, saw her, and increased its speed, still dragging Harcos with it.

Askari pulled her bow from across her back and an arrow from the quiver, slipping the machete into its sheath.

"Get back here, you scoundrel!" she yelled.

She shot an arrow. It whizzed through the air as she pulled a second from her quiver and smacked the rarohan right in the rear.

The rarohan stopped, turned around, and growled at her, like a coyote protecting its dinner from being stolen by another member of its pack.

Askari froze. It was going to come for her any second now, and there weren't any other warriors around to help. She could run away, leading it back to the others, but it might abandon her and grab Harcos again. She could attack it, but what were her chances of being able to kill it? It dropped Harcos' arm and began to stalk toward her. There was no time to think. She took a deep breath and let the arrow fly. It buried itself in the garg's skull; the creature collapsed to the ground. Askari ran forward and began to hack at its neck. She had somehow managed to pick the dullest machete in the armory, but after a few minutes, the job was done.

"Harcos!" she exclaimed, running over to him. He lay unconscious, blood gushing from a wound in his shoulder. Askari ripped a strip from her shirt and wrapped it around his arm the best she could, then heaved him up over her shoulder and stumbled back toward the others.

When she arrived, Agi had organized a sweep to make sure all the rarohan had actually abandoned the hunt.

"What happened?" she asked as Askari set Harcos on the ground.

"He got thrown and then dragged off, and he's still alive, but I'm scared of the blood loss and the poison," Askari said.

"We'll have a team carry him back to camp," Agi said.

"What happened to the rarohan?" Askari asked, while trying to tighten the bandage she had made around Harcos' shoulder.

"I think we killed the pack leader—or well, Zaj did specifically."

"Askari did a great job of being bait," Zaj joked.

Askari glared at him for a moment and then shrugged. It was true. She had distracted it while Zaj chopped off its head. "Anything for you," she muttered.

"When the sweep team gets back," Agi said, "we'll carry the wounded and dead back to camp, inform the elders of what happened, and move out as soon as possible. Askari, you head back with Harcos, and Zaj, you're with Erzci."

"Deaths?" Zaj and Askari asked at the same time.

Agi's face grew serious. "Yes, Janko is dead."

Askari felt a cold chill. Janko was everyone's favorite—always cheerful, always encouraging, always optimistic. She swallowed and took several deep breaths. Dead. Janko. Dead.

The thought followed her as she strode back toward camp. She held one end of a long sheet where Harcos lay unconscious, while Lyront held the other. Dead. Janko was dead. He had a wife and two kids. He led the singing in the evenings around the fire. And he was dead.

Word had apparently arrived back in camp ahead of them. Janko's wife was sobbing and holding on to her two children for dear life. Leka and the other medics had set up an area where they could rapidly treat the injured, while other community members packed up the main medical tent and supplies.

Askari set her end of the sheet down gently. Leka rushed over to examine Harcos, who was still unconscious.

"He'll be okay," Leka said. "It looks like he hit his head, and this wound isn't deep."

Askari nodded, relieved. Trying to keep her eyes from staring at the poor widow and her children, she sank to the ground next to Harcos and put her head in her hands.

"Hey," a soft voice said, and she felt a hand on her shoulder. It was Shujaa.

"Hey," Askari replied.

"You okay?"

"Sort of. Janko is dead and we didn't kill all the rarohan. They could come back at any time, kill any of us. Hunt us. Eat us."

"It'll be okay." Shujaa sat down next to her, holding out some damp rags for Askari to use to wipe the rarohan blood from her face and arms. "We're going to get out of here, and everything will be fine."

"When are they sending out a team to track down the rest of the rarohan?" Askari asked.

"They're not. They think it will be safer and wiser to move locations, get out of rarohan territory as soon as possible."

"But they killed Janko!" Askari said. "Doesn't anyone want revenge? Not to mention, rarohan aren't exactly known for letting their prey walk off."

"Everyone wants revenge," Shujaa said, shrugging. "But Elder Elol says that revenge is a good way to get more Baratok killed. He says the wisest course of action is to stay our anger and focus on keeping the baby safe. He thinks we killed enough of their pack that we'll be able to get out of range before they recover."

Askari sighed. "I have a bad feeling about all of this."

"Askari!"

Askari glanced up to see Elder Kira standing in front of her tent, a short distance away.

This was her chance! She could argue that she should be allowed to stay. Askari stood slowly, taking deep breaths to calm herself as she ducked inside. The same five sat in a half circle.

"Sit," Elder Kira said.

Askari sat.

"You fought well today," Elder Faro said, "and according to some of the other warriors, saved both Sasa's life and Harcos'. We thank you for that."

Askari bowed her head respectfully.

"After discussing the situation," Faro continued, "we have decided that we will send you off with extra food and arrows to make your journey easier, as a thank you for your service to this community today."

"What?" Askari exclaimed, looking up abruptly at the solemn faces of the elders in front of her. "I still have to go? Saving two lives wasn't good enough to make up for a couple of minor mistakes with no real consequences?"

"Askari," Kira said harshly, holding up her hand to silence Askari's sputtering protests. "Your behavior was in direct disobedience to the rules we have established for the good and the safety of this community. What do you expect us to do? Wait until you lead a monster back to camp before we punish you? No. We built this community out of nothing, from the first day the world as we knew it ended. We fought, clawed, and killed to get where we are today. We structured this community the way we did to keep everyone safe, to build a next generation, to hope that the human race will last beyond us. And we will not let one selfish young warrior ruin that."

"Janko didn't live," Askari muttered under her breath, knowing the comment was inappropriate and immature. But she was so angry, she could barely stay seated, let alone stay quiet.

Kira ignored her and raised her chin so she was looking down her nose at Askari. "The easiest way for you to learn why we do things the way we do is to go off on your own. To have to struggle to survive like we did. As a Baratok, you are responsible not only for yourself, but for everyone here. You must learn to obey."

"What if I die?" Askari spat. "What will your lesson be worth then?"

"If you die," Kira said, crossing her arms, "then you were not as strong as we hoped you were." She stood and gestured for Askari to stand as well. "While you were fighting, Vica packed provisions, including knives, food, a bedroll, some extra clothes, and the like. You may see her, and then leave immediately. You should have eight hours or so until sundown, enough time to travel a good number of miles on your own."

"What about the rarohan? What if they come back?"

"You have had enough training to evade them," Kira said. "Climb a tree or something. We can take care of ourselves. We wish you well."

"Yeah, right," Askari said, her ears hot. She turned and stormed out of the tent, not looking around her, ignoring everyone bustling around the camp. She strode to Vica's tent, where the head of scavenging and food preparation stood waiting. Vica was round and comforting, and everyone turned to her for advice. She was sort of like everyone's mother or grandmother, even to those whose parents were still alive. She had a large backpack prepared with a bedroll attached, and a fresh, sharp machete that she traded for Askari's dull one.

"I'm sorry, Askari," she said. She did look sorry, her sad eyes peering up at Askari from underneath her wild and curly hair. "You know where we are headed, so you will find us again in a week or two."

"Yeah," Askari muttered. She took the bag and blade from Vica. "Thanks."

She glanced over her shoulder one last time, at the hustle and bustle of the Baratok people preparing to move, and then strode into the woods.

CHAPTER 3: THE GAMBA

ASKARI WOKE THE NEXT morning to a drop of water on her nose. She opened one eye and stared up at the lush, green canopy overhead. Then she felt another drop. And another. And another.

She barely had time to fold up her bedroll and repack her bag before the skies opened up and the rain flooded down. The heavy, relentless downpour gushed through the covering of leaves and soaked everything underneath, including her. She pulled on her jacket—which was, of course, already wet—yanked the hood up around her face, and began to trudge eastward, in the general direction Elder Faro had sent her.

Sleep had not come easily the night before. All manner of strange noises had woken her, real and imagined, and she dreamed that the rarohan had come to consume her flesh again and again, and then that the nagy had come back to life and was crashing through the forest searching for her. She had jerked awake numerous times and had to remind herself of why she wasn't sleeping under a tent, and why there was no light from the hot campfire that would normally burn day and night in the center of their camp, and why she was alone in the middle of nowhere.

In weather like this, the community would have stayed put, no matter how many rarohan they hadn't managed to dispose of. Even the monsters hated rain, preferring to hide out in a cave or a hole or a den or wherever in this kind of deluge. Askari tried to keep her eyes out for a rock overhang or a particularly tight-woven thicket, but right now she could barely see her hand in front of her face, let alone much of the woods around her. The only thing left to do was keep moving.

To pass the time, Askari began to recite lessons in her head. Since many in the community couldn't read, they were taught orally, and were required to memorize and recite rules, stories, and guidelines in front of their elders before they could progress in their training. She began with the *Five Rules of Monster Engagement*.

"Rule One, if you can see it, it can see you," Askari recited. "Or smell you or hear you. If you can't see it, it can still see you." One of the community members had put this to a song, but she hated it for being too cheerful with an annoyingly catchy tune, so always refused to sing along. "Rule Two, only stand and fight if you cannot run. Take the path of least resistance. Rule Three, community first, individuals second. A community is equal to the sum of its individuals. Rule Four, avoid, avoid, avoid. Rule Five, all monsters will try to kill you. Monsters are not your friends."

The Rules had always bugged her a little bit—not because they didn't work, but because she thought they were short-sighted. If they were allowed to interact with monsters once in a while, maybe, just maybe, they would learn something useful that would make survival a hair easier. But the elders believed that the risk of losing a community member was too great and forbade anyone from seeking out monsters on their own or choosing to fight one when they could feasibly run away.

Askari knew that in the old world, people had farmed animals, like cows. The Baratok still had some animals, horses mostly, and some other communities allowed dogs. She wondered if there was a monster they could tame or farm—after all, in their travels they had heard of many gentle monsters that left humans alone and sought out meals from the wild animals in the forests. But in her community, that would be highly frowned upon. Monsters were monsters; people were people. They were meant to kill each other. Askari had to admit, though, she had never encountered a monster that hadn't tried to eat her, so perhaps the elders were right about this one.

Monsters were, by and large, an odd type of creature. The elders said they didn't act like native animals, though Askari didn't have enough interaction with native animals to know what the differences were. Some people (Harcos, usually) speculated on where the monsters had come from, but Kira strongly discouraged that discussion. The main myth Askari had heard from other travelers involved an alien invasion and some kind of virus. She thought that seemed unlikely. The general consensus was that no one knew why monsters acted the way they did or where they had come from. What mattered was survival.

She recited the Rules a few more times, and then moved on to the thirteen types of monsters.

"Small monsters, water monsters, large monsters, poison," she said. "Insect monsters, floating monsters, disguise monsters, paralyzers. Ghost monsters, human monsters, mountain monsters, pack, and don't forget about the cave."

This classification system had always bugged her too, at least once she began to think about it. It mixed together size and method of killing with their preferred environment and their appearance. If she had made a system for understanding monsters, she would have simplified it into something more like: location—or where they tended to live; size—with subcategories for tiny, small, medium, big, and gigantic; appearance—which would include human-looking ones or ghost monsters that disappeared or the ones that disguised themselves as something else; and then method of killing—which would include poison and paralytic agents, but also teeth, claws, fear, or generally ripping things apart.

As she trudged through the forest, drenched, cold, and generally uncomfortable, she worked her way through her main lessons: *Ways to Kill a Monster, How to Bind a Broken Bone, Seven Strategies for Not Dying, Poisonous Monsters and What They'll Do to You, Safe Places to Camp, How to Set*

Up a Camp, How to Light a Fire, Teamwork Basics, Fighting as a Group, Community Rules, and probably a dozen more. She found the muttering to be a kind of stress relief; filling her mind with familiar ideas was comforting.

The downpour let up after three or so hours, and Askari breathed a sigh of relief. It had lessened to a mild drizzle, and even though she was soaked through to the bone and freezing cold, at least she could walk upright, without hunched shoulders. Plus, she could see her surroundings more clearly, the dripping wet trees and slimy moss, shiny rocks peeking out through the sagging undergrowth. Plants drooped so low to the ground that it was much easier than usual to climb over them—that at least was a positive.

It hadn't rained this hard in weeks, and Askari had not seen it coming.

I should have, she reflected. All the signs were there. Ants had been making little dams to protect the entrances to their empires. Mid-afternoon yesterday, the wind had picked up, and even in the forest, gusts had surprised her several times; the trees had groaned and bent, their leaves flipping over to show their light undersides to the sky. Clouds had rolled in, but she couldn't see them well from under the canopy and had assumed they were light, non-rain clouds. The forest itself had gotten quieter and quieter—there had been fewer birds, fewer squirrels, and much less noise. Likely, everyone had gone into their burrows and holes to wait out the storm, except for her, of course. She wished she had a burrow or a hole.

Another mistake like this and she might as well lie down and let the gargs come and eat her. Part of her wanted to give up anyway, but she had a mission, and she was going to complete it or die trying. She thought that this might be her opportunity to show Elder Kira that their rules and way of living was not the only way, that the new generation might have a few ideas worth trying. But she had to survive first—because that's what the elders held over her head. *We survived,* they said. *You have it easy compared to us. And if you break the rules, you'll die.*

All day yesterday, Askari had seethed with anger. How dare they force her to leave? They had disguised it by telling her they were sending her on a mission, but it was exile, plain and simple. She could die out here, alone, and they knew it! They could have given her latrine duty. They could have locked her up in a wagon. But out here, she could get eaten by a monster or drowned in a river or fall off a cliff—it clearly didn't matter to them if she ended up dead. She had contemplated never going back, but her friends were there. The only family she had ever known.

The anger had burned and scalded in her stomach, and her neck was sore from the tension. And Kira—she knew Kira took pleasure from sending her away. Kira had always hated Askari for some reason, and this—well, Askari was going to survive if only for a chance to torment Kira another day.

But that was yesterday. Today, all she could think of was Janko. The way his wife had wept when she heard the news of his death. His children's wide-eyed stares, wondering how and why this had happened to them. She could see his smile in her mind, and heard him say, "Sun's up, smiles out!" as he had only the morning before. His death wasn't her fault. He had been on a different team, fighting different rarohan. But somehow, she felt like if she had been smarter or faster or *anything*, maybe she could have saved him. Maybe if she hadn't tracked down Harcos, and instead stayed behind, she could have saved him. Of course, then they would have lost Harcos. Or maybe it was the universe paying her back for her disobeying the rules of the Baratok.

And because of this foolhardy quest she was on, she would miss his sending. All Baratok dead were burned, their ashes sent to become one with the world again. It was always a heavy occasion, filled with sorrow for the person they had lost, and joy that life would be easier for them now. She wouldn't be there, but she could still wish him the best.

She paused for a moment and closed her eyes, listening to the woods around her. The squirrels had begun to appear from their nests, and the birds who enjoyed being out in a light drizzle now chattered and fluttered about. She could hear the wind still whistling, the leaves rustling overhead, and drops of water drip drip dripping to the forest floor. But there was one other sound mixed in with all the rest, a steady low bubbling murmur. What was it?

A river. Askari's eyes snapped open. She was near the river that Faro had pointed out to her on the map. That was a good sign—she was making solid progress, faster than she had anticipated. Once she reached it, she would follow it upstream for a few miles, and then make camp for the night.

Wandering over to a nearby rock, Askari sat down on it heavily. She hadn't eaten this morning, not wanting to get her food wet in the downpour. She pulled a dry piece of bread from her backpack, which had somehow managed to stay largely free of water, and crunched down on it. They had also sent a lump of pemmican—enough for two days, but not much more than that. She would have to stop and hunt at some point today or tomorrow though, if she wanted to keep up her strength.

The bread tasted stale. She frowned at it. They had clearly given her old food that would probably have been thrown out in a few days anyway. Another surge of anger rushed through her—she had saved the lives of two warriors and all she got was stale bread? She fought back the anger and focused on scanning the woods around her. She hadn't noted any signs of any monsters yet, so that was a good sign, probably. It could also mean that the majority of monsters had vacated the area due to the presence of a larger, more fearsome monster—but she wouldn't dwell on that. If that were the case, she would kill the garg or die trying, and that was that.

She observed plenty of plants in this part of the forest, but she didn't recognize most of them. Shujaa would have been helpful. Maybe some of these were food. Harcos would probably know too. She did recognize some of the trees—mostly oak and maple, with a few pines mixed in, many of them old or dead. That would make it easier for her to find kindling, at least.

Askari spent the next few minutes staring at a large, shiny black mushroom that grew several feet away. She had been taught time and time again to stay away from all mushrooms, given that so many of them turned out to be poisonous. And whenever they cooked mushrooms at home, they were little dinky things, not giant ones like this. She wondered if mushrooms liked rain. Did they have personalities? Opinions? Or were they just like the rest of the plants in the forest?

She sighed and stood up, re-latching her bag. She had to keep moving or either a garg would find and eat her, or else she would never complete her mission and die anyway. The rain had let up entirely at this point, and she could even see rays of sun had begun to peek through the clouds. It was still pretty dark on the forest floor, but it was nice to think somewhere might be drying out a little.

As she neared the river, she noticed another mushroom, big, black, and shiny, like the one before.

"Must grow in this area," she muttered to herself, frowning a little. There was something off about the mushroom, but she couldn't put her finger on it. Askari wished she had paid more attention during her botany and foraging lessons. She stopped walking and stared at it for a few minutes, and then turned and continued on her way. She didn't know anything about plants, so as long as she stayed away from it, she should be fine.

She walked a few more feet toward the river and saw another mushroom. This one quivered briefly, like it had just been brushed by something moving past it. Frowning, Askari turned and looked back at the previous mushroom. It was gone.

Her frown deepened as she walked slowly past the new mushroom, keeping an eye on it over her shoulder. What exactly was it? A weird plant? A hallucination? As soon as she was past, the mushroom miraculously sprouted ugly hairy legs and scurried behind a tree.

"Oh, good grief," she said, rolling her eyes. She wracked her brain trying to think of what kind of garg this would be. It was a small one, and not something her community had come across, at least not that she knew of. It might have been mentioned in a lesson though, or maybe she had seen a picture of it in a book. A mushroom-shaped head with hairy legs. She needed a better look at it.

Askari continued walking through the forest, watching for the mushroom. Sure enough, not too much farther ahead, she saw it sitting perfectly still, as if it had been there the entire time. She bent over and picked up a long stick with one hand, while quietly sliding her dagger from its sheath with the other. She slowly moved closer, then reached the stick out and poked the mushroom creature with a quick jab.

The garg stood up and hissed at her, drool dripping from six-inch-long fangs. It had one eye in the center of a bald, slimy head, which was mostly taken up by its enormous mouth. It had long legs, like a frog, but was covered in a thin, scraggly hair, and the mushroom hat appeared to be attached to its head.

"You're a gamba!" she exclaimed, a grin breaking across her face. She had heard about these. The last time the Baratok had encountered a smaller group of travelers, they had told stories of mushroom-hatted gargs. She pursed her lips, trying to remember what else the travelers had said. All they had said was that the gambas ate meat and would stalk their prey until it slept, then attack, going straight for the jugular.

"Glad I noticed you before I went to bed tonight," she said. Then she hissed back at it, the way it had hissed at her, and waved her arms to make her look bigger. It gave a little bark-yip and scurried off into the trees.

"I probably should have killed it," she said to herself. "Oh well. Next time."

Askari trudged through the woods for several more hours until the sun was just over the cusp of the tree line. She could see a break in the trees ahead, and the rush of the river was quite loud now. A moment later, she stepped out onto a rocky ledge, set a few feet over the river. It was spilling over its banks, no doubt because of the rain that had passed through that morning. On the opposite shore was another rock ledge, but this one had dry ground underneath. She could use it as shelter to camp for the night—if she could somehow get across the river.

Mud squelched and sucked her feet down as she mucked along the edge of the riverbank. She had a feeling that no matter how hot it was the next day, she wasn't ever going to be dry—or clean—again. Then, to her right, she saw the gamba. It was sitting almost hidden behind a log, waiting for her to pass by.

"I see you!" she exclaimed, waving her hand at it as if to shoo it away. "I'm gonna poke you with my stick again if you don't go away."

The mushroom ignored her. Askari walked past it, carefully keeping an eye out to make sure it didn't attack. She didn't want to be immobilized if it had some kind of paralytic agent in its saliva or fangs.

"You stay back," she warned, swinging her stick at it.

Again, as soon as she had passed by it, the gamba leaped into the air and disappeared into the woods.

"It's not a very subtle garg, is it?" Askari muttered.

The next moment she heard something growl deep in the woods. "Aw, great garg," she muttered. "What now?"

She moved close to a tree and peered around it. The mushroom was in a heated battle with... something. Askari squinted to try to see what the other creature was. It had big ears, that much she could tell. Big ears and gross-looking wiry fur, with enormous hands. It didn't really look like a monster, more like some sort of unfortunate rodent that had gotten stuck with the short end of nature's stick. It did appear to have fangs, though, and blood-red eyes, and it was a little smaller than the gamba. Part of her brain thought it seemed familiar, like she had seen it somewhere before. It appeared to be losing the fight.

Askari watched for a few minutes as the creatures tumbled and growled and tried to rip each other's throats out. She debated for a minute if she preferred one to win. On one hand, the gamba was kind of cute and had been her friend for the last few hours. On the other hand, as soon as she tried to go to sleep, it would try to rip her throat out. At the same time, she didn't know anything about the red-eyed rodent at all. But it was small, and she felt sorry for it.

She picked up a rock and tossed it from one hand to the other. She should probably stay out of it. Or... she could always let fate decide. Taking careful note of where the ball of hissing fur was, she pulled back her arm, closed her eyes, and threw the rock as hard as she could.

It hit the mushroom hat and the gamba went down. Instantly, the other creature was on top of it, gobbling away.

"Gross," Askari said. She watched for a minute, then shook her head and turned away. At least somebody in the forest wouldn't go to bed hungry tonight. She continued picking her way down the edge of the riverbank. A few hundred feet down, she found a ford, barely peeking up from the high water. It looked like someone had made it ages ago, with slippery green slime covering the rocks, but it worked, so she carefully picked her way across and headed upstream toward the ledge she had seen. She would make some food from the supplies Vica had given her, try to get a little sleep, and then rise early to hunt rabbits in the morning.

It was pitch black when she woke up, with only the sounds of the night around her. She squinted at the sky, but between the ledge she was sleeping under, the canopy of trees, and the cloud cover, the stars were far from visible. All she could see was the dull red glow of the fire coals. Frowning, Askari listened carefully, trying to figure out why she had woken up. She rolled over, and then sat upright with a shout.

Glowing red eyes stared at her in the darkness.

"What—what—" she gasped, trying to move away from it, despite her legs being tangled in her bedroll. She felt around for her knife.

The creature in front of her began to make an odd clicking noise with its tongue. It darted forward and grabbed at Askari's mouth with its long fingers. It was a strange size, she noted—smaller than a dog but larger than a cat. Askari pulled the bedroll out from around her legs and scrambled away. The creature let out a sigh and then scurried after her. Askari turned, trying to get out from under the ledge and into open ground, but before she could, it grabbed her by the hair and pulled her back.

"Stop it!" Askari yelled, landing on her rear with a thump. "What are you doing?"

The creature scampered up onto Askari's chest and stared her in the eyes with a scowl. Askari closed her eyes, expecting an attack, but it didn't come. When she opened her eyes, it was staring at her, then it began to wave its finger and make an odd clicking noise, almost as if it were scolding her. Askari froze. This was odd behavior from a monster. Or a rodent, for that matter, if in fact it wasn't a monster after all.

She shoved the creature off her chest and got up on her knees, aiming to launch herself out from underneath the ledge. It grabbed her by the hair and pulled her back down to the ground again.

"Okay, okay!" Askari exclaimed, rubbing her head where the hair pulling had hurt her scalp. "I get it! I shouldn't leave. What do you want?"

The red-eyed creature ran to edge of the rock ledge and peered around it, then scurried back to Askari, pointing and clicking. Askari had no idea what to do. She had grown up learning that all monsters were bad, that all monsters would try to kill you. But this garg wasn't trying to kill her. At least, it wasn't trying particularly hard. Of course, it might not even be a monster. Maybe it was a rodent that she hadn't ever encountered before.

She tried to think through the problem. On one hand, it could be some kind of trap. Then again, gargs (and rodents) usually weren't that clever. On the other hand, it could be that the monster-rodent was trying to help her. She couldn't see that well, but she remembered that the strange creature fighting with the mushroom earlier in the day had red eyes. Could it be the same one?

Leaning forward, she tossed some fire starter on the coals, still hot from the night before, and then blew on them softly; they glowed brightly and burst into flame. A few minutes later, she had a small fire burning beside her. The creature was now visible—ugly, hairy, big hands, enormous ears, and glowing red eyes. It had five fangs protruding from its lips; one of them was curved outward. It was definitely the creature from earlier.

It clicked again, pointing out into the darkness around them.

"I don't know what you want," Askari whispered. She grabbed a larger, dry stick covered in dead leaves she had been saving for the morning, and held it over the small flames, praying it would catch on fire. A moment later, it burst into flame, bright, hot, and hissing in the damp night air. She swung it around and leaned out from under the ledge. Then she gasped.

Beady black eyes stared at her from the darkness, pair after pair, each with a differently patterned mushroom hat.

"What the—?" Askari exclaimed, scrambling backward until she was backed up against the rock ledge, her heart racing. She was trapped.

The gambas hissed at her, a low *ssssss* mixed with a deep growl, their teeth glistening in the firelight. The ugly red-eyed creature hissed back at them, staying close to Askari. Had it come to her for help? Or to warn her? Or for some other, more nefarious reason? Either way, Askari had to do something to get out of this—and fast. Or else she was gamba dinner.

She thrust the flaming branch toward the closest gamba. It didn't seem afraid, just glared and scowled at her. Maybe they didn't know what fire was. She did it again, and this time the flames touched the garg. It let out a hissing scream that pierced the night and then burst into flame. A moment later, the gamba was gone, vaporized.

The mushroom hats began to stomp their feet and howl. Askari aimed for a second gamba, this time not hesitating. The gamba screeched and scurried backward, doing its best to avoid Askari, but it couldn't. It too caught fire and disappeared in a lick of flame, leaving behind only a small pile of dust and a strange fishy smell.

Fire. It would definitely do the trick. It made sense—the oily substance that covered their bodies must be flammable. That was the only thing that could explain the sudden combustion. She jabbed the flaming branch forward again, and this time, the gambas backed up rapidly.

The red-eyed creature clicked and chattered, dragging a third dried branch toward the fire. This one also had some dead leaves on it. That was good. If she had two flaming branches, she had that much more chance of getting out of here. They chattered and squealed, jumping back away from the blazing stick.

While they didn't like the fire, they also weren't running away scared. That made Askari nervous. She could evaporate a few of them, but there were more than enough gambas to overwhelm her if they decided to all work together.

"Get out of here, you nasty little gargs!" Askari exclaimed. She glanced over to see the red-eyed creature was dragging in still another dried branch. It was clearly a clever animal, and that little bit of intelligence was making her a tad bit uncomfortable.

Askari looked at the flaming branch in her hand, then at the red-eyed creature, then back at the branch. Without a second thought, she tossed it into the crowd of gambas.

Such a sound she had never heard in her life, a cacophony of squeals and shrieks, whining and screaming and scurrying. The loudest sound reminded her of two trees rubbing together, but much louder and more drawn out than trees. The gambas ran as fast as their little feet could lope through the dead leaves and underbrush. One gamba had gotten caught underneath the flaming leaves. It screamed and crackled, until it vanished in cloud of dust.

Askari didn't hesitate. As soon as the branch left her hand, she grabbed her bedroll, tied it to her pack, and threw it on. Then she grabbed the next flaming torch and held it out, while the red-eyed creature tried to get the remaining branch to catch flame.

"I'm coming!" Askari yelled. "And you had better get out of my way or else you'll all be dead gargs!"

She swung the torch around as she stepped out from under the ledge, and then screeched as one of the gambas leaped from the top of the ledge onto her head. She flung her arms around trying to get it to let go, but it hung on tightly. Finally, she grabbed it by the mushroom hat—it felt squishy and slimy in her hands—and flung it into the crowd of gambas on the ledge. They shrieked and tumbled over each other, trying to get away from her.

"You are very bad assassins," Askari said, taking a few deep breaths to calm herself. If they had worked together from the start, they could have easily overwhelmed her in an instant. She hoped they didn't figure that out before she had a chance to get away. She bent down and picked up the second flaming branch as the red-eyed creature scurried up her legs to her shoulder and settled onto her backpack, hanging on with its strangely human-like fingers.

Askari swung the fiery branches in a wide circle around herself, aiming to hit as many of the gambas as she could. The flames left spots on Askari's eyes, but she strode forward confidently, watching as the gambas scrambled over each other to try to get away from the fire.

One ran up and tried to bite her leg, but she kicked it as hard as she could. It went flying. She headed toward the stream. She didn't know how big gamba territory was, but she had to walk until she was in a spot that was too hot or too dry for them to follow. Or at least until it was daylight and she could actually see.

She walked faster and faster until she was moving at a jog slow enough that her torches didn't blow out, but still fast enough to keep ahead of most of the gambas that scurried around her feet. She listened as she neared the river; the flames were barely enough to show her the ground in front of her, let alone to see where she was going. She thought maybe she should put it out so other creatures in the woods wouldn't find her, but she had a bad feeling that the gambas could see in the dark, which gave them the advantage. So, she took a deep breath and kept running. She tripped a few times, and her hands began to feel hot, like they were burning. She was pretty sure she was bleeding somewhere, but none of it mattered. If she wanted to survive, she had to keep going.

The red-eyed creature hung on to her backpack, staying in a low lump behind Askari's head. It was making a whining noise, and Askari felt almost as badly for it as she did for herself.

As she jogged, the ground began to incline. It became more difficult to run; her heart pounded in her chest. She reached the top of the hill only to find a wide-open clearing with no trees except one large one in the center. Overhead, she saw nothing but blackness—no moon, no stars. Then, it began to rain again. It was a light drizzle, which wouldn't have bothered Askari in the least, except that her torch began to fizzle.

The next moment, the flames went out. She skidded to a halt, blinking at the world around her, but all she could see were spots on her eyes. Panic welled up in her abdomen, a fear so intense that it was all she could do to not start running as fast as she could.

Something grabbed her ankle. She kicked it, and the gamba squealed. She tried to move backward, closer to the large tree. Maybe she could climb it, get away from these creatures, survive until morning. Something grabbed her other ankle. She kicked that, but it was useless. The gambas were closing in, climbing on each other, climbing her. She could feel their slimy little hands with their human-like fingers grabbing on to the fabric of her pants. She could hear them chattering, making gasping noises, then a sound like a coughing, wheezing laugh. The red-eyed creature was quivering, curled up into the tiniest ball on Askari's backpack.

Askari was pretty sure she was going to die. Death by gamba—unique, to say the least.

Then the sky rumbled, and she could feel the gambas that were climbing her freeze for a second, all listening to the woods around them. Askari listened too, to the rain hitting the leaves of the trees, the rumble of thunder in the distance, and the weird breathing of the gambas. She wondered what they were hearing that she wasn't.

Thunder rolled again, this time closer.

Without warning, a loud crack ripped through the night. Askari shrieked and leaped back, falling onto a heap of gambas. Bits of tree exploded everywhere, raining down on Askari and the gambas, and the main part of the trunk burst into flame. The uppermost branches flew outward into the forest. Askari scrambled to her feet and began to run, but fell again as a branch slammed into her arm and knocked her to the ground.

The gambas squealed and screamed. Askari rolled over, only to see the strangest sight—a chain reaction of burning gambas. The gamba closest to the tree burst into flame, then the one next to it, and the one next to that one—and each of the gambas in the pile that had tried to climb Askari burst like popcorn, *pop, pop, pop*! and were gone in an instant. The rest of the gambas began to scream and wail before scampering into the woods and vanishing into the darkness.

The red-eyed creature screeched and tried to hide under the hood of Askari's coat, and Askari breathed in sharply as some of the oily substance on her skin burst into flame and disappeared, leaving little burn marks behind. She noticed that the woods around her smelled like scorched fish.

The tree was now a glowing red flame, burning from the inside, smoke rising into the air. It cast light around them, and Askari saw that not a single gamba remained. Luck. That was all. She was alive because she had gotten lucky. She swallowed, trying to hold back a sudden feeling of nausea.

The red-eyed creature began to yank on Askari's hair and chatter.

"I'm going, I'm going!" Askari exclaimed.

She picked up the dried branch she had dropped and stuck it into the tree to make a torch once again. The rain was light, so hopefully the torch would burn until the sun rose. Her arm throbbed where the branch had crashed into her—she was definitely going to have a bruise. But that didn't matter now. She just needed to go. To take the chance the universe had given her.

Taking a deep breath, Askari looked once more at the tree, thankful the lightning had hit it and not her, and then strode into the darkness.

CHAPTER 4: THE POK

A FEW HOURS LATER, a tiny piece of dawn peeked its head up over the horizon. Askari had managed to keep her torch alight through the drizzle, but now she dropped the flaming branch on the damp ground and stomped it out with her foot. Though the soft light of morning still cast shadows over everything, she could now see the forest around her. There were no gambas in sight—not behind her, not in front of her, not beside her. That was the good news. The bad news was that she had no idea where she was. In her desperate midnight run through the woods, she had lost the river. The only things she could see around her were trees, and the river's steady gurgle of water had been replaced by the sound of a light breeze rustling the leaves.

Askari slowed down, allowing herself to breathe a little more easily. She kept a wary eye around her, but exhaustion was setting in. Her arm throbbed. She didn't know how long she could go before passing out right where she stood. It didn't matter, though—she had to keep going, had to keep walking. She would look for shelter, a safe place to rest, but she wouldn't stop until she found it.

The creature curled up on her backpack suddenly began to chatter, and Askari smiled and held out her arm. She had forgotten about her new friend. It ran down to her forearm, perched like an extremely ugly and large squirrel, and stared at her. It had blood-red eyes with little black lines running through them and enormous ears, each as big as its head. Its body was covered with a stiff, wiry fur, and the fingers on its hands looked eerily similar to a human's. A prehensile tail ran up Askari's arm and hung on to her backpack, and the creature gazed up at her with a curious expression—wide eyes, silly grin, teeth sticking out of its mouth, one crooked and facing away from the others.

"Hello," Askari said. "Thanks for waking me up. Those gambas would have eaten me, no doubt."

It chattered something incomprehensible and waved its arms around.

"Do you have a name?" Askari asked. She tilted her head sideways and examined it more closely, now that it was daylight. She felt like she had seen a drawing of this kind of creature before, but she couldn't remember where. Big ears, wiry fur, human-like fingers, strangely intelligent.

"Hmmm," Askari said, wracking her brain. A memory from her childhood suddenly flashed into her mind.

She stood in the center of camp, her mother frowning down at her. A creature with red eyes and big ears sat in a nearby tree. "You stay away from it," her mother scolded.

"We don't even know what it is! What if it's a monster? It might lead you off somewhere and eat you!"

"But I want to keep it, Mom!" Askari had whined. Then her mother grabbed her by the arm and pulled an angry little Askari toward their tent.

"Still don't know what you are," Askari said, grinning at the memory. "Could be monster, could be rodent. But if all monsters are evil, then... you must be a rodent."

The red-eyed creature chattered again and scurried back up her arm, settling in on top of her backpack.

"I should name you," Askari said. "How about... Red?"

That felt a little lame, she thought, and kind of obvious too. Red because it had red eyes?

"What about..." Another memory suddenly flashed into Askari's mind.

She was alone in the woods, sitting in a soft mossy spot under a tree. The red-eyed creature stared up at her, eyes gleaming and ears alert. Little Askari held a corncob doll with a painted face and clothes made from leaves and flowers.

"We will be friends and have tea," little Askari said, smiling. "And then we will fight the monsters!"

The creature chattered, and then reached out and grabbed the doll from Askari's hands.

"Give that back!" Askari exclaimed, scowling.

The creature pondered her for a second and then popped the entire corncob into its mouth, leaves and paint and all.

What was that doll's name? Askari frowned, trying to remember. Something easy that rhymed—Dolly? Molly?

Polly! That was it. She shrugged, trying to shake off the memory. She tried not to think about life before her mom died—it hurt too much.

"How about Polly, then?" she asked. "After my doll? Just don't do anything that'll make me regret keeping you, Polly."

Polly chattered and clicked happily. Askari felt that was the closest she was going to get to approval from the creature.

Askari walked for what felt like an eternity, though she knew it was likely only a couple of hours. The sun rose high in the sky, and the forest was steamy and muggy as the water from the day before began to evaporate. Polly lay asleep on the top of Askari's backpack, and she herself felt almost as though she were sleepwalking.

As she was contemplating whether it would be worth it to lie down right where she stood and sleep until she couldn't sleep any more, despite the chances of a gamba or ten having followed her from the river, she stumbled into a clearing, in the center of which loomed a barn.

It was old, clearly from the pre-monster times. It had chipped and peeling red paint in some spots, but most of the wood looked rather grey and old. A smaller room jutting off of the back had almost entirely caved in, but the doors on the front seemed solid enough. As long as no creatures were living in or around it, it would make for a fine place to sleep for a few hours.

Polly stirred on Askari's shoulder as Askari tried to shake the sleep out of her eyes. What were the elders' rules for exploring buildings? She had never paid much attention to this set of rules. They were nearly impossible to implement on her own, and depending on the situation, could either be overkill or lacking. But it was all she had.

"One, check the perimeter," Askari muttered to herself. This rule had always annoyed her. Who decided the perimeter? Some monsters would travel miles for food, while others wouldn't leave their own small territory. Plus, the more space you explored, the more you had to keep track of. But that didn't matter right now.

She surveyed the edges of the clearing and saw nothing, but that wasn't enough. She began checking for footprints, flattened grass, excrement, or any other signs of gargs or large animals.

"Two, review the surrounding area," she said when she had finished her initial once-over. Except, she couldn't very well do that on her own. These rules were clearly not designed for individuals traveling alone—she would have to put some thought into developing her own set of guidelines. Reviewing the surrounding area was a team effort, where everyone pitched in any knowledge or memories they had. They would recall monster dens, or if someone had died or been attacked nearby, and try to scout out for at least a three-mile radius. If the elders had a map of the area, they would compare it to what they could see in front of them.

"Three, scout the building." She could do this one. Taking slow, steady strides, Askari began to walk in a spiral pattern toward the barn. She looked for similar things she might have found on the perimeter—tracks or excrement, for example—and listened as well, in case anything was scurrying or growling or making any noise. If something was living in a barn like this, it was likely either a daytime monster out hunting or a nighttime monster—in which case it would be sleeping. She crossed her fingers that it was neither, and that she could sleep long enough to get some of her energy back.

The grasses in this clearing were bright yellows and greens, and patches of warm red flowers grew in clusters. The robin's-egg blue sky hosted white puffy clouds that cast gentle shadows on the ground below. The other side of the barn had a fence, mostly falling down, where the original owners had probably kept some kind of animal, and she was glad to see the back wall still intact.

Askari finished her spiral and ended at the barn door. She pulled on the handle. With a loud creak, it opened just wide enough for her to enter. Light from the outside slid in through the cracks in the wall and roof, making visible motes of dust that ran like streaks through the air.

Polly leaped off Askari's backpack and began to run around, climbing the walls and peeking in crevices. It was mostly just dirt in the barn. There were stalls big enough for horses, and old equipment that Askari didn't recognize. Some had big blades, others had what she thought were motors—actual working motors were rare these days given that it was so difficult to get electricity or fuel. At the opposite end of the barn from the main entrance, a large sliding door was hanging off its hinges, leaving a wide-open hole. It wasn't ideal, but she didn't see any garg excrement, scratches in the floor, or signs of destruction besides the regular wear and tear. She could sleep in one of the stalls so she wouldn't be easy bait for any garg that happened to be strolling by.

In the back of the barn, a narrow set of stairs led up to the top floor, which was a big empty room with a trap door in the center and a sliding door on one wall that looked to be permanently open. She could see most of the meadow from here. It seemed like a safe enough location, where she could rest for at least a few hours.

Finally satisfied, Askari headed back downstairs. She picked the cleanest stall, laid out her bedroll, and fell asleep.

Askari stretched, yawning as she woke to the sound of rain beating on the roof over her head. Apparently, the storms were not done yet; she felt lucky to have found shelter. It was hard to tell what time it was, since the clouds made it so dark, but she guessed she had slept for five or six hours, putting the time around mid-afternoon. She would need to hunt soon as she was about to run out of dry food, but it wasn't wise to head out in this storm—not when she was safe and dry already.

She could explore the barn more, though, and maybe find some kindling to start a fire. Then she heard a scratching noise. She ducked down in the horse stall and froze, waiting to hear where the noise was coming from. The noise drew closer and closer until it was outside the stall door. She looked up and shrieked as the ugliest face she had ever seen loomed over her with enormous ears and red eyes.

"Polly!" Askari gasped as all the memories rushed back in. "I forgot about you. Again." She took a few deep breaths to calm herself. "Where have you been?"

The creature jumped down into the stall and dropped a large rodent at Askari's feet. It had a round grey body and a long narrow face, with two black and two white alternating stripes going from its nose to its ears. It had a fluffy tail and was quite dead, its insides spilling out all over the floor. Askari had never seen this type of animal before, but that was no surprise—it was likely a nighttime ground dweller that Polly had scrounged up while it was napping.

"I guess we'll cook then," she said, grinning at her new companion. Polly chattered and twittered for a moment, then disappeared back over the top of the stall.

Askari pulled the stall door open and stepped out into the main part of the barn. She had been pretty tired when she arrived, so it was almost like seeing it for the first time. The roof was surprisingly well-sealed, and there were only a few places where the rain leaked in. The side door hung off its hinges, so Askari headed over that way—it looked like a good place to light a fire.

She poked around for a bit. Just outside one door was a heap of stones, probably used in some kind of wall that was no longer there. After brushing away a layer of dust from an area on the cement floor, Askari dragged several of the stones in to make a barrier for the fire. Dried, dead leaves had piled up inside along the walls, likely put there by the wind and aided by the open doors. Those would be great fire starters.

In the far end of the barn was an extra room. Askari glanced in and noticed an old refrigerator. She tugged on the handle, but it was stuck shut. She was disappointed—she had always wanted to look in one. She headed back with an armload of dried logs and began to build a fire. In no time, she had little wisps of flame licking up from a pile of dead leaves. Then she skinned the rodent Polly had caught, stripped the meat, and began to cook it. Polly scampered down the stairs and plopped down by the fire; she stared at the meat while drooling and licking her lips.

When it was finally cooked through, Askari took a bite. It tasted odd, she decided. It was richer than she was used to, with a slight tang of... something. Polly didn't have any issues whatsoever—she gobbled hers down as fast as she could. Askari tossed the remaining innards into the meadow.

When she had finished eating, she cleaned her knife and small plate, then packed everything neatly away.

"As soon as it stops raining," Askari said, "we'll head out. I'd love to sleep here all night, but it's not safe to stay in one place for too long." She decided it would be a good time to doze, so using her backpack as a pillow, Askari lay down next to the fire and drifted off to sleep.

She was awakened by a loud screech.

"Polly?" she asked, sitting straight upright. The sound had come from inside the rotting barn door. Askari leaped to her feet and stared at two soaking wet figures trying desperately to close the large door that hung precariously from its hinges. They had pushed it partway shut and were bracing it with wooden boards that had been lying on the floor nearby.

"Help me!" one of the people exclaimed, bending down to lift another log, while the other strained to keep the door shut.

"Shujaa?" Askari asked, stunned. "Harcos?" A surge of excitement rushed through her—she wasn't alone!—followed immediately by a rush of fear. Had they been kicked out of the Baratok? Sent on a fool's errand like her? What had they done? Why were they here?

"Will you just help us?" Harcos yelled.

Askari ran forward and helped Shujaa lift the beam. They leaned it up against the door, which held it shut. Harcos let go and ran to drag another piece of wood across the door.

"What's going on?" Askari asked.

"It's a pok," Shujaa said breathlessly, reaching for another plank of wood. "And it's not far behind us."

Askari rushed over to the stalls and began to yank on the doors, hoping the rusty hinges would come loose. Harcos came to help, and few moments later, they had a large pile of wood and boards braced across the door.

"What's in this place?" Harcos demanded, surveying the room frantically.

"It's an old run-down barn," Askari responded. "There's a lot of dead wood, machines, an old refrigerator, a cot..."

Harcos shook his head. "I need to look around."

He started in the main part of the barn, opening and peering in each stall. Shujaa followed him down the aisle between the stalls, looking in the ones on the opposite side.

"Just trash," she said. "Some papers, an old hose, a rusted gardening implement of some sort…"

"Same kind of stuff over here," Harcos said.

He made his way back toward Askari, who was standing near the farm machines. "This is a tractor, I think," he said, pointing at one of the larger ones. "And that's a lawn mower."

"What's a lawn mower for?" Askari asked.

"Cutting grass short," Harcos replied.

Askari frowned. "Why on earth would you want to do that?"

Harcos shrugged. "I don't know. Bugs? Fewer hiding places for gargs?"

He headed into the downstairs room with Shujaa close on his heels. Shujaa brushed past him and began to open the old cupboards.

"Hey, what's that?" Harcos asked, pointing at some old cans stacked neatly in the far cupboard.

Shujaa squinted and read slowly, "Paint… insecticide… kerosene…"

"Grab that," Harcos said and then turned to Askari.

"Is there an upstairs?"

"Yes, but are you going to tell me what you're doing here?" Askari asked, frowning at her friend.

"After we deal with the pok." Harcos exited the room and peered around the corner before taking the steps two at a time.

"I don't see any pok," Askari muttered.

"It was chasing us," Shujaa said, brushing past Askari and heading up the stairs. "They don't like water, and we crossed the river, but it will catch up soon enough."

Askari followed the two of them up the stairs.

"Hay!" Harcos exclaimed. "Brilliant!"

"Why? Askari asked. "It's dead, and so old it's probably not even good for feeding horses anymore."

"But it'll still burn," Harcos said, his voice filled with excitement. He grabbed a bale and threw it down the stairs. It burst apart, covering the floor and steps with a layer of musty, dried grass. A cloud of dust billowed. "Go spread it out," he said. "All over the floor. I'll keep throwing it downstairs."

Shujaa dashed down the stairs and began to kick the hay around the barn.

"I think there was an old broom in one of the stalls," Askari said. She strode across the barn and opened the stalls, one at a time. "Here it is!"

For the next few minutes, all were silent as they focused on their tasks. Harcos sent bale after bale of old, musty hay tumbling down the steps, and Shujaa and Askari hastily spread it across the floor.

Then Askari stopped. "Wait a second," she said. "What is this for?"

Shujaa frowned. "We're setting the barn on fire, obviously."

"Yes," Askari said, "but why? Poks aren't afraid of fire."

"But they still burn," Shujaa replied.

It was a trap. Somehow, Shujaa and Harcos planned to get the pok in the barn and then burn it down, with the pok still inside. It was dangerous and stupid—but then again, there weren't that many ways to kill a pok.

Askari swept the hay toward the door and studied the now barricaded opening. This was where they were going to let it in, most likely, which meant this was where they would have to start the fire, to prevent the pok from rushing out into the rain again. She heaped the hay up against the walls and around where the coals from her cooking fire still glowed.

Then she stepped toward the door and peered out into the rain through the gaps in the barricade. She gasped. Tentacles dripped down from the pok's face as it stared back at her. It was much taller than her, with spiky black fur and giant pincers.

An image flashed into her memory: *She was five, and it was so big. The feelers slithered and reached, searching for her. It was so close, and she knew she was going to die. "Help me, Mommy! Help!" she screamed.*

Askari shook her head to clear it of the memory. A pok had killed her mother. She had desperately tried to forget—forget the monster, forget her past, forget it all. But here she was, face to face with a pok, and with the memory.

"Aw, garg's brains," Askari muttered. Then she yelled as loudly as she could, "It's here!"

Polly burst in from the outside through the other door that was barely open, soaking wet and screeching to high heaven.

"What is that?" Harcos asked, horrified.

"That's Polly," Askari said, "and that's the pok!" She pointed toward the door.

Harcos sprinted down the stairs and grabbed the lighter fluid from Shujaa. He began to squirt it all over the hay.

"Okay, we have to get the pok in, and then exit through the back," Harcos said, "and then at least one of us has to run around and make it back to this entrance, so we can set the hay on fire. Got it?"

"Got it," Askari and Shujaa said simultaneously.

Askari glanced back toward the door and gasped. "It's gone!" she exclaimed.

"Just looking for openings," Harcos said. "Shujaa, was there anything else flammable? Oil or gas or something?"

Shujaa ran back into the room with the cupboards and began to empty the bottles onto the floor. "Found a bottle of motor oil!" she called, tossing it to Harcos.

Askari scrambled to gather up her backpack. Just because they were making a hasty escape didn't mean she could afford to leave her only resources behind. She turned around to see if Harcos needed any help, and then screamed. The pok was coming down the stairs.

"It got in upstairs!" she yelled. "Shujaa, hurry!"

The pok landed at the bottom of the stairs, now effectively preventing Shujaa from leaving the small room she was in.

"Over here!" Harcos yelled. "Over here!" He waved his arms, backing toward the exit, trying to attract the pok's attention. It wasn't working. The pok glared into the room where Shujaa was, making a strange and discomfiting clicking sound.

"Over here!" Askari joined Harcos' chorus. After all, weren't two meals better than one?

It still wasn't working. The pok was trying to get into the room, though it was too big for the door, but Askari had a feeling that if it was motivated enough, it could push through the rotting doorframe without too much trouble.

Askari slid her bow over her head and grabbed an arrow from her quiver. Without hesitation, she let the arrow fly, hitting the pok solidly in the tail. The pok screeched and spun around, locking its eyes on Askari.

"That's right!" Askari yelled. "I'm over here!"

It stomped forward, barely giving Askari time to take in its six thin, spindly legs and long narrow greyish-blue body. Two arms, each with massive pincers, reached out toward Askari. Its eyes were sunken into its head like strange yellow beads, and a mass of feelers hung down from where its nose should have been, rubbery and slimy, twisting and slithering in all directions. A tail like a scorpion's curled up and over the creature's body, poised to strike.

Askari let another arrow fly, missing the monster's face by a hair. She shot again, this time aiming for the monster's belly. She hit, but the arrow bounced off like the garg was made of metal.

"Garg's blood," Askari swore.

Polly appeared out of the darkness beneath the garg's belly and began running up and down and all over the monster, trying to attack. The monster seemed mildly distracted by her efforts, but as soon as its eyes locked on Askari again, it began to move forward, one step at a time. Askari could see Shujaa edging out of the room, staying close to the wall and being as quiet as she could.

Shujaa reached the door and tried to move some of the barricade. A piece of wood crashed to the floor. The pok spun around and locked its eyes on Shujaa.

"No!" Askari yelled, taking aim and shooting the pok again. Polly screeched and scrambled up and over the pok, landing on its face. She opened her mouth and took a big bite out of one of its eyes. The pok shrieked and tried to attack Polly with its face tentacles.

"Go, Shujaa!" Askari yelled. Shujaa rushed forward, trying to remove enough of the barricade that she could fit through. As she did, she kicked some of the coals of Askari's fire out into the hay, which immediately began to burn.

"Askari, come on!" Harcos was already at the other door, about to step out into the rain.

"Coming!" Askari said, walking backward, keeping her eyes fixed on the pok with one arrow notched in her bow.

She was almost to the door when Polly leaped off of the garg and sprinted toward Askari across the barn's wooden floor. The pok spun around and stared at Askari. Askari froze. On one hand, if she moved too fast, the pok would attack and she might not make it out alive. On the other hand, if she didn't move fast enough or waited too long, it might also nab her. The key was to let the fire get big enough that the pok couldn't escape upstairs or through the side door.

But Askari had thought too long. The garg took three long steps forward, looming over Askari. The feelers were crawling, slithering about in the air over Askari's head. Askari sank to the ground and began to crawl backward.

She felt like her five-year-old self, scrambling to get away, horribly aware of the fact that the monster was going to kill her this time, and her mother wasn't here to save her.

But she couldn't think of that now; she had to act. With one hand, she reached down and pulled the machete out of its sheath. She stabbed upward at the pok's belly. It shrieked and stumbled back, giving Askari enough room to scramble to her feet. She swung the machete toward its leg, slicing off the bottom part of one foot. It screeched and spit. Askari ducked, trying to remember if pok mucus was acidic or paralytic or something else awful that would immobilize her.

"Run, Askari!" Harcos yelled. "Run!"

Then the scorpion's tail swung up and over, straight at Askari. She threw herself to her right and landed hard on the wood floor of the barn. The spike on the tail thudded into the floor only inches away from her face. The pok yanked its tail back up and swung it down again; Askari rolled to her left, successfully avoiding the tail for a second time. On the pok's third attempt, Askari found herself lying on her back, staring up at the creature's tentacled mouth swirling and feeling the air above her. Slime dripped down onto her face, and if she hadn't been so busy trying to save herself, she might have gagged.

As fast as she could, she swiped across the pok's face with her machete, slicing through its feelers. It reeled back with an unholy howl that made Askari's bones shake as pieces of tentacle landed on the floor around her face and hands. But she didn't wait. She dragged herself to her feet and ran as fast as she could to the back of the barn, slipping through the door where Harcos and Shujaa stood waiting. The pok, still screaming, charged toward the door, but the opening was only a few feet wide, so it slammed into the wooden slats, unable to fit through.

"The fire's not big enough yet," Harcos whispered. "I'm going to go fan the flames." He ran around the side of the barn, and a moment later—Askari had no idea what he did—there was a loud roar and the barn was ablaze, the heat making the rain and water sizzle, smoke rolling into the sky above them. Inside the barn, the pok's shrieks and screams pierced the night, slicing through Askari's eardrums right down to her brain. Polly appeared in the crack of the door and scrambled up onto Askari's backpack.

"Let's go," Askari said as soon as Harcos reappeared.

They began to run, pausing only to glance at the blaze behind them.

"Burn!" Askari hissed. Then she turned and ran as fast as she could, away from the barn and into the forest with Harcos and Shujaa on her heels. Then, all at once, something knocked Askari to the ground; a boom rent the air. When she sat up and turned around, she saw the entire barn engulfed in flames with an enormous white pillar of smoke billowing over it. Harcos and Shujaa scrambled back to their feet.

"The machines," Harcos whispered. "They must have caught fire, been under pressure—something."

"Good riddance!" Askari yelled toward the fire, toward the pok. She knew it wasn't the same pok that had killed her mother—that one was long dead, killed by Askari's grandmother. At least, that was what Faro had told her. But the more dead poks, the better. She clenched her teeth, pushed down the strange flood of emotions that threatened to overwhelm her, and stomped off into the rainy evening followed closely by her friends.

CHAPTER 5: THE KOVER

As soon as they were clear of the barn and were sure the pok hadn't escaped to follow them through the woods, Askari turned to Harcos and Shujaa.

"What are you doing here?" she asked, wondering for the hundredth time if they had gotten kicked out like she did. She could understand Shujaa, maybe, for having gone out to pick juneberries, but what had Harcos done?

"We snuck out," Shujaa replied, shaking her head. "There was no call for what the elders did, sending you off on your own like that. At very least, they should have asked for volunteers to go with you. Surviving on your own in this world is extremely difficult, and the punishment was more than harsh—it was unjust."

"I heard everything they were saying," Harcos said. "I eavesdropped on the tent after you left. There was more than enough reason to allow you to stay—after all, you saved my life!"

"And probably mine too," Shujaa added.

"Plenty of Baratok have broken the rules," Harcos said, "but the elders give them latrine duty or whatever. Nothing you did actually ended up putting the community in more danger than they were before, and you saved some people in the process, like me and Shujaa. And Sasa."

"Kira wanted you sent off," Shujaa said. "The others argued against it They said it was an unnecessarily harsh punishment, but they didn't want to go against her."

"Why does everyone listen to her, anyway?" Askari asked, shaking her head. She didn't understand it. Kira was the grumpiest of the elders, always giving out the harshest punishments, always angering the others—but for whatever reason, they almost never opposed her.

"I don't know," Harcos replied, "but once we heard that, we decided you needed help, so we packed up some food and left."

"I think Vica knows," Shujaa said. "She was nearby when we raided the food wagon, but she didn't say anything."

"Aren't you worried they won't let you back?" Askari asked.

Shujaa shrugged. "They can if they want, but I think they might have a regular uprising on their hands if they tried."

"Here's the thing," Harcos said, crossing his arms defiantly. "You're right. Not about everything, but about some of it. A lot of it. The elders are so cautious that we can't make progress. We can't learn about the monsters. We can't make life easier on ourselves, or even think about settling down somewhere. They've decided that their way is the only way, and I'm not convinced. Remember that time one of the scouts thought they saw a ringat on a cliff three miles ahead?"

"Yeah," Askari replied, "and they made us go ten miles out and around, routing us through a massive storm."

"Everybody got sick," Shujaa added, shaking her head.

"If they had sent someone to go check it out—" Harcos said.

"—or to kill it," Askari interjected.

"—then we wouldn't have gone through the storm, and we wouldn't have gotten sick."

"There are dozens of examples like that," Shujaa said, shrugging.

Harcos nodded. "Basically, we've decided that if they kick us out, we'll find somewhere else to go. Or build our own community. But we didn't want you to die alone out here."

"I feel the same," Shujaa said, "and while the circumstances I came from were, well, less than ideal, I saw other ways of running a community, and I know for a fact that their way isn't the only way. Plus, I didn't want you to die. And three alone in the wilderness is much better than one."

Askari looked intently at Shujaa. She had been a child slave and escaped, traveling alone in the wilderness for weeks. She had only been nine at the time. Then the Baratok found her, removed her collar, and took her in as one of their own. Askari skipped forward, threw her arms around Shujaa, and then flung one arm out to drag Harcos into the hug. "You two are the best human beings I could imagine."

They walked almost all night, stopping once to eat a little. Shujaa fell asleep for a short time on a log, during which Askari kept watch and Harcos also tried to sleep. Polly watched with her, but curled up to sleep on Askari's backpack as soon as they were moving again. They hadn't talked much, but all agreed that they shouldn't stop for too long, on the off chance the pok hadn't actually died.

Askari shook her head—they were all starting to sound like the Baratok elders.

The sun rose the next morning, and soon all the remaining clouds from the storm had burned away. The rays felt warm where they poked through the canopy of trees, but the air was still cool enough to make Askari shiver in her wet, muddy clothes. Shujaa and Harcos were more awake and more cheerful now that the sun had come up.

"So who's your friend, then?" Harcos asked, reaching out to poke a finger at Polly, who was relaxing on Askari's backpack. She hissed at him and nipped at his finger.

"Hey now!" Harcos said, frowning.

"This is Polly," Askari said. "She saved me from some evil mushrooms yesterday, and now we're friends."

"What is she, though?" Harcos asked again. "Some kind of garg?"

Askari shrugged. "I don't know. A rodent I think. After all, all monsters are bad, right? And she saved me, so she clearly can't be bad, and thus, not a monster."

"Hmmm." Harcos leaned forward to take a closer look. "Your logic is... less than sound. She wasn't afraid of the pok. She attacked it, and it didn't even notice her. I've ever met a rodent that wasn't afraid of gargs." He reached out to pat her head, but pulled back as Polly hissed again. He held his hands up in surrender. "Fine," he said. "I'll leave you alone."

"Polly," Askari scolded, glancing over her shoulder at the creature. "These are my friends. Be nice."

Polly glared at them, then turned around huffily to face the opposite direction.

About half an hour later, they stumbled onto an old road. It was mostly overgrown, with bushes and plants growing out of the cracked and broken asphalt, but they could still see remnants of the white and yellow paint that indicated the center and edges of the road. The strangest part was that it was still full of cars—old-style wagons that ran with motors, used before the Cataclysm. They were mostly rusted, and many of the windows had been broken through. Trees grew out of the seat cushions.

The road was packed. Askari could imagine how it had been, everything moving swiftly and happily, until the monsters appeared out of the blue. Everyone must have run away—or died. Askari peered cautiously up and down the road, and then began to walk down one edge, keeping an ear out for sounds of monsters.

The Baratok tended to avoid roads. Elder Kira always said it was too easy for the largest monsters to move quickly on them. Askari thought it wouldn't hurt to try—so much open space would make things a lot easier for their wagons, too. This road, on the other hand, looked like it wouldn't be easy for anyone to move along, monster or human.

"This is so weird," Harcos murmured, "imagining all the people who were trying to go somewhere, and then couldn't. Just abandoned it and fled."

"I wonder what kind of garg chased them off." Askari looked in both directions, up and down the road. It was so packed with rusted metal and rubber wheels, she had trouble imagining a monster being able to make its way down the road even without all the trees that had grown in.

"Maybe it was a pack of something smaller," Shujaa suggested, "like the gyiks we saw on the Tuske. They could probably squeeze between the vehicles and jump through the windows to get at the people inside."

Askari stood, staring at the scene in front of her. She didn't often spend a lot of time thinking about how the world was before the gargs came, but it was unsettling to think of how many people had died, been eaten, had just given up. The world used to be, according to the elders, heavily populated. There were millions and billions of people—Askari couldn't even imagine how big that number was, let alone how many people that would be. Where would they all live? In buildings, presumably. She shook her head. It was incomprehensible.

"We should probably move," Harcos said. "Before something shows up to eat us."

"Of course, you're right," Askari said. "I was distracted, thinking about dead people. Before we go, though, now that it's light, I need to get my bearings. This road is the first landmark I've found that might actually help me figure out where we are."

"You're lost? Since when?" Harcos asked. "The barn was right on the way. This road heads straight into the village."

"Really?" Askari exclaimed. She pulled off her backpack, knocking a still-miffed Polly to the ground, and pulled the map out.

"There." Harcos pointed to a line that led northwards toward the village. "This is the road we're on now. It leads directly into town. If we head in this way, on the road or beside it, we should get to the village by midday."

"That's perfect," Askari said, returning the map to its pocket in the backpack. Polly immediately scrambled back up and resettled into her sleeping position. "I was hoping to arrive sometime today, so I guess getting chased by gambas didn't get me too far off track."

"Gambas?" Harcos asked incredulously. "Those are pretty rare."

"They weren't rare where I was. There were probably a hundred of them, all trying to eat me." Askari shook her head. "If not for Polly and a serendipitous lighting strike, I would be dead." She reached into her pocket and pulled out a piece of meat from the night before and fed it to Polly, who eagerly scarfed the treat down.

"So what exactly do the elders want you to find?" Shujaa asked. "Harcos made it sound all crazy and mysterious."

"There's a book that was supposedly left for them at some kind of message place," Askari said, "like those post offices that Elder Faro always talks about. He used to work at one or something? Anyway, I'm supposed to get the book and bring it back. It sounds like maybe they use these places to communicate with each other."

"Communicate with who, though?" Harcos asked.

"I don't know—other communities, maybe?" Askari suggested. "Friends from the old world?"

"So, does that mean someone from our community regularly makes this trip, then?" Shujaa asked.

Askari frowned. Did it?

"Maybe they only get it when it's convenient," Harcos suggested. "Like if they happen to be nearby."

"Which would mean they don't actually need the book." Annoyed at the thought, Askari began to flex her fingers, making fists and then releasing them.

"A test, then." Shujaa shook her head. "They wanted to see if you could survive. Ridiculous."

Askari could feel some of her exhaustion fading and relief taking its place. Her muscles loosened, and the pain from her scratches and bruises was less noticeable. It was so good to not be alone any longer. And it felt good to complain.

They continued to walk, chatting about the community, Askari's mission, and whether or not Askari deserved to be sent away. Harcos tried to be friendly with Polly, but she hissed, glared, and clung tightly to Askari's backpack.

"So you really don't know what she is?" Harcos asked, pulling his hands quickly away.

"I don't," Askari said. "But she's friendly, and apparently loyal."

"I want to be friends with her, so I can study her. How did you get her to come to you?"

"I didn't. Well, not exactly." Askari shrugged. "She was fighting a gamba, and I threw a rock and killed it. Then she showed up a few hours later to return the favor, except she saved me from a hundred gambas, not one."

"It's amazing," Harcos said, shaking his head.

"She saved my life." Askari smiled over her shoulder at the creature sitting on her backpack. "And she fed me last night, too. Even if she does end up being a monster, I think I'll risk it."

A moment later the road took a steep turn to the left and down, but was completely blocked. In front of them lay two cars, one upside down with another on top of it. Two more cars had veered off to either side, colliding with trees. The vehicles were smashed, their headlights broken, and doors ripped open. The mess completely blocked the road.

"This must be what stopped traffic," Harcos said, gesturing toward the old, rusted four-car pile-up.

"I wonder what caused it," Shujaa said. She moved closer to the vehicles littering the road, bending down to peer underneath and through the windows.

"A garg?" Askari suggested.

Past the accident, a village spread out below them, house after house filling up a large verdant valley. Trees and plants had grown up between the houses, their trunks and branches pushing through walls and collapsing roofs. Old metal vehicles sat along the sides of the road, rusty shells of their former selves, still parked where they had been left so many decades ago.

"This is it!" Askari exclaimed.

They moved forward, carefully navigating past the crushed vehicles, and gazed down into the valley ahead of them. It was quiet; there was no movement visible except for the wind lightly brushing against the trees and grass.

"So, the stuff they taught us for checking out abandoned buildings doesn't really work here," Harcos said, pausing at the top of the hill and surveying the houses below. "Even if there are monsters in this village, there are hundreds of places for them to hide. I don't think patrolling the perimeter is going to make much of a difference, and there's no way we can check inside every building to see if something is hiding."

"We probably shouldn't walk in on this road, though," Shujaa pointed out. "We might get ambushed."

"Yeah, let's try to sneak out and around through the woods," Askari agreed, "and maybe surprise anything that is waiting to surprise us."

They turned into the trees, ducking under low-hanging bushes and trying to avoid thorny brambles that threatened to trip them. Polly leaped off of Askari's pack and scurried up into a tree, disappearing in the thick canopy.

"Where'd she go?" Harcos asked in a whisper.

"Doing her own scouting, I'd imagine," Askari whispered back.

They fell into a single file line, with Askari at the front, Harcos in the middle, and Shujaa at the back. Moving as silently as possible, they made their way around to the opposite side of the village. As they walked, they stumbled across two more roads leading out of the town, but those were also overgrown with weeds and trees.

"I don't see anything," Harcos whispered after a half hour of trekking, "or hear anything either."

"Don't know how you could with all the noise you're making," Shujaa muttered.

"I weigh more than you!" Harcos protested.

"Hush," Askari interjected, stopping to look at them. "I think we should sneak down into the town now. We haven't seen any signs of gargs yet, and this is about as random a spot as any. Keep your eyes open and listen for anything that sounds like danger."

Shujaa and Harcos both nodded as Askari turned left and began to make her way down the hill leading into the valley. Askari could see a short distance ahead of them; houses on either side of the road led toward the center of town.

The first building they came to was a small house, painted blue, with a sagging front porch and what looked like a tree growing up through the center of it. The front door hung from its hinges and its windows had been completely smashed in. The front porch steps were rotted out, and the floors inside were spotted with dark holes, rotted through. Askari felt her interest pique. She was curious to see what kinds of things the people from the before time owned—maybe they had a refrigerator. They hadn't often been allowed to explore inside houses when they ventured nearby with the Baratok, and she knew this was her chance.

Thus far, she hadn't seen any signs of monsters—no excrement, no slime, no large holes in any of the buildings that couldn't be explained by age alone, so she gestured to the others to follow her to the next house.

"Wait," Shujaa said, pointing to something ahead of them in the street. "What are those?"

Askari frowned. A series of three boards ran end to end from one side of the street to the other, almost like a bridge—except that there was nothing underneath it. She frowned. It looked deliberate.

"I don't know," she said.

"Me either," Harcos replied, "but it can't hurt us."

"No," Askari replied, "but it might be indicative of something that can."

With one more glance at the strange bridge, she turned into a large yard with a gate along the perimeter. It was only one story and had a ground-level porch. Askari pushed on the gate. It opened with a loud creak. Shujaa and Harcos froze, and Askari craned her neck to see if anything was coming to eat them. They stood for a moment, and then Askari pushed it open the rest of the way and stepped through.

The front door, red with three tiny windows at the top, lay flat. Askari stepped over it and gazed at the room. A moldy carpet covered the floor, complete with grass growing on it; an over-turned blue couch with a floral print took up most of the room; a tall, stately clock stood regally in one corner, made of dark red wood with shiny gold panels on the inside sparkling through the dirty glass.

Askari moved further into the house, examining the ceiling and poking around corners, checking for monsters. She paused next to the fireplace—photos sat on the mantel covered in dust. One showed a laughing baby, her face covered in some kind of food. The next photo was of a happy couple sitting on a swing—the woman was pregnant. A third photo showed the woman in a beautiful white dress, standing next to the man in a black suit. They stood beside two other couples, both of them older, and all smiling happily.

"Hey, in here," Shujaa whispered from the other room.

Askari turned her attention toward the kitchen, where Shujaa stood pointing at a small metal box. "What do you think this did?" she asked quietly.

Askari reached out and pulled on a handle. A door opened. There were buttons on one side with numbers and some words.

"What does it say?" Askari asked.

"Popcorn," Shujaa read slowly. "Kitchen timer. Defrost."

Askari shook her head. "I don't know," she said. "Some kind of cooking thing, I would imagine. There's a stove there, and a refrigerator." She moved over to the fridge and pulled open the door, gagging as the putrid smell assaulted her nose. Inside was mostly covered in mold, but there were still some bottles that sat, untouched. "What does it say?" Askari asked, covering her nose and blinking as her eyes watered.

"That reeks!" Shujaa exclaimed, pinching her nostrils shut. She leaned forward and squinted at the bottles. "I think that says... ket... chup? Ketchup? Like to catch up? I don't know what that one is. The next one says mustard. Mustard is a plant—we collect the seeds for flavoring food. The other bottles say Italian dressing, strawberry jam—we make that sometimes! —and milk."

"Harcos, do you know what ketchup is?" Askari asked, turning to see where he had gone off to.

He poked his head around the corner. "I think it's some kind of sauce made out of tomatoes. Elder Dano sometimes mumbles about it during dinner."

"Huh." Askari took one last look in the fridge and then shut the door. She would have to check out some other refrigerators to see if other people had different things in them. How strange it was to see how the old world lived. They had so many things, but she thought it must be especially nice to open a box and just have food there, without having to hunt and skin and cook it. Looking in a refrigerator hadn't lessened her curiosity in the slightest—if anything, it had increased it.

They made their way through the house, opening doors and peering into the different rooms. The house had two bedrooms, though both mattresses were rotted through, and a tree had rooted itself in one; a bathroom with a toilet, sink, and shower; and another room which Askari thought was probably for thinking or something—it had a short table and a chair, and there were papers spread all over everything.

When Askari finished exploring the house, she came back out to the living room to find Harcos staring at the wall.

"What are you looking at?" Askari asked.

"What do you think this is?" Harcos asked, gesturing to a black square that appeared to be attached to the wall, with a long tail hooked into the wall near the floor.

Askari shrugged. "A box?"

"But why is it on the wall?" Harcos asked. "It must be for looking at, but it's just black—why would you look at it?"

"Maybe it does something," Shujaa suggested. "If you had electricity or something, you could turn it on."

Harcos nodded thoughtfully. "I'll have to ask one of the elders when we get back."

"So, what's our game plan?" Askari asked, turning to look out the front window of the house. The road they had come in on was still quiet. "We need to make sure the village is safe to wander around in, but our first priority is to find the book. Elder Faro told me to look for a building marked by a blue sign with a white bird head on it, sometimes with a red line."

"Did he tell you if there were words?" Shujaa asked.

"No. I can't read," Askari reminded her. "Do you want to see the map? Maybe it says there." She pulled off her backpack, slid the map out, and handed it to Shujaa. Harcos leaned forward and peered at the map over Shujaa's shoulder.

"Post Office," he read.

"Yeah, that's what he called it," Askari said.

"Where do you see that?" Shujaa demanded.

He pointed to the map.

"Oh, okay," she replied. "Well, I think we can find that, especially if it has a sign."

"In terms of a game plan," Harcos said, "we'd probably find the place faster if we split up. That said, I think it's safer if we stick together, at least for now. We should poke into some other houses too, to see if there is anything we can salvage, though it's unlikely. Most of these houses have probably already been looted, and if all of them have broken windows and broken-down doors, then I doubt there will be much left untouched by weather."

"We can find a place to camp for the night too," Shujaa added. "If the village ends up being monster-free, we could have a roof over our heads."

"Then let's walk into the center of town," Askari said decisively. "We can start there. To be on the safe side though—" Askari pulled her bow from across her back and notched an arrow, kicking herself for not doing this much, much sooner. One of these days, she was going to forget something really important, and wake up inside the belly of a giant garg. It was a good thing Elol wasn't here. They would all be on latrine duty for a week (or three).

Shujaa pulled out two knives, and Harcos, a machete he wore strapped to his waist.

"Good call," he said, grinning. "Elders would string us up if they knew we hadn't been on the ready this whole time."

"It'll be our secret," Askari said, winking.

They stepped out of the house and started to walk down the street. All of the homes in this area were similar, most one-story, some with or without a basement, painted various shades of white, brown, and blue. After passing a few, Askari began to notice the doors. They were all a little different— some were red or black or wooden; some had windows while others didn't; some had glass doors in front of the wooden door; even the doorknobs varied. Askari wondered if the door said something about the person who lived in the house. Maybe a brightly colored door meant that the person who lived there had a bright personality, or a black door meant the person was more reserved.

Then Askari wondered if she would ever have a door—if the community would ever find a way to settle in among the monsters, or if they would be on the run forever. Staying in one place might get boring, she thought, but at the same time, it would probably be easier.

"There are more," Shujaa said quietly, pointing down the road.

Askari frowned. Again, a row of boards led from one side of the road to the other—like a bridge over nothing. "Strange," she said.

"Look," Harcos exclaimed, drawing her attention away from the strange boards. "Sorry," he said, dropping his voice to a whisper. "But look! A library!"

"Where?" Shujaa asked.

To their left was a tall building that was similar to the houses. There was a large, unbroken window on the front with letters across it, and a door with both a ramp and a staircase leading up to it.

"It says 'library'!" Harcos had a huge grin. "Can we go inside?"

"Sure," Askari said, shrugging. They hadn't seen any signs of monsters, and it certainly wouldn't hurt. "What's a library?"

"A place with books," Shujaa replied.

Harcos jogged up to the front door and jiggled the handle. "It's locked," he said sadly.

"We could break the window," Askari suggested.

"No!" Shujaa and Harcos said in unison. They looked at each other and laughed.

"Why not?" Askari frowned. It wasn't like anyone lived here or owned this stuff. Who would care?

"Because if we damage the window, we leave the books open to weather," Harcos said. "They would be ruined after only a few months. We can't take them all with us now, but there's a wealth of information in there. We don't want to ruin that. We might need it one day."

"Why don't we look around back for a different entrance?" Shujaa suggested.

"Good idea!" Harcos turned and headed around the side of the building. "Found another door!" he called.

Askari followed Shujaa toward the door, and then stopped short. A beautiful painting covered the side of the building. It was of an ocean or a lake, but you could see below the water's surface. There were all kinds of interesting-looking fish, some with pink spikes and others that just looked like orange blobs. On top of the water, birds floated, and some kind of fire-breathing garg flew in the sky. There were mountains in the background. The paint had started to chip and peel, but Askari still thought it was amazing.

"Do you think those fish are monsters?" Askari asked.

Harcos paused and stared at the painting for a minute. "I don't think so. See these ones down here? I think they were painted by little kids. See how the lines are kind of jagged and awkward? Looks like it was painted by a bunch of different people, kids mostly, well before the gargs came."

Askari nodded, and then turned to follow Harcos and Shujaa inside the building. Some of their community members carved wood or painted with flower dyes, but the thought that a whole group of people might make art together was something she would have to ponder.

It was pretty dark in the hallway they entered, but when they moved into the front room with the big windows, more than enough light allowed them to see. A big desk stretched down one wall with strange metal and plastic boxes on it. A large table surrounded by comfortable chairs took up some space near the desk. The rest of the room was mostly filled with shelves, and on the shelves were thousands of books.

Shujaa's face lit up. "Books," she whispered, eyes wide, a smile stretching across her face. "They're so beautiful!"

"You guys can—" Askari began, but was interrupted by a shrieking sound coming from the back of the library. The three of them turned to face the sound.

A small ball of fur exploded into the room, and Askari relaxed a little.

"Polly!" she exclaimed. "You about scared me to death!"

Polly scrambled up onto Askari's backpack, reached her hand around Askari's face, and covered her mouth.

"Mmph!" Askari tried to pull Polly's hand away from her face.

"I think she's telling you to be quiet." Shujaa dropped her voice to a whisper.

Polly let go of Askari's face and began to make frantic gestures toward a door on the other side of the room. Moving silently across the carpeted floor, Askari pulled open the door, machete in hand. It was dark, but she could see enough to tell that a set of stairs led upward.

Testing each tread carefully, Askari began to ascend. At the top of the stairs, she stepped out into a huge room that was the same size as all the rooms downstairs combined. Chairs filled the center of the hardwood floor, all facing a large dais. On the wall over the dais hung a painting of a great eye, staring out into the room.

"Creepy," Askari whispered, her voice echoing. To her left, tables lined the wall. They were covered with all kinds of strange things—a crown, some pamphlets, a robe, a goblet. Swords hung on the walls above them.

"Whoa," Harcos whispered from the top of the stairs. "What is this?" He walked slowly forward, leaving footprints in the layer of dust that covered the floor.

"Looks like a museum," Shujaa said. She pointed to a sign on the wall. "It is. And a meeting place, apparently."

"Lamplighters Society," he muttered under his breath. "I've never heard of them." He peered at the crown and then picked up one of the pamphlets, stuffing it into his pocket.

Polly leaped off Askari's backpack and scampered toward a tall window that overlooked the town, then paused, gesturing for Askari to follow. Askari strode over with Shujaa and Harcos at her heels. Polly climbed up on the windowsill.

Askari peered out the window, promptly gasped, and then clapped her own hand over her mouth.

It was the biggest garg she had ever seen—dozens of feet long, covered with spiny needles, leaving a trail of slime in its wake.

No one spoke, but they all knew what it was: a kover. Reminiscent of a massive slug, the creature was whispered about so it wouldn't give children nightmares. It was slow but deadly. Its slime contained a paralytic agent that caused anyone who touched it with their bare skin to be paralyzed.

The slime-coated needles that ran down its back could shoot out, hitting anything within a fifty-foot radius. A kover would consume any living thing that crossed its path, if not now, then later. It was known to retrace its steps, hoping to find victims that had been unwittingly trapped by its slime. This type of garg was impossible to kill—they said that even if you chopped it into pieces, each one of those pieces would simply grow into another.

They stayed silent. Kovers were all but blind, but their hearing rivaled none. They would move slowly toward their prey forever, until they eventually caught and consumed it. The three warriors would have to wait until it was far enough away that they could easily run before they spoke, and even then, they would have to keep moving to stay ahead of it. Accomplishing their mission and getting out of town had just become infinitely more difficult.

Time slowly passed. Askari stared at the kover, hardly daring to breathe as it crawled across the ground past the library. Every few feet it would pause its forward trajectory and put its head up in the air, turning it, listening. Then, it would once again begin to move, head forward, dragging its massive bulk behind it, the trail of slime glistening in the sun.

Askari glanced at Shujaa, belatedly wondering if the kover could hear her eyeballs move. Shujaa stood frozen, staring at the garg with an expression of fear and awe. One of her fingers twitched. It occurred to Askari that she didn't know what gargs Shujaa had seen as a slave before joining the Baratok. She had only been nine when the Baratok found her, and they had happily taken her in, as their lifestyle made having children particularly difficult.

Harcos was as still as anyone could be, his face impassive. But Askari knew his mind was working, thinking, planning. They would need a way to get out of this, and he would have something to say about it—once they could talk again.

Polly sat on the windowsill in front of Shujaa, both hands up on the glass, staring at the kover while sitting completely still, as if she couldn't tear her eyes away. It was good this little creature was so clever, Askari thought, or else they might all be dead right about now.

Glancing back out the window, Askari held back a sigh. It hardly looked as if the kover had moved at all. They were going to be here for a while.

They stood completely still for over an hour before Harcos finally turned and whispered so quietly Askari almost couldn't hear him: "My legs are tired."

"We should go," Shujaa agreed in a hushed voice. "We need to find the post office, get whatever was left there, and leave as quickly as possible."

"I had an idea while we were waiting," Harcos said. "We're in a library! We should see if we can find a map of this town that will show us where the post office is. That way we can head directly there, and then get out of town as fast as we can."

"Great idea," Shujaa said, turning toward the exit. Polly ran past her and disappeared down the stairs.

Askari followed, glancing over her shoulder in time to see Harcos snatch up a couple more pamphlets from the table and stuff them into his pocket.

"What are you looking at?" he asked innocently.

"Nothing," Askari replied, and followed Shujaa into the main part of the library.

Since she couldn't read, Askari kept watch out the front door while Harcos and Shujaa searched the library for maps.

"Found them!" Shujaa said just a little too loudly, immediately clapping her hand over her mouth.

Harcos carried one to the front desk and laid it out.

"We're here," he said, pointing to a building on the map. "The post office is over there. Four streets west, two streets north."

"We're in luck, then," Askari said. "It looks like the kover went the other way."

Harcos folded up the map and stuffed it into Shujaa's backpack. He then removed his own backpack and pulled out a small glass bottle. Before Askari could ask what it was for, Polly appeared from the darkness and scampered up onto Askari's backpack.

"There you are," Askari whispered. She reached out, flipped the lock on the front door, and then pushed it open as slowly and quietly as she could. The door squeaked a little, which made everyone freeze and cringe, but they hustled through. Askari pulled it closed it behind them.

"Uh oh," Harcos said, gesturing at the street in front of them.

Askari stepped forward and then halted. The kover had gone all the way around the library in a large circle, leaving a wide trail of slime and creating a trap for anyone who tried to leave.

"We're wearing shoes," Askari said. "It should be fine."

"What if there's a tiny hole in your shoe?" Harcos asked. "Or what if you step in it, then take your shoes off later and accidentally touch the slime? Or kick one of us? Or—"

"Okay, okay, I get it," Askari said, sighing. "What do you want to do? We might be able to jump it."

"Maybe you could," Harcos countered. "But the slime river is at least fifteen feet across! I couldn't do it."

"Me either," Shujaa said.

"Then we make a bridge," Askari suggested.

Shujaa's eyes lit up. "Like the ones we saw earlier—made out of boards!"

That explained it. Someone else had been here and had tried to avoid the trails of slime left behind the kover. She hoped the slime lost its potency as it dried; otherwise, there was little hope of them escaping unscathed.

"Good idea," Harcos exclaimed. "What do we use?"

Askari looked around. There was a cement sidewalk around the library with trees growing out of it. Otherwise, it was all plants.

"We could check inside," she suggested.

"Whatever we do, we should do it quickly," Shujaa said. "Let's just make noise and then run. It's going to hear us one way or another."

"In that case..." Askari strode over to the side of the library and tugged at a piece of siding that had begun to come lose. She yanked as hard as she could, and the nails screeched as they slid out. Harcos came over to help, and a few minutes later they had made enough noise to wake the dead, not to mention let every monster within several miles around them know where they were—but they had enough boards.

They laid the first board down, and then Harcos walked carefully and slowly over it and laid down another, covering the second half of the slime river. Then, Askari and Shujaa followed, being sure to keep their balance. Tripping and falling could mean the end, not just for one of them, but for them all.

"Where do you think it went?" Shujaa was moving slowly across the slime river because she kept looking up and around, as if worried that it would return.

"It's slow," Askari reassured her. "We'll be able to run if it shows up again."

Once they had safely crossed, Harcos turned and slid the bottle and a spoon from his pocket, bent down, and began scooping the slime into the bottle, careful not to touch it or get it on the outside.

"I want to study it," he muttered as both Shujaa and Askari shook their heads, and then turned to keep watch while he finished. When he finally slipped the bottle into his pack, they headed downtown, keeping their eyes peeled for the kover or signs of any other gargs.

"What do you think it eats?" Askari asked. "People can't come here that often, can they?"

"Probably a lot of deer and rodents," Shujaa said.

"But the Baratok sent you here for a reason," Harcos added. "It's entirely possible other communities send messengers here who get eaten. We shouldn't assume this garg mostly eats animals. It might very well be quite experienced at human hunting."

They moved through the streets trying to be quiet, but knowing it was impossible to be completely silent. Askari wondered if it could hear their hearts beating or their blood rushing through their veins—or their brains, thinking. Could it predict where they would go or what they would do? She shook her head to clear away the thoughts. She needed to be focused on their environment, not worrying about what a garg might or might not do.

The houses in this section of town were much bigger than where they had been exploring before. They had large wraparound porches, and a couple even had towers. One house was in the shape of an octagon, which Harcos found particularly interesting. They didn't stop to look, however, until they arrived at the center of town, only one block away from the post office. A big green lawn spread out in front of them.

Askari frowned.

"How come this isn't overgrown?" she asked, squinting. The grass was a dull green surrounded by a nice black fence. In the center of the green, a tall lamp post rose up, lit.

"It's lit," Shujaa added. "The lamp."

"Amazing," Harcos said, shaking his head. "The grass is fake." He bent down and tugged on it, and a square piece pulled up. "And if I were to guess, I'd say the lamp post is solar powered and still has a working battery."

"But it's been decades," Askari argued. "Shouldn't it have broken by now? Or shouldn't wind or rain or something have knocked it over or damaged the bulb?"

Harcos shrugged. "Maybe someone keeps fixing it."

"It's all very interesting," Shujaa interrupted, "but we really should keep moving."

"You're right," Askari said. She gave the fake grass one more suspicious glare, then turned and followed the others toward the post office.

The sign was faded, almost to the point of being illegible. In fact, if Shujaa hadn't pointed out the word "POST" painted in big, bold letters, Askari might not have even noticed the logo of the bird painted next to it. It was chipped and faded, and since Askari couldn't read, she might have walked by it a dozen times before ever stopping to look inside.

A bell dinged as Harcos opened the door.

"Great," Shujaa muttered. "We might as send up smoke signals—hey kover, we're over here!"

"Let's hurry," Askari said.

"What were your instructions?" Harcos asked.

Askari reviewed the room. One wall was covered with squares, each labeled with what she thought were numbers. The main part of the floor was empty, but there were countertops along the window. At the far end, two large windows looked into the back of the shop.

"I think that's where people would sit and help you," Harcos said, pointing to the windows. "And they stored the mail back there."

"What are you talking about?" Askari asked.

"A post office," Harcos replied. "People used them to send mail. Like letters and presents and things?"

"Oh," Askari said. "I never would have thought to do something like that."

"People lived far away from their family and friends back in the old days," Harcos said. "They couldn't always see each other, so the post office allowed them to communicate."

"I thought they could like, talk magically on a... a..." Askari frowned, wracking her brain. "Phone?"

"Yeah," Harcos said. "But sometimes they wrote stuff down and sent it, or if they wanted to send gifts, they used the post office too."

Askari knew that forty years wasn't that long—after all, Elder Timo claimed she was over seventy years old. But it seemed like such a different world—unimaginable to her.

"Faro told me that if there were any messages, I would find them by..." Askari closed her eyes and ran through the lines she had memorized. "Enter the building and turn right, then walk along the counter to the very end. Open the door leading into the back, and you will see a basket on the floor, just inside. Any messages will be in the basket."

She opened her eyes. Shujaa had already began to walk toward the door. She tugged on the handle.

"It's stuck," she said.

"Are you sure it's not locked?" Harcos asked.

"I can't tell."

Askari followed them. She and Harcos each took a turn pulling on the handle. Polly decided at that moment to leap off Askari's backpack. She pulled herself up onto the counter and ducked through an opening in the window.

"Do you see the basket?" Askari asked, leaning as close to the glass as she could to see if Polly had found anything.

A moment later, a scraping sound came from the door, and then it opened a tiny crack. Harcos reached out and pushed it open the rest of the way.

"You're a good garg," he said, leaning down and handing her something he had pulled from his pocket. She grabbed it immediately and gobbled it down.

"What was that?" Askari asked, frowning.

"Just a treat, never you mind," Harcos said. He stepped through the door and looked around, and then gestured for the other two to follow him.

Sure enough, on the floor beside the door was a white basket. There was one thing in it. Askari reached down and picked it up. It was a kind of book, but it looked homemade, not like the books the Baratok owned which she had been told were made by machines. The pages were made of paper but stitched together. The leather cover had a drawing of a nagy. It was rough, and Askari thought it could've used a few more details, but it was a nagy nonetheless. There were also words on the cover.

"What does it say?" she asked, handing it to Shujaa.

"Monsters of the New World, Book One," Shujaa read, "by Doctor Minda Byrd."

"Who is Minda Byrd?" Askari asked.

Shujaa didn't respond; instead, she opened the book to the first page. Askari peered over her shoulder and saw a sketch of a gamba.

"I got attacked by a whole legion of those," Askari said.

"It says here they have regions they live in, and while they're solitary hunters, they will come together if they fear a significant threat," Shujaa read.

"I can't wait to read this!" Harcos exclaimed, eyes alight with curiosity. "But we probably shouldn't right now."

"You're right," Shujaa said. She closed the book and turned to Askari. "Turn around. This is your job, so you hang on to the book."

Askari let Shujaa pack the book safely away, and then turned back to the front of the post office. "Let's get going."

At that moment, Polly scrambled up onto Askari's backpack and placed her hand over Askari's mouth again.

"Uh oh," Harcos whispered.

They watched through the windows as the kover slowly came into view, tilting its head around, listening.

"It heard the bell," Shujaa whispered.

"And it can hear us now," Askari said. "Is there a back door?"

"Let's look," Harcos said.

They moved into the darkened back room, and Harcos found a door without too much trouble. Sure enough, as he opened it, a trail of slime greeted them, this time within inches of the building.

"We need another bridge!" Shujaa exclaimed.

Askari hadn't taken much time to poke around, but it didn't look like there was much that could be useful. Most of the room was empty except for large shelving units that took up a lot of the floor area. There were packages ready to be mailed out on the far end, and a few letters that had never been sent, in addition to baskets and some generic supplies she didn't recognize.

"Could we make shoes out of the baskets?" Askari asked. "There are plenty of them lying around."

"That might work as a bridge too," Shujaa pointed out. "We could step in one and then lay the next."

"It might take too long, though," Askari pointed out, "at least if the kover is anywhere near us. And we'd need a lot to get all the way across."

"Bridge, bridge, bridge," Harcos muttered to himself, walking around the room looking up, down, and generally craning his neck in every direction. Then, he stopped.

"I've got it!" he exclaimed.

"What?" Askari and Shujaa asked in unison.

"Cardboard!"

"Good idea!" Shujaa exclaimed, just as Askari asked, "What's cardboard?"

Shujaa and Harcos both ran over to the shelf covered in unsent packages. Shujaa grabbed one and ripped it open. Little white pieces of—something—fell all over the floor as she dumped out its contents. "Clothes," she said. "Should we take any of this stuff?"

"If we can fit it, yeah," Harcos said ripping open another box. "Might as well. There's some kind of bag with a zipper in here too. Let's stuff that full. I'll carry it."

"You take the stuff," Shujaa ordered Askari, "and put it in that bag. We'll make the bridge."

"What's cardboard?" Askari asked again.

Shujaa held out the stiff brown papery material that the packages had been wrapped in. "It deteriorates pretty quickly in the rain, but it'll last forever in here," she said.

"What about slime?" Askari asked with a worried expression. "We don't want it deteriorating while we're standing on it."

"It should hold up long enough for us to cross over," Shujaa answered.

"How do you know all this?" Askari pressed.

Shujaa sent her a quick glare and then went back to ripping boxes open. "I just do."

By the time they decided they had enough cardboard, Askari had loaded up the zippered bag with clothes, vitamins, pain killers, a couple of books, a hammer and measuring tape alongside a pair of work gloves, three toy dolls, a huge puffy winter coat, a case of forty-two bars of soap, tissues, several tubes of chapstick, some journals and photographs, two solar-powered flashlights (if they worked, they would be extremely valuable), a card game, a pair of shoes, socks, rope, and hand sanitizer. They discarded a box full of something called DVDs, which even Harcos didn't know what they were for, a pile of magazines that were all the same (though Harcos did grab one copy for later perusal), a battery-operated clock (with no batteries), a bunch of wire things they didn't recognize, some flat metal equipment, mountains of papers, and a large stuffed toy duck, which they all wished they could take with them, but since it was about the size of Shujaa, it didn't seem prudent to carry on a mission through the woods.

"Let's go," Harcos said, gathering up the stack of cardboard he had been building. Polly was playing in the packing materials, little white things about the size of peanuts that now covered the entire floor. Some of them were sticking to her fur and hiding in her ears.

"Wait." Askari held up her hands. "What's our plan? We need to find out where the kover is first—it doesn't make sense to run out there and put the cardboard down, only to have it crawl by and leave another layer of slime down again."

Harcos nodded. "Good point. Let's open the door and see where it is. Then, hopefully we can toss down the cardboard, run across, and get out of here as fast as we possibly can, all while the kover is on the other side of the building."

"Yeah," Shujaa said. "I'm not sure we have a lot of other options. Unless something decides to make a racket on the other side of town."

"I'll open the door a crack," Harcos volunteered, "and see where the kover is, if it's back there at all."

"We'll wait behind you with the cardboard," Askari said. "Hey, is this stuff thick enough for armor?"

"No," Shujaa replied. "The kover quills would cut right through it."

They walked over to the door, each carrying their burdens. Polly scampered along the ground behind them, apparently unconcerned about the danger that lurked outside. Askari wondered if she had forgotten, or if the packing materials were just that much fun.

Harcos pulled the door open a crack and peered out.

"Seems okay," he said in a whisper, "but let me check both ways."

He pulled the door open as Polly scooted under his feet to peer out the door. Carefully, he leaned out and looked first to the right, then to the left.

"*Duck!*" he exclaimed, yanking his head back inside. He pushed the door closed, almost crushing Polly. Askari bent down and pulled the little animal back through, and Harcos slammed the door as a series of *whumps!* hit the outside of the building.

Polly whimpered.

"What was that?" Shujaa asked.

"It shot at us!" Harcos replied, his eyes wide. "I thought for sure I was going to get hit."

"Do you feel anything?" Shujaa asked, examining his head from all angles, and then checking his arms, legs, and torso. "Any missing sensations, pain, anything?

"No," Harcos replied.

Polly whimpered again.

"Oh no!" Askari exclaimed, kneeling to check the animal. "She got hit!"

"What?" Shujaa and Harcos bent down to look at Polly, who was now squirming all over the ground, trying to yank a quill out of her face.

"Gloves!" Askari exclaimed, and began to dig through the bag of stuff they had collected from the packages. A moment later she pulled out heavy leather gloves. She put them on and then said, "Polly, be still!" The creature froze as Askari reached out and plucked the quill from her nose.

Harcos quickly materialized another bottle and held it out to Askari. She dropped the quill into it.

"Why don't you keep wearing those gloves?" he said. "Don't touch any of us with them. Maybe grab me a few more quills from the door when the kover is out of range?"

"How will we know?" Shujaa asked.

"Well, I've been timing it since we saw it at the front of the post office," Harcos said. "It took it twenty minutes to circle the building. That means in about five minutes we should be good to go out, and we'll have ten minutes or less to cross the slime and get out of sight, as quietly as possible of course."

"Okay, we can do that," Askari said, nodding. "But we're not wasting time with quills."

"Just one or two?" Harcos begged. "While Shujaa and I lay the bridge?"

"Just do it," Shujaa sighed. "We don't need all three of us for that. I'll take the bag of stuff though, so you can carry Polly."

"Okay," Askari replied, nodding. "Fine."

Harcos counted another three minutes, and pulled the door slowly open, carefully avoiding the quills. He peered in both directions.

"Clear," he whispered, and pulled the door open the rest of the way.

Askari didn't waste any time. She yanked five quills from the door where they had punctured surprisingly deep, and passed off the bottle to Harcos as he finished laying the cardboard. Then she handed the bag to Shujaa and picked up Polly, who was still pawing at her nose.

They made their way across the cardboard bridge and into the road, and began to jog as quickly as they could through the town.

"We have to watch out for other trails of slime," Harcos whispered to them. "There's no telling how many circuits the kover has made around this building."

Sure enough, one street over, the slime filled the road in front of them. Harcos ripped three boards off a nearby house and made another bridge across the slime. Then they began to jog again.

They encountered four more trails of slime, and Askari began to notice a pattern of sticks, branches, boards, and stones all placed randomly in streets and on grass throughout the town that matched the two bridges of boards they had seen earlier in the day. They passed three locations where quills were embedded in the walls of buildings or that had shattered the windows of houses. Other people had been here, and other people had encountered the kover. Askari wondered how many of them had died.

Then she began to worry about Polly. What if she died from the slime? What if she couldn't eat or move ever again once it started to take affect? She scratched Polly behind the ears and tried to focus on escaping. Then, without warning, Polly sat up and leaped out of Askari's arms.

"Polly!" Askari cried.

"Hush!" Shujaa scolded. "Polly will be fine."

"Did the quills not hurt her?" Harcos asked, looking intently at Askari. "She doesn't seem paralyzed."

"No," Askari said. "She scratched her nose the whole time. I thought it would only take a minute."

"She's so small though," Harcos said, frowning. "I assumed it would be instantaneous."

"Well, it wasn't," Askari snapped, "and now she's gone."

"She'll find us again," Shujaa said, "but we have to go. Now."

Askari nodded and followed the two of them the rest of the way through the village, toward the road where they had come in. They passed the library and then the two houses they had explored. Nothing looked like it had changed, and even the slime trail had dried so it was almost invisible. Askari shivered. How many things had they walked by that had remnants of slime on them? How many times had they almost died? There was no way to know.

Then they heard a loud crashing sound and a roar coming from the opposite direction.

"It must be Polly," Harcos said, "creating a distraction. Let's hope she makes it back to us. In the meantime, we'll make the most of it by hurrying up!"

He picked up the pace, rushing through the last street and out to where the road was covered with brambles.

All at once, he came to an abrupt halt.

"Oh."

"Oh what?" Askari said, catching up to him. Then she too came to a halt. In front of them loomed a creature Askari thought she would never see again: the pok. Its tentacles were charred and still smoking from the fire, and one of its legs dangled where Askari had cut it off. Its eyes flamed an angry red, and it hissed and spit at them.

"I guess we can't go that way," Harcos muttered. He turned on his heel and sprinted back into town.

CHAPTER 6: THE HULLA

LIGHT, FLUFFY CLOUDS floated in the bright blue sky while the sun's rays highlighted the perfect emerald green of the oak leaves. A light breeze gently ruffled the branches, making the leaves ripple and the trees sway. But Askari didn't notice any of it. All she could think about were her feet. They hurt. A lot. The raw rubbing on her right pinky toe, the dull throbbing in her bones, the strange tingling feeling in her heels—not to mention the way her whole body ached each time her feet slammed against the ground. She couldn't remember ever having run this fast in her life.

The houses around her flew by in a blur as she gasped for air, lungs burning; she began to count the tall wooden poles whooshing past—twenty-two, twenty-three, twenty-four... she wasn't sure how much longer she could run at this pace, and as soon as she paused, even for a second, the pok would be on her and she would be dead. She had no idea where Harcos and Shujaa had gone, but she was acutely aware of where the pok was: behind her. Right behind her. A hair's breath away. If she hadn't chopped off one of its legs at their last encounter, it would have caught her by now.

All the while, she was fighting back memories. *"Help me, Mommy!"* she could hear her child-self scream. *Tentacles curled and prodded, feeling the air around her face, and then her mother dashed forward, throwing herself between Askari and the pok...* but no! She couldn't think about that now. She had to focus on the end goal—to save herself.

The houses flew by. She thought weaving between the buildings would make it harder for the pok, but it skittered up and over them and back down the other side. She was beginning to feel helpless. She had been the fastest runner in the Baratok, other than Zaj, and one of the only ones who could have even hoped to survive for a few minutes, but she couldn't keep this up. She needed a diversion—something to distract the pok long enough for her to hide.

Then she heard shouting.

"Over here!" someone yelled. "Hurry!"

It was a woman's voice, but definitely not Shujaa's. Someone else. A stranger. It didn't matter though—it wasn't as though Askari had a lot of choices. She took a sharp right and ran toward the voice. The pok, surprised, ran past Askari, but it didn't take long for it to change direction. But by then, Askari was pounding up the steps of an old boarded-up house, gasping for breath as the door slammed shut behind her. She heard about twelve locks slide into place as she collapsed to the floor.

"I've never seen anyone run that fast," the voice said.

Askari looked up, blinking as the air swirled in front of her eyes. As her vision cleared, she saw a wizened old woman staring down at her. The woman's greying hair was cropped close to her head, and her skin was a couple of shades darker than Askari's. She wore a loosely-fitted tan shirt and blue pants.

Askari tried to respond but could only cough, and instead focused on taking deep breaths to help calm her racing heart. Her lungs burned, and the world spun around her, slowly settling until the floor no longer moved. She reached up to wipe the sweat from her neck.

"Would you like some water?" the woman asked.

Askari nodded, slowly dragging herself to her feet. They were in a sort of entryway to the house; a set of stairs led up on her left. To the right was a large room with one boarded-up window and shelves on every wall, all crammed with books. A chair sat in the middle beside a table with a box of candles, a notebook, and a pen on it.

The woman led her further into the house, to a room where she had set up a makeshift kitchen. There was a table and a refrigerator that appeared to be running—Askari felt a surge of excitement at having a chance to peek into a working one. A painting hung on the wall where the window would have been, had it not been securely boarded up with multiple layers of boards. There was even a rug on the ground, though it could have used a good cleaning.

Askari's eyes widened as the woman turned on the sink. It worked! Water gushed out into a cup.

"Is it safe?" Askari asked haltingly as the woman held out a cup.

"Yes," she replied. "I drink it every day—I'm not dead yet." She took a sip to demonstrate, while staring at Askari over the lip of the glass with eyebrows raised, and then handed the glass to Askari, who downed it as quickly as she could.

"Slow down," the woman said, crossing her arms, "or you'll give yourself a stomachache."

A scrabbling noise came from where the window should have been. Askari turned abruptly.

"It's the pok," the woman said, "searching for a way in. It won't find one, don't worry."

"Who are you?" Askari asked, turning her attention back to her host. She had never heard of anyone living and surviving completely on their own. Either there was a group nearby that Askari was unaware of, or this was one tough lady.

"I would like to know the same thing about you," the woman responded, raising an eyebrow. "Unfortunately, we don't have much time, with a pok crawling all over the house trying to get in. For now, you can call me Minda. And you are—"

"Askari."

"—Askari, good. Baratok?"

"Yes." Askari was surprised. How had she known? There wasn't time for questions, however—Minda jumped right into planning.

"Fine. Now, in order to deal with the pok, we need to create a diversion. I want you to follow me."

Askari couldn't tell how old Minda was, but she figured the woman was probably at least sixty, similar in age to the Baratok elders. But Minda didn't seem to give two beans about her age. She quickly left the kitchen and headed toward the stairs, taking them two at time. Several of the treads appeared to have been repaired, but Askari still followed as quickly as she could, hoping she didn't fall through. Once on the landing, Minda led Askari to a door that opened to another set of stairs. These had also been repaired and appeared to lead to an attic. A bit of light shone through cracks in the roof, but otherwise, it was completely dark.

"What are we doing?"

"I told you," Minda said, "creating a diversion."

She pulled out flashlight—a working one!—and aimed it into the darkness of the attic.

In the center of the room hung an enormous grey—thing—with a cross engraved in it. It was a little more than half as tall as Askari, and was suspended from a chain attached to the beam running down the center of the house.

"What is it?" Askari asked, stepping closer to peer at it.

"A bell I dragged over from the church," Minda replied.

"What are we doing with it?"

"Creating a diversion." Minda glared at Askari for a moment. "Don't you listen?"

She stepped forward and yanked on the bell pull. The clapper clanged against the sides of the old tarnished instrument. Askari clapped her hands over her ears—the sound reverberated in her head, making her eyeballs rattle and teeth clench. The sound slowly dissipated, but Askari still felt like her brain matter had turned to jelly.

Minda yanked on the bell pull and it clanged again, the sound deafening in the small space. Then she turned and led Askari back down the stairs and onto the landing.

"Sorry about that," Minda said when the door was shut behind them. "I forgot to warn you."

Askari could still feel her brain sloshing around in her head. Minda led her back down the stairs—again, two at a time—to the main part of the house. Askari shifted her backpack around, thinking about taking it off, but if she needed to move quickly, it was better that she had it with her.

"Now," Minda said, "we need to get out of here." She pointed to the front door. "There's a peephole. Go see if the kover is in sight yet. I'm going to get my things."

Askari strolled over and put her eye close to the small glass circle. She could see the grasses outside, the houses across the street, and some old broken-down vehicles parked nearby.

"I don't see—" she began, and then leaped back away from the door with a shriek, tripping and falling to the floor. The pok had appeared on the porch, magnified by the peephole. Minda laughed as Askari pulled herself up from the ground. The pok began to pound against the front door, its spiked tail thudding into the solid wood.

"It was just the pok," Askari said with a scowl, dusting herself off.

"I figured. The kover will be here any minute, though," Minda said. She had attached a long knife to her belt and now wore a small backpack. "We should go."

Askari nodded.

Minda strode back toward the kitchen, but stopped about halfway there and pulled open another door. This one revealed another set of stairs, this time leading down. Minda didn't pause, but called over her shoulder, "Close the door behind you."

Askari glanced one more time at the kitchen—the refrigerator was only a few steps away—and then shook her head. It wasn't important. There was a pok after them, for garg's sake. She pulled the door shut behind her. As soon as they were plunged into darkness, Askari heard a clicking noise and suddenly the staircase was ablaze with light.

"Light?" Askari breathed. She skipped the rest of the way down the stairs. A bulb hung from the ceiling, glowing a warm orange light. "How?"

"It's called solar power," Minda said, "but we can't talk about that right now. I'm going to show you a tunnel, and once we're in it, we can't talk. We don't want to distract the kover, and as I'm sure you know, they can hear even the smallest sound."

Askari nodded, looking around the basement room. It was bare, cold, and dirty, but there were a few surprising decorations. The paintings had clearly been brought in from elsewhere. One was of a family with two children, a mom, a dad, and a dog—big, white, and fluffy. Another almost looked like a child's drawing done in colored crayon of a house and a river and a family of stick figures. Askari stared at it. She felt like she had seen it before—but no, she thought. She was probably mixing it up with one of the Baratok kids' drawings.

The rest of the room was about what she would have expected—strange metal machines that she didn't recognize that connected to the house with pipes and wires, a cement floor covered with dirt, and a few wooden chairs stacked in one corner. Boxes upon boxes were heaped on the floor and against the walls.

"What is all this stuff?" Askari asked.

"I've been scavenging," Minda replied, striding across the room to an old rickety door that had been reinforced with boards and nails. She undid a series of locks and pulled it open to reveal a dark gaping hole. Then, she clicked on her flashlight to reveal a low, narrow tunnel.

"Hit the white switch on the wall," Minda whispered as she entered the tunnel, "and close the door behind you."

Askari reached out and smacked the switch with the palm of her hand, but nothing happened.

"You have to push it up," Minda whispered, gesturing with her hand.

The room behind them went dark as soon as Askari flipped the switch, so that only the light of the flashlight illuminated the tunnel.

"What is this place?" Askari asked in a whisper.

"There used to be a bar in that basement," Minda replied, glancing over her shoulder at Askari. "The tunnel was used during Prohibition. But that was a long time ago and not relevant at the moment."

"What's Prohibition?" Askari asked.

Minda aimed the flashlight in her face. Askari blinked.

"Clearly the Baratok education these days is less than stellar." Minda shook her head and turned back around. The tunnel was quite dusty. "It doesn't matter. What did I say about talking?"

Askari fell silent and followed Minda, her shoulders stooped, the walls of the tunnel feeling like they were about to cave in on her any minute, though she could see places where someone—Minda, most likely—had reinforced the beams with tree branches and nails. Periodically they came across the skeleton of a rat or some other small rodent, and Minda would kick it out of the way. Spiderwebs hung down from the ceiling; Minda batted at them as they moved through.

Askari felt her mind wander. Where were Shujaa and Harcos? What if the pok had abandoned the house and went after them? What if they had stumbled across the kover in their desperate attempt to escape the pok and were now dead? And where was Polly? She had run off when the pok appeared, disappearing into a tree. Askari knew Polly could fend for herself, but she still felt nervous—after all, Polly had been injured. Plus, wasn't Polly her responsibility now?

The tunnel felt like it went on forever, and Askari began to breathe more heavily, nervous that they would never get out of this small, cramped space. She tried to remind herself that to leave, all she had to do was turn around and go back—but it was dark back there, and she couldn't see where they had come from. So she followed, one step at a time.

Finally, Minda stopped. She reached overhead and pulled on a string which released a set of stairs that sank down to the floor. A small amount of light filtered down through the opening above. Slowly, carefully, Minda climbed up. The stairs creaked once and Askari realized suddenly that this might be the most dangerous part of their trip. What if the kover heard them and was close? They could be dead in minutes, depending on where this tunnel had taken them.

Askari eyed the opening. She thought she could jump and grab the edges—or she could if she weren't wearing a backpack. It didn't matter—she would take the stairs as carefully as she could, following Minda's example.

When Minda reached the top, Askari followed, skipping the steps Minda had skipped and treading as lightly as possible. She made it squeak twice, but when she looked up, Minda nodded with approval.

They stood in a small shack, its windows boarded up similarly to the way the house had been. Only a little light leaked through the cracks in the wall and roof. It was filled with cans of what Askari assumed was paint and some old machines she didn't recognize. Askari strode over to the door and peered through the peephole that someone—Minda, probably—had installed here. All she could see was a house and some trees. No monsters, no people, no Polly.

Minda slid back the locks holding the door in place and opened the door slowly. Askari silently begged it not to creak. It didn't, and Askari followed Minda out, blinking in the sunshine. They were in a neighborhood, surrounded by other houses, and the shed appeared to be in the backyard of another old boarded-up home. They didn't go in this house though, as Askari assumed they would; instead, Minda led her around one side and out into the street. She checked in both directions, and began to walk confidently past the rotting porches and rusty swing sets, stepping over the cracks in the pavement and the little excitable trees that desperately tried to root themselves in the road.

Askari wanted to ask what they were doing, what the plan was, but she didn't dare speak, not out here in the open—not when they didn't know where the kover was.

A couple blocks down, Minda turned first right, then left, the right again. Askari listened intently, trying to pick up any sound that might indicate where Shujaa and Harcos were. Where would they go once they realized the pok was chasing Askari? Would they go to the library? The post office? Would they try to come up with a plan to save her? Or would they decide not to risk themselves, and head out of town as quickly as possible?

She didn't know. She wouldn't blame them if they had left, though it would be rough to be alone again. It was nice having friends around, not to mention people who could read.

I should learn to read, Askari thought. *If we make it out of this, I'll ask Shujaa to start teaching me.*

Minda stopped, holding up a hand. She tilted her head, listening. Askari heard it too—a rustling of leaves. It could be anything, or it could be—

Askari gasped as something landed right on her head, scrambling to grab at her hair.

"Polly!" she exclaimed in a loud whisper. "Shhhh!"

Minda had her knife out in a flash, pointed at Polly's neck.

"No, no!" Askari hissed, trying not to shout. "She's a friend! A friend!"

Minda lowered her weapon and scowled at Polly.

Polly scurried down Askari's arm and wrapped her arms around Askari's neck. Her fur was prickly and uncomfortable, but Askari got the distinct impression that Polly was scared.

"It's okay," she whispered, scratching the creature's head. "What's wrong?"

Polly pointed up at the sky.

Askari and Minda looked up at the same time. Above them, a flock of creatures hovered almost silently.

"Hulla," Minda breathed. "It's like they can see the garg-ridden future or something." Garg-eating monsters of the sky, hulla came and waited when they knew death was imminent. They fed on monster carrion—and human too, when they could find it—and thrived on death and destruction. Their wings had feathers as sharp as knives, and their talons could rip the head off a nagy. But the most disturbing thing about them was their faces—human faces, skin so thin you could see their bones, and eyes that would make the bravest person shudder.

A shriek pierced the air, coming from the opposite direction of the hulla.

"The pok," Minda said, turning toward Askari. "It sensed the kover. We must keep moving."

"Why don't you get in my pack?" Askari whispered to Polly. "It'll be fine. We just have to find Shujaa and Harcos."

Polly pointed to their left, jabbing her finger in the direction they had come from. She chirped.

"Are they that way?" Askari asked.

Polly nodded.

"That's a smart minket," Minda said, nodding with approval. "Let's go." She turned and strode in the direction Polly had indicated, scanning the buildings around them and keeping one eye on the sky in case the hulla decided to make a move.

"A minket?" Askari whispered, glancing back at Polly, who had crawled inside the pack. Her head and enormous ears were sticking out of the top. Askari hadn't heard of a minket before. She would have to ask Minda for more information when they were safe.

After a short distance, Polly chirped again, this time pointing to their right. Minda turned toward an old, rusted vehicle, long, narrow, and painted bright yellow, though the paint was now chipped and peeling.

"A school bus," Minda said, seemingly pleased. "Solid exterior, multiple exits, easy to see. Smart." Minda stepped forward and pulled open a door at one end. Harcos and Shujaa sat crouched in the front seats, staring at Minda, their blades at the ready.

"Come on," Minda said. "We have to get out of here."

"Who are you?" Harcos asked.

"We'll explain later," Askari said. She turned and began to survey the town around them, watching for any signs of monster activity. For the moment, everything was quiet, but Askari knew that wouldn't last long.

Harcos and Shujaa scrambled out of the bus dragging their backpacks—Harcos had even somehow managed to hold on to the bag of things they had scavenged from the post office.

"Where are we—" Harcos started to ask, but then ducked as a hulla dove down from the sky, passing over them in a great gust of wind.

"Back inside, back inside!" Minda exclaimed, shoving Harcos back up the stairs into the school bus. A moment later, the rest of the flock of hulla dove down, screaming at the top of their lungs. It was the strangest noise—human, but like a dozen people all screaming with sore throats at the same time, pitifully, painfully. Askari barely had enough time to pull the school bus door shut behind her before one of them scraped its claws across the bus's roof.

"Quiet!" Minda said, ducking down so she couldn't be seen through the windows. Polly scurried to the back of the bus and peered out, clicking and chattering.

"What does she want?" Minda hissed.

"She wants us to look, I think," Askari whispered. On her hands and knees, she crawled down the bus aisle between the seats and peered out the back window. It was dirty and rather hard to see through—but then she saw it, the kover, sliding toward the house Askari and Minda had just vacated.

Askari turned and looked at the others. "It's the kover. It's here."

"Garg's blood," Harcos whispered.

"What about the pok?" Shujaa asked.

"Wait," Minda said, hushing them again.

Askari turned her attention back out the window, trying to breathe as quietly as possible.

The kover moved painfully slowly, though she supposed it wasn't all that surprising. It probably weighed as much as ten other gargs combined, and it had to drag all of that weight across the ground. But just because it wasn't fast didn't mean it wasn't deadly. It was methodical, careful, powerful.

Then Askari gasped. From nowhere, the pok appeared, launching itself through the air and landing on the back of the kover. The kover roared, a low rumbling, spitting sound, a noise Askari hadn't heard before. The pok reared back its head and then drove its tail spike into the kover's flesh. The kover roared again, releasing a stream of quills from its back, several of which embedded in the pok's belly and face. The pok screamed and bent down to take a mouthful from the kover, its tentacles slithering and crawling all over the kover's slimy skin.

A distant part of Askari's mind noted that while the pok seemed enormous when looming over her, now, compared to the kover, it looked small. It could easily run up and down the kover's back, and the pok's tail spike barely even registered when it drove down into the kover's flesh.

"We should go now, while they're distracted." Minda had appeared behind Askari and was watching the fight with curiosity. Askari frowned a little—this had been Minda's plan? To get the pok to fight the kover? It was risky, and the elders would have been totally against it. After all, pitting monsters against each other was a sure way to get yourself killed; it was a strategy the elders highly discouraged.

Shujaa still sat huddled in the front, staring at the sky, jaw clenched tightly with a worried—or possibly determined—scowl on her face. Harcos was fixated on the fight, eyes wide with horror and awe.

"I've never seen anything like it before," he whispered.

"Get your bags." Minda pushed past Harcos toward the front door. She jumped down the steps, landed in a measured stance, and began to jog down the street away from the fight.

"Go, go!" Askari commanded, pushing Harcos toward the door and reaching out to help Shujaa stand. They stumbled out of the bus in a pile; Minda was already a good distance down the street. She turned and looked over her shoulder, waving at them to hurry up.

Shujaa began to run first. Harcos followed in her footsteps, still clutching the bag of scavenged items. Askari bent down so Polly could more easily climb up onto the top of her backpack, and glanced one more time at the monster battle taking place a short distance behind her. The hulla hovered overhead, their eerie human faces cackling and shrieking, gleefully watching the battle between the kover and the pok. The pok had scrambled off the kover's back and was running in circles around it, periodically reaching out with its pincers to slice or stab at the soft fleshy sides of the bigger garg. Askari couldn't tell which was winning—though, in the end, the hulla would ultimately come out ahead.

Askari shook her head. This was one battle where she didn't care who won, as long as she was long gone when it was over. So, she ran, one foot in front of the other, one step at a time, her backpack bouncing and sweat dripping down her face. She glanced back one more time before she turned a corner, only to see a hulla staring right at her. It smiled.

Askari felt goosebumps ripple down her arms and neck. She swallowed, then turned her attention back to running. Hulla were the most unsettling of gargs, there was no doubt about that. But right now, she just needed to run.

Minda halted on the edge of the village, breathing heavily. Harcos collapsed against a tree, and Shujaa bent over with her hands on her knees to breathe more easily. Askari took a few deep breaths, coughed once, and then turned toward Minda.

"What's the plan?" she asked, heart still racing.

"I'm going to lead you far enough away from town that you don't have to worry about the kover or the pok or the hulla," Minda said between breaths. "But then you're on your own. You can go back to wherever it is you came from."

"Who are you, anyway?" Harcos asked, looking up from his spot on the ground. Sweat dripped down his face, and his hands were covered in dirt.

"Minda," she replied.

Shujaa frowned. "As in Minda Byrd? Doctor Minda Byrd? From the book?"

Minda sighed. "Yes, from the book. Now if you've all caught your breath, we should get moving."

Askari had not made the connection earlier, but it made sense. Minda Byrd, the person who drew the pictures of monsters, put them in books, and left them for people to find, was living in the town where the books were supposed to be. She must know a lot about the monsters if she spent all her time drawing them and writing down how they lived, what they ate, and how to kill or avoid them.

"Doctor Minda Byrd?" Harcos repeated, a huge smile building on his face. "I might have some questions for you, if you don't mind."

"We need to get going," Minda pressed. "Later."

"Of course, of course." Harcos offered his water bottle all around, and after everyone had taken a drink, they started moving through the forest, this time at a much slower, more reasonable pace. The woods were silent—all normal activity of squirrels, birds, and other forest dwellers had been suspended, likely due to the battle that was raging a few miles behind them. Periodically they heard a screech or a rumble, or they saw a hulla rise high above the trees for a moment before diving back down. Hulla were known to try to interfere in monster fights if they thought they could guarantee a meal—Askari figured that was probably what was happening.

They broke through the thick undergrowth onto a trail and the going became much easier. Minda was leading them away from the city, north. It wasn't exactly the direction they needed to be going in, but if Askari was visualizing the map in her head correctly, they were walking parallel to the river, which ended at an enormous lake. That would make for a good place to camp and regroup; then they could head south again toward where the Baratok community should be.

"Stop," Minda said suddenly. She looked up, craning her neck in all directions. Askari looked up too, while Shujaa and Harcos turned back-to-back and focused on the forest around them. They all stood as still as possible and listened.

Something dropped through the trees ahead of them, crashing and grunting the whole way. Askari readied her bow, notching an arrow and scanning the trees. A hulla appeared, its face that of a young woman, but with gaunt features, skin stretched across its bones. It fluffed its feathers and then turned its attention to the humans.

"Don't shoot," it said.

Askari gasped, and Shujaa let out a little muffled shriek. They could talk?

Minda scowled at the creature. "Git!" she exclaimed, making a shooing motion with her hands.

The hulla leaned in and stared at Shujaa, then Harcos; it winked at Minda, and finally turned its attention toward Askari. It stared into her eyes, and Askari felt trapped, as if she were hypnotized, as if she couldn't move from that spot.

"Going sssssso soon?" it asked.

"Git!" Minda said again.

The hulla tilted its head, staring at Askari. "I know you," it said.

"Go away!" Minda exclaimed. She stepped forward, waving her long knife at the creature.

The hulla jerked slightly, shifting its attention toward Minda. It smiled.

"I guess we owe you one now," it said, its grin widening.

Minda scowled at the creature, who immediately turned its attention back to Askari.

"Thank you for dinner, Assssskari," the hulla hissed. It let out a cackling shriek and leaped into the air, disappearing through the canopy.

For a few moments, no one moved or spoke.

Finally, Minda took a deep breath. "I hate them. I really hate them. But we need to move. We have several more miles to go before dark."

And once again, they began to walk.

CHAPTER 7: THE FULEK

ASKARI WAS RELIEVED when, just after the sun set, Minda led them into a clearing with a house in the center. She wasn't sure she could walk much longer without falling over with exhaustion. She was hungry, tired, sweaty—all she wanted to do was sit down for a few minutes. But Minda hadn't let them rest once during the hike through the woods, no matter how difficult the terrain had gotten.

It was clear the area had been taken care of recently—the lawn clipped, the house painted. The windows were boarded up and the fence in disrepair, but it was much nicer than any house Askari had seen in a long time, including the one Minda lived in.

"What is this place?" Harcos asked.

"It's a safe haven for wanderers," Minda replied. "We have a few tricks to keep the gargs away. We take turns maintaining it."

"Who does?" Harcos asked, staring intently at Minda.

She shrugged. "Lamplighters, who else?"

Harcos fell silent, a frown settling across his features.

"It smells odd," Shujaa commented.

It did, Askari had to agree. It had a woody and resinous smell but with a sweet scent built in, like rotten caramel or burnt molasses. A sickly flowery smell might describe it, like when one of the Baratok kids made a perfume out of rose hips, and then it went bad.

Minda led them up old front steps onto a wraparound porch. Boards were nailed over the downstairs windows, and Askari could see signs of repair everywhere—replaced boards on the steps and porch, a solid tree trunk holding up a sagging part of the porch roof, fresh paint of different colors splashed across the walls. Rocking chairs sat along the porch in various locations, facing the lawn and forest. Flowers dotted the hillside and white clouds floated in the deepening purple sky of twilight.

"It's gorgeous here." Shujaa craned her neck, looking in all directions.

"Yes," was all Minda said as she picked up a flower pot and removed a key from beneath it. She unlocked the front door and led them inside.

Askari glanced over her shoulder at Polly. She had woken up and now looked around curiously at the house. Before Askari stepped over the threshold, Polly leaped off her backpack and vanished into the tall grass.

The floor of the front room was solid hardwood, and clean too, as if someone had recently swept it. Large area rugs added color to the living room on their right, which was filled with soft-looking chairs and couches. Paintings hung from the walls, and a neat pile of wood sat next to a fireplace.

"Can't gargs get in that?" Harcos asked, pointing at the chimney.

"It's grated," Minda replied, her tone implying she didn't appreciate him second-guessing the house's safety. She strode into the kitchen and tossed her bag onto the table. "What've you lot got for food?"

Shujaa began to unload her provisions onto the table. "Bread, pemmican, dehydrated beans, dried apples, wild carrots, some herbs..."

Askari stopped listening and started exploring again. Past the living room, a set of stairs with several repaired treads led to the second floor. She cautiously ascended and peered into the rooms. She counted seven bedrooms, each with one or two beds, blankets, and extra clothes. The windows were boarded up like the ones downstairs, but curtains hung over them. As she stepped into each room, a light flickered on. Her eyes widened—cables ran out the windows. They must somehow be solar powered.

"I need to learn how to make those," Harcos said, coming into the room behind her and pulling the door closed soundlessly.

Askari turned to look, first at him, then at the door. "Why did you close the door?"

He dropped his voice to a whisper. "We need to talk."

"About what?"

"Minda."

"What about her?" Askari frowned. "She seems like a decent person. She saved my life, and yours too, technically."

"But who is she?"

Askari glared at him. "Does it matter?" Askari thought that by now it would be pretty clear to Harcos that Minda wasn't a slaver or a cannibal, or she would have tried to eat or capture them already. She was simply a person who had been kind enough to help them out of a tight spot.

"First of all, she lives alone," Harcos began ticking his suspicions off on his fingers. "Second, she lives alone and is still alive. Third, she knows a lot about gargs—and writes books? In the world we live in? Ridiculous. She also mentioned the Lamplighters as if she were one of them, and she knows how to make electric lights from solar power."

"None of these things make her particularly dangerous," Askari argued. "Just strong. Innovative. Smart. Plus, who are the Lamplighters and why do you care?"

"Remember that weird room upstairs in the library?" Harcos asked. "That was the meeting place of the Lamplighters Society. All I know about them is what's in the pamphlets I grabbed." He pulled it out of his pocket and began to read aloud: "The Lamplighters, where scientists come to learn. Look no further for the perfect opportunity to meet, network with, and learn from professional and amateur scientists alike. Attend weekly lectures, cocktail parties, and debates. Partner with other Lamplighters on projects and research—anything from hydroponics to engineering to the

Land of Szornyek. There's no better place to learn that from each other!"

"That doesn't sound so bad." Askari raised her eyebrows and crossed her arms. "Besides, what does it have to do with anything? That pamphlet is decades old."

"She knew who they were!"

"So what?" Askari was starting to get annoyed. She got it—people could be dangerous. But weren't they all kind of in it together? They were all fighting gargs, all trying to stay alive in a world filled with gigantic human-eating monsters— why was Harcos being so suspicious all of a sudden?

"Why, though?"

"She's old." Askari shrugged. "Old people remember stuff about the old world that we don't. That's probably all it is."

"But I'm not talking about the old world," Harcos said, shaking his head. "I'm talking about now. The Lamplighters, according to her, are maintaining this house. That means that this old-world organization is current—still operating. Who are they? And why have we never heard of them?"

Askari frowned at her friend. She didn't know who they were and she didn't really care. "Look," she said. "Minda saved us. She didn't eat us or sell us to slavers. She's one of the good guys. Now, I'm not sure what you're trying to say, but—"

"I'm just saying that she might have saved your life," Harcos interrupted, "but that doesn't mean we can trust her. That's all."

Askari raised her eyebrows and gestured toward the door. "You left her alone with Shujaa, though, so you can't be too worried."

Harcos gave her a brief glare, and then spun around and strode out of the room. Askari rolled her eyes and followed, taking the stairs two at time.

Shujaa and Minda were unloading the food they had in their bags onto a large table in the kitchen.

"All I've got is stale bread rolls and a bag of pemmican." Askari pulled her bag off and began to rummage through it. "I was going to try to hunt yesterday or today."

"I've got stale bread, too," Harcos said. "And jerky."

"I have some vegetables and there are some seasonings here—I propose we make a soup." Minda looked at Shujaa.

"I have some fresh herbs too," Shujaa said, nodding. "Soup would be easy and good. Is the water here safe?"

"Yes," Minda replied. "We test it regularly."

She and Shujaa began to putter around the kitchen, pulling out dishes and ingredients, while Askari helped Harcos set a fire in the fireplace. In no time, a warm blaze lit up the room that was now mostly dark, and a pot of soup bubbled over the flames. Askari's stomach was grumbling—she hadn't had a hot meal in ages. It might have only been a few days since she had left the Baratok, but it felt like weeks.

"What's your plan?" Minda asked, stirring the soup. She tasted a little with a spoon, and then added a little more salt into the pot.

Askari shrugged, leaning back in a chair and staring at the flames. "We have the book and now we have to get back to the Baratok."

"I should be able to calculate where they will be compared to where we left them, based on how fast they travel," Harcos said. "We just have to figure out the best spot to cross the river."

"I can help with that," Minda said. "I recommend you go a little farther north before heading west. There is a ford right before Sea Monster Lake. It should take you most of the day to get there."

"Is there a sea monster?" Harcos asked.

Minda gave him a hard look. "Of course there is. What do you think it is, the '70s? It's a capa—big, beautiful, and loves human jerky, though it mostly eats weeds. I recommend bypassing the lake, though, and camping near the ford. Avoid the sea monster—that's your best bet."

"That's always our best bet," Askari muttered. She hadn't ever really thought about it before, but it was true. The Baratok always preached avoidance. Don't go near this monster, don't go near that monster—don't do anything that might accidentally put you in front of a monster—it was ridiculous. Sometimes it might make sense to pursue a monster—for example, if it stole a child, or if its scales could be used as knives. But the Baratok were cautious. They would never even entertain such a possibility.

A scratching sound came from the front door.

"I bet that's Polly," Shujaa said, standing up to let the creature in. Polly pranced into the room and proudly dropped a large rodent at Askari's feet.

"Another one?" Askari asked. This one didn't look quite the same, though—it was round, fluffy, and brown, and it had rather large teeth.

"A woodchuck," Minda said. "Well caught, Polly. She's done this for you before?"

"Yeah, she caught me one yesterday," Askari said. "It had black and white stripes on its face—about this big." She held her hands a couple of feet apart.

"Sounds like a badger." Minda picked up the dead rodent and turned it over. "Woodchucks are tough to eat, but have a great flavor. The trick is, you've got to boil it first, then fry it." She produced a knife from her belt and positioned the woodchuck belly up.

"You're going to get blood on the floor blanket," Shujaa said. She went into the kitchen and brought in a large pan, bending down to hand it to Minda. Then she stood back to watch the procedure with her arms crossed.

"It's called a rug," Minda said, placing the pan under the woodchuck.

"Can I ask you a question, Minda?" Harcos asked as she began to work.

"Go ahead." She made a few quick slices and pulled the skin off, then began to remove the organs one at a time.

"Why should we trust you?"

Askari glared at Harcos for a second, and then she looked at Shujaa, who shrugged and nodded in agreement with Harcos.

A small smile flitted across Minda's face. "Took you long enough to ask," she said. "And the answer is that you have no reason to trust me."

"You saved us," Askari protested. "From the pok and the kover, then you brought us to a safe haven, and now you're making dinner."

"Those aren't reasons to trust me," Minda said. "Those are just things I've done. If I were a slaver, I might be luring you here, getting you to let down your guard and fall asleep. Then I could drug you and have my slaver friends come and take you away."

Shujaa uncrossed her arms and curled her hands into fists, taking a step back from Minda with an angry frown. "Is that what you're doing? Because I'd die first."

Minda smiled again. "No. I actually am trying to help you. I used to be a Baratok."

"Why should we believe you?" Harcos asked. He stared at Minda's face, unblinking, as if searching for any sign that she might be lying.

"Again," Minda said, "no reason. But you can ask me anything about the Baratok and I'll answer to the best of my abilities."

"Why did you leave?" Askari asked. She was suddenly quite curious. Did Minda get kicked out? Did she leave because she wanted to?

"It's a long story," Minda said. She began to slice cuts of meat from the woodchuck carcass and tossed them into a pot of water, pausing as if in thought. Then she said, "We had a disagreement. About the way things should be done."

"Only one disagreement?" Shujaa asked.

"Okay, we had a lot of disagreements." Minda shrugged. "Mostly between me and Kira. The others tended to be more reasonable."

"How long ago was it?" Harcos said.

"Oh, maybe fourteen years now," Minda said. "Or fifteen."

"List the elders." Harcos said.

"Harcos!" Askari said. "You don't have to quiz her!" She could feel herself becoming more defensive—Minda had saved their lives. There was no need to be rude.

"Assuming they haven't died since I was there, or added new ones," Minda said, ignoring Askari's comment, "their names are Elol, Timo, Faro, Sheo, Dano, Vica, and the Kira we all love and adore."

Harcos laughed at the sarcastic statement. "She's a keeper, that's for sure."

"Is she the one who sent you three on this assignment?" Minda asked. "To get the book?"

"She sent Askari," Shujaa replied. "We sneaked off after the fact."

"That was quite big of you," Minda said. "Why?"

"It was kind of impulsive, to tell you the truth," Harcos said. "We were angry at their choice of punishment for

Askari. It seemed harsh—like they were sentencing her to death. It's not like she killed anyone. And they sent her off alone, in the wilderness—for what? A book?"

Minda nodded, a thoughtful expression on her face. "It does seem harsh, yes."

"The best way for her to survive," Harcos added, "was to have help. So, we packed our bags and left."

"Maybe they knew Minda was here," Shujaa suggested. "Maybe they knew Askari would only be alone for a few days."

"Maybe," Harcos said. "But knowing Kira, it wouldn't have mattered. Anyway, we probably shouldn't have left, but it's worked out so far. And if we hadn't, Askari would be dead, so I don't regret it. Not yet anyway."

"I wouldn't have found the book either," Askari added.

"What did you do to earn such a punishment?" Minda asked Askari.

"Broke a few rules." Askari shrugged. "I kept sneaking off to practice tracking, and I followed Shujaa because she disappeared while everyone else was busy with Fia and the baby."

"You must have broken a lot of rules," Minda said.

"I don't know," Askari replied. "It didn't seem like that big of a deal."

Minda laughed. "It rarely does. But the rules are for the good of the community. If one can break them, soon everyone will... or so Kira thinks. I was a proponent of more flexibility— we didn't get along."

It was nice, Askari thought, to talk to an adult who actually agreed with her thoughts about the strict rules and regulations of the Baratok community. And Minda had survived alone for a long time—although, now that Askari thought about it, maybe Minda hadn't always been alone. Maybe she had left with friends, and they were all gone now. She frowned a little. Fifteen years was a long time ago—Askari had only been a kid. Maybe...

"Minda," Askari asked the old woman, "did you know my mother?"

Minda looked at Askari for a moment and then sighed. "Yes." She stared toward the meat that was now sizzling in a pan over the coals and said softly, "And I'm more sorry about her death than you can know."

Askari fell silent. She debated asking Minda for more detail—what she had been like, how well she had known her, if they had hunted together—but she couldn't do it. The memories the pok had brought to the surface were too fresh, too painful. Besides, she had already quizzed all the other elders for information about her mother—Minda probably wouldn't have anything new.

Everyone sat in silence while the meat cooked, until Shujaa announced, "I think the food's done!"

The rest of the evening they spent chatting about this and that, eating, and enjoying the fire. The soup was hot and delicious, and the woodchuck was surprisingly good and perfectly tender. Polly got an entire leg to chew on, because as Minda said, "She's a good dog."

"What's a minket?" Askari asked, realizing this might be the last chance she got to ask any questions.

"It's a friendly garg," Minda said.

"Those aren't real!" Shujaa exclaimed.

"Yeah, the Baratok have been pushing that myth for a long time," Minda said. "Saying all gargs are bad helps them build the narrative that their rules make sense. But really, it's just a story to prevent children from doing anything stupid. Gargs need to eat, just like everyone else. And if humans are available, they'll eat you. If not, they'll eat animals or other gargs if they can. There are a number of species of gargs who could potentially be domesticated—some even eat plants, believe it or not. There is as much variety in gargs as there is in native animals. Minkets are an example of this—they do what's easiest to get food and simultaneously survive in this garg-eat-garg world. Polly here apparently thinks she's less likely to die if she sticks with you. Did you help her?"

"I saved her from a gamba," Askari said, shrugging. "And then she saved me from a lot of gambas."

"That'll do it."

Askari pondered this rather new concept. A monster that was helpful? Good? She hoped what Minda said was true, that Polly was really trying to help, but a little voice in the back of her head wondered if Polly mightn't show her true monstrous nature as soon as Askari's back was turned. But at the same time, Polly had attacked a pok for her and caught her food—why would she betray her? Askari shook her head to clear the thought. Polly would never hurt her. She would do everything in her power to keep Polly happy—that's all there was to it. Besides, everything in life was a risk, and this was a risk she was willing to take.

Once the fire had died down, they headed upstairs. Each one chose a room and drifted off into a comfortable sleep; Polly curled up in a ball beside Askari's leg.

Askari jerked awake in the middle of the night and clapped her hands over her ears. A high-pitched screech filled the air, slicing into her brain like a sharp knife. She jumped out of bed and peered out into the hallway. Harcos and Shujaa were standing outside their own rooms, both covering their ears with horrified expressions on their faces.

"What's happening?" Shujaa exclaimed, eyes wide.

"Where's Minda?" A suspicious frown crossed Harcos' face.

That moment, her bedroom door opened, and she peered out with drooping eyelids. "Go back to bed."

"How are we supposed to sleep with this noise?" Shujaa exclaimed.

"Better question," Harcos interjected. "What is happening?"

"It's the security system," Minda muttered. "It'll stop in about twenty minutes or so."

"And we're supposed to believe you because...?" Harcos asked in an annoyed tone of voice.

Minda looked at him, shook her head, and then went back into her room and closed the door.

"I can't sleep like this!" Shujaa said again.

"What kind of security system?" Askari asked.

"The one that keeps gargs out, I would imagine," Harcos replied.

All at once, the noise stopped. It was followed by four short screeches, then silence.

"Finally!" Shujaa exclaimed. "I hope it doesn't go off again." She turned to go back into her room, but Minda reappeared, this time looking less sleepy and more concerned.

"That wasn't supposed to happen," Minda said. "Get your weapons and meet me in the kitchen." She disappeared back into her room.

The three stared at each other for a moment and then rushed to do as Minda had instructed. Polly was awake, sitting up on the bed acting nervous. She chittered and talked while kneading the bedspread with her fingers.

"It'll be okay, Polly," Askari said, trying to comfort the minket as she grabbed her bow and arrows from the chair on the other side of the darkened room. Her machete was under her pillow. She pulled her shoes on too, in case they had to go outside, then followed Shujaa into the kitchen. Minda was already there with a sword and three spray bottles filled with some kind of liquid. She had lit an oil lamp and set it on the kitchen table; it cast a warm, flickering glow over the room.

"What's going on?" Harcos demanded.

"Our security system," Minda said, "is actually a garg."

"What?" Harcos exclaimed.

"It is called a fulek." Minda ignored his exclamation. "Fuleks are grass and plant eaters, which makes them an easy target for larger gargs—except for the fact that they release a chemical spray which causes most gargs' skin to melt. Some type of acid, we think. We imported a family of fuleks to live around each property the Lamplighters manage. They spray their acid around, which encourages most gargs stay away. The disadvantage is that humans are also susceptible to the acid, plus they make that noise every night when the sun reaches the zenith on the opposite side of the planet."

"What... how...?" Harcos didn't know how to phrase his question.

"Research. That's how we know." Minda strode over to the window and leaned forward to peer through a peephole someone had installed. "The screeching usually lasts twenty minutes to a half hour. That only lasted a minute or less, which means there must be some kind of problem."

"What kind of problem?" Harcos asked.

Minda shook her head. "I don't know."

"What are we supposed to do?" Askari asked. "It's dark. We can't see anything."

"I don't know," Minda replied, frowning. "This has never happened before."

They stood around the kitchen table. Askari wracked her brain trying to think of what they should do. The Baratok had never prepared her for this kind of problem, and they definitely didn't have a set of rules for what to do when it happened. They had never taught improvisation when it came to overall strategy, though Elol had encouraged it when training them in hand-to-hand and other types of combat.

"Improvisation," Askari said out loud.

"What's that?" Minda asked.

"We need to improvise," Askari replied. "The Baratok didn't really teach us how, but I think if we can improvise how to improvise, we can figure something out."

Minda stared at her blankly.

"Polly!" Harcos exclaimed.

"Where?" Askari turned toward the stairs. She had left the minket upstairs in her room—Polly hadn't seemed particularly inclined to come down.

"No," Harcos said, "I mean, maybe she can help us."

Askari raised her eyebrows and then shrugged. She went to the bottom of the stairs and called up, "Hey Polly! Come here! Want some woodchuck?"

Harcos produced a strip and waved it in the air.

"Come here!" Askari called again.

Polly scampered down the stairs and climbed Harcos' leg, settling on his shoulder. She swiped the meat from his hand and began to gnaw on it. She was becoming friendlier with him by the day.

"Hey, Polly," Askari said. "Um..." She wasn't sure how to continue. How was Polly, a minket—an animal—supposed to understand such a complex question? What was she supposed to say? Hey Polly, the fulek alarm system isn't working and we don't know why, can you help?

Instead, Askari screeched.

Polly jumped, digging her claws into Harcos' shoulder, and scampered down to the ground to hide between his legs.

"I'm sorry, I'm sorry!" Askari exclaimed. "I didn't mean to scare you! We're trying to figure out what happened to the fuleks."

Polly glared at her, red eyes glowing in the darkness of the room. After a moment, she spit on the ground and then ran toward the front door.

"What's she doing?" Minda asked.

"I have no idea," Askari replied. "But we should follow."

"We fan out, though," Minda said. "Askari, you lead—I'll take the left, you two share the right. Keep an eye out for any signs of any animal, garg, or human—understand?"

"Got it," Harcos and Shujaa said together.

Askari pulled open the door. A cool breeze gently bent the necks of the tall grasses close to the house, and the trees swayed. The moonlight lit most of the tidily chopped grass between the house and the woods, so it was easy to follow the minket as she scampered out the door, across the porch, and into the lawn. Askari could hear the sounds of Harcos' feet in the grass, but Shujaa and Minda moved completely silently. Beyond them, there was nothing but the wind—not even birds or frogs. She shivered.

Polly turned left off the front porch and guided them around the house. Askari followed a safe distance behind, in case anything jumped out of the shadows and snatched Polly up for a late-night snack.

Behind the house, Askari could see the shape of a large, old shed. It looked like it had been shored up, probably by the Lamplighters as well, but the front door was open and creaking in the wind. Polly stopped short, stared at the dark opening of the shed, and then squealed and made a beeline back for the house.

Minda stepped forward, taking the lead. She gestured for the others to be silent and then crept forward, sword in one hand, solar-operated flashlight in the other. Askari tiptoed closer, trying not to step on anything that might make noise. Then there was a loud CRACK behind them.

Askari spun around to see Harcos with a sheepish look on his face. He had stepped on a stick. Minda scowled and waved at him to be quiet.

The screech came again. It was high and piercing, and much louder than it had been in the house. Askari ducked down and slapped her hands over her ears, grimacing in pain. It was not a pleasant sensation. Minda had done the same, she could see. The sound stopped abruptly, like it had before, and Minda pointed toward the shed.

She moved softly forward, gesturing for Askari to come close, and for Shujaa and Harcos to stay back and watch around them. Askari moved forward.

"I'm going to flip on the light," Minda murmured. "You get on the other side of the door and watch."

Askari moved as quickly and silently as she could, and positioned her head so she could see into the shed. Minda flicked on the light, aiming it into the shed. The light spread over a strange sight.

On the floor, a large garg with ears like a rabbit and a round, furry body was lying on one side. Its long, gangly legs were stretched out in all directions, and a tail rested on some kind of fabric. In front of the garg, three miniature versions lay silent, unmoving.

The garg let out another screech. This close, Askari thought her brain might explode. She clapped her hands over her ears and squeezed her eyes shut, waiting for the noise to end. When it did, Minda re-aimed the light into the shed, taking stock of the situation. Then, without hesitation, she turned to Harcos and Shujaa.

"Go!" she exclaimed. "Get water, blankets, and two oil lamps. Run! As fast as you can! Lamps first! Askari, hold this." She shoved the flashlight into Askari's hand and darted into the shed, kneeling by the garg. "Shhhhh," she said softly, moving her hands along the creature's belly. "Shhhhh, we're here to help."

"What is it?" Askari whispered.

"It's the fulek, of course," Minda replied. "And it's giving birth. I think one must be stuck."

"These babies don't look too good," Askari said quietly.

"I know."

Harcos appeared a moment later with two glowing oil lamps. He set them on shelves in the shed, and the orange light made it much easier to see. He seemed to understand the situation almost immediately. "Is one stuck?" he asked.

"I think so," Minda replied. "Do you have blankets and water?"

Shujaa appeared at the door. "Here," she said.

"Okay," Minda replied. "Here's what I need. One of you needs to help me with this baby. One of you needs to try to bring those three back to life. And one of you needs to guard the door, to make sure no other gargs show up and try to start eating the fulek and its pups. Who is doing what?"

"I'll take the babies," Shujaa volunteered. That made sense, Askari thought. She was more experienced with medicines and had worked with the healers and the infants in the community on more than one occasion.

"I'll help with the birth," Harcos said. "I've helped with the horses before."

"I'll guard, then," Askari said, feeling quite relieved. She would have had no idea what to do with either the babies or the birth.

"Get the bottles," Minda said. "They have extra acid in them. Spray it around—a pregnant fulek won't have had acid for at least a few days now. They stop producing it close to birth to minimize the risk of injuring their young."

Askari sprinted back into the house and grabbed the bottles. Polly was sitting on the floor, looking up at her with wide eyes. "I want you to come with me," Askari said, "if you're not too afraid. We have babies to protect."

The minket glared at her and stayed put.

Askari spent a few minutes squirting the acid onto the grass around the house and lawn, and then took up her post outside the shed. The door was still open, letting in moonlight, so she could hear them talking about the best way to get the baby fulek out. It was apparently breech, meaning it was coming out backward and its long legs were getting in the way. Someone would have to stick their hands inside the garg to get it out the right way. Askari shuddered and focused on the lawn around her.

The scene around Askari remained silent as the others worked—only the wind made noise. Every so often the fulek would scream, and Askari would grit her teeth and cover her ears, focusing on keeping her eyes peeled for danger, even though she couldn't hear anything. Then the sound would stop, and her head would spin for a moment, the shriek still echoing in her skull. After the fourth scream, the sound wouldn't stop echoing. It kept going, softer and softer, but thudding back and forth, and then breathing, soft, shallow...

Breathing. Breathing that was not coming from inside the shed. She shifted her stance into a crouch, staring into the darkness around her. A light covering of clouds had floated in front of the moon, so it was much harder to see than before. She flashed the light into the darkness, only to illuminate glowing eyes in the bushes nearby. Something was there.

"Git!" she yelled.

"What's happening?" Minda called.

"There's something here!"

"Close the door!" Minda ordered.

Shujaa jumped up and pulled the door closed with the fulek, its babies, and the humans inside. Askari was alone. But not alone enough.

She focused all of her senses in the direction of the glowing eyes, and heard a low rumble.

"Git!" she yelled again, brandishing her machete. The clouds blew past and the moon reappeared as a massive creature padded forward. It had glowing eyes and rippling muscles. Its sharp teeth shone in the moonlight when it pulled back its lips and snarled.

"A cougar," Askari breathed. She had never seen one up close before. She once thought she had seen one on a far-off ridge, but it had been too far away to know for sure. Only a few Baratok claimed to have ever been even a few hundred feet away from one—and this cougar was standing right in front of her.

Askari froze, watching the cougar as it looked back at her. She tried not to blink, tried not to break eye contact. Quickly, she ran through options in her mind. She could run, lead it away from the fulek mother, but she was worried it wouldn't follow. It probably knew there was easy food in the shed, and why would it chase down prey when it could simply wait for the door to open? She might be able to scare it away if she yelled and made noise, but that could also draw other predators from the surrounding area who might have been following the sound of the fulek's screams. Or she could attack.

Without hesitation, Askari leaped forward, brandishing her machete. She jabbed toward its face. The cougar growled and leaped backward, then paced to one side, looking, watching her. She leaped forward again, jabbing the machete toward it. Askari swallowed. She had fought dozens of gargs, but she didn't know what to do against a regular animal. She didn't even want to kill it—the big animals were rare, as they had major competition for food.

Then the cougar attacked. It was fast, faster than she would ever have imagined. And it could jump a long way. She skipped back, narrowly avoiding its claws, but it kept coming; the next moment she tripped and found herself on her back with the cougar standing over her. It had one paw holding down her hand with the machete in it. The cougar roared, teeth glinting in the moonlight. She began to pummel its chest with her free hand, but the cougar didn't even notice. Drool dripped from its fangs to her face. She swallowed—if only she could get her hand free, then she could fight back.

Then something appeared behind its head, hissing, spitting, attacking.

"Polly!" Askari breathed.

The cougar tossed its head back, trying to throw the creature off. Askari began to pummel the cougar with her feet and free hand as hard and as fast as she could; its claws were digging into her machete hand, and she could feel herself beginning to bleed. She groaned a little but refocused on the fight above her.

Polly held on, arms wrapped around the cougar's neck. It roared and hissed, flailing its neck to get Polly off. Then, Askari watched with amazement as several inches of claws emerged from the back of Polly's hands. They were long, sharp, and looked like they could kill something in an instant. Polly pulled her hands across the big cat's neck, ripping open the skin. The lion reared back, roaring and freeing Askari's hand. She scrambled to her feet and made herself as big as possible and roared as loudly as she could, holding her machete over her head, preparing to bring it down onto the cougar with all the force she could muster.

The cougar froze in a crouch, staring up at her with wide eyes, blood pouring down its neck and back. It glanced at the shed for a moment, and then turned and took off into the darkness. Polly tumbled off its back into the grass and ran back to Askari, who knelt and gathered the little minket into her arms.

"Thank you, thank you, thank you," Askari murmured, hugging Polly tightly.

Harcos poked his head out of the shed. "We did it!" he exclaimed. "We saved two of them, and safely got out the one that was breech!" Then he looked around. "What attacked?"

"A cougar, I think," Askari said. "Polly helped me run it off. I don't think it will attack again. I hope, anyway."

"Seriously?" Harcos' eyes widened in surprise. "I've never seen one of those."

Minda poked her head out of the shed door. "I want to take the fulek and its babies into the house—it's much more secure there, and warm. We have to do it quickly though."

Shujaa stepped out with a basket covered in blankets; it was making squeaking noises.

"Harcos," Minda said. "We'll make a stretcher out of that blanket—a sling, sort of—and carry in the mother."

Harcos disappeared back into the shed, and Askari stood up, machete at the ready. Once Minda and Harcos had the mother secured, the group made their way slowly across the lawn, with Askari looking in every direction for anything that might appear from the darkness. She was worried that the cougar might still be lurking, but they didn't see any sign of it.

They made it safely to the house. Harcos ran back for the oil lamps and closed up the shed, while Minda and Shujaa settled the fulek and its babies into a pile of blankets. The babies squeaked, while the mother lay on the floor unmoving, eyes drooping, clearly exhausted.

When Harcos returned from the shed, Askari locked up the house behind him.

"Where's the dad?" he asked. "Shouldn't it be around?"

"No," Minda replied. "As far as we can tell, fuleks are both male and female. A family is a group of siblings usually, possibly with a parent or two parent-children groups together. I don't know where the other fuleks we brought here went—I'm hoping nothing went wrong with them. I'm going to stay here for a few days to make sure the parent is safe, and then check in with some of the other Lamplighters to see if anyone knows what happened."

"Is there anything else we can do?" Harcos asked.

Minda shook her head. "Get some sleep—I'll crash down here."

"There's no security system now," Askari said. "What if something attacks?"

Minda shrugged. "Then we fight. But we'll be no good if we don't get any rest. Go to sleep."

Askari headed back up the stairs, eyes drooping, and fell asleep with Polly curled up next to her leg.

Minda was the first one awake the next morning. Askari stumbled downstairs to find her cobbling together a makeshift breakfast using leftovers from the night before and stale bread. The fulek was awake as well, and washing its babies as they made strange little chirruping noises.

"Oh good, you're up," Minda said, turning. "You need to get going pretty soon. I hope you slept well."

"Better than an alva in the snow," Askari said, yawning as she pictured the furry bear-like garg that slept for most of the year and only awoke to feed in the spring. "At least once the screeching stopped, that is. A bed is nice. Much better than sleeping on the wet ground under a ledge surrounded by gambas."

Minda looked at her for a minute and shook her head. "What are the elders teaching kids these days? You need a refresher in basic survival skills," she said bluntly. "Try sleeping in a tree next time."

"It was raining!" Askari protested.

"Better wet and uncomfortable than dead." Minda reached into her bag and pulled out another book. "I added some notes to this last night, and I want you to give it to Faro with the other. I'm not quite done, but close enough."

Askari took it, studying the cover. There were some letters she couldn't read, and a picture of a ringat, a kind of rock-like garg that was good at hiding.

"What does it say?" Askari asked.

Minda frowned. "Can't you read?"

"No, I never learned."

"What are they teaching you?" Minda muttered again. "It says, *Monsters of the New World, Book Two*."

"Oh, that makes sense," Askari replied.

"Yes, it does. Now get that to Faro, you understand?"

"I understand."

Harcos appeared at the bottom of the stairs. "Leftovers!" he exclaimed, grabbing a slice of cold woodchuck meat and gobbling it down.

"I'll pack up whatever is left," Minda said, moving around the kitchen quickly. "You can take it with you. Anything that animal catches you, make sure it cooks through to kill any bacteria. I would be very annoyed if you died from a fever so soon after I saved you from a pok and a kover."

Shujaa appeared at the bottom of the stairs with bags under her eyes. "I hardly slept," she said. "Those bed things are weird. I ended up on the floor. Give me my bedroll under a tree any day."

"Well, that's what you'll get tonight," Harcos said, grinning.

"How is the fulek?" Shujaa asked.

"It's fine," Minda replied. "The parent and the three living babies all appear to be healthy, as far as I can tell. I'm going out to collect some food for them when you leave, and will stay until I'm sure the parent is strong enough to take care of the babies. They grow pretty fast."

"Anything we should do before we leave?" Harcos asked.

"No, I'll take care of it," Minda said, almost impatiently. "If you ever encounter another Lamplighter house, just do what we did when we got here, but backward. Clean up, close the grates, lock the doors, hide the key—it's pretty simple."

"How many of these houses are there?" Harcos asked.

"Dozens," Minda replied, striding over to the front door and pulling it open. "You'll know them because they'll have a picture of a lightbulb carved into the door." She pointed at a strange drawing that had a sort of bubble on top that shifted into a tube at the bottom, with three loops drawn in the center. "Now, I want you all to listen to me carefully. I've marked a trail on this map for you to follow—I've been living here for years, and this is the safest route."

"Easy enough," Askari said, stuffing the food Minda had packaged into her backpack.

"One more thing before we go," Harcos said.

"Of course." Minda raised her eyebrows.

"Who are the Lamplighters?"

Minda looked at him carefully, a small frown on her face. "You haven't heard of them?"

"No," he replied.

She stared at the three of them intently for a moment, first Harcos, then Shujaa, then Askari, and then said slowly, "I don't know much, other than that they are a group of people studying the gargs, who work together to create safe spaces to do research and work. But don't tell the elders I said anything. If they kept it a secret, they must have a reason."

"The elders know about the Lamplighters?" Harcos asked.

Minda nodded and then changed the subject. "You three need to leave—it's a good distance to get to the ford. But before you go," Minda finished, "I have a message for Kira. I want you all to listen very carefully and repeat it back to me."

Askari nodded at the same time as Harcos and Shujaa.

"Tell her: 'I didn't tell. It's not them, it's me. Don't be a jerk.'"

Askari tried not to grin as she repeated it back to Minda. She wasn't sure she would be able to say it to Kira's face, but she also knew, as Minda glared at her, that she would be hard-pressed to choose between facing this glare again and facing Kira's, and right at this moment, Kira's seemed a lot easier to stomach.

"Now go!" Minda exclaimed, shooing them off the porch.

"Thank you," Shujaa said politely. "You saved us, and we appreciate that."

"Yes, thank you," Harcos said, following Shujaa down off the porch.

"I'd be dead if it weren't for you," Askari said, waving at Minda.

"In more ways than you know," Minda muttered. She sat down in a rocking chair and watched as they strode away from the house.

"What a relief to spend a night in a house," Harcos said as soon as they were out of range of Minda. "It felt safe, like my tent back home."

"So, our plan is to follow this map to the ford?" Shujaa asked.

"We'll camp there," Askari replied, "and cross the river the next morning. We should be crossing paths with the Baratok on the plains sometime the day after tomorrow."

"That's what I would estimate, too," Harcos added.

"Alright, then," Shujaa said. "I guess we'd better pick up the pace."

CHAPTER 8: THE GYIKS

THEY WALKED ALL day without seeing any signs of monsters, crossed the ford late afternoon, and traveled another couple of miles through the woods before setting up camp in a small copse surrounded by dewberry bushes loaded with fruit, a nice treat after all their traveling. Polly brought them four chipmunks to skin and cook. They tasted a little like chicken, Askari thought, but weren't as good as the woodchuck they had been snacking on all day.

They woke early the next morning and continued through the forest. Harcos spent the day speculating about the Lamplighters, until both Askari and Shujaa threatened to tie him up and leave him as dinner for some lucky garg. He walked in silence for the rest of the afternoon until Shujaa finally said, "How much longer until we reach the Plains of Tork?"

"Can I see the map?" Harcos asked.

Askari pulled it out of her bag, and Harcos pointed to a spot somewhere in the middle of scribbles of trees.

"We're still in here somewhere, I think," he said. "See that rock? I thought we would pass it yesterday morning, but we only passed it about an hour ago."

Shujaa groaned. "I thought we would be back by now!"

"We should plan on camping another night," Harcos said, "and hopefully we'll reach the plains tomorrow."

He was right. They camped that night in a clump of pine trees. Polly brought them a porcupine. It was probably the most awful meat Askari had ever eaten. Stringy, greasy, and smelling like something a monster would eat, none of them could finish it. They pretended to love it, and then Harcos buried the leftovers just outside camp while Polly was napping. They filled up on dewberries and leftover strips of meat from the last two nights instead.

"I hope she brings us a bird next," Shujaa said. "I could really go for some roasted crow."

"I'd be happy enough to not to have to skin dinner every night," Askari replied, scratching the spot between Polly's ears as she lay curled up in Askari's lap.

"So, what's the plan?" Harcos asked. "We hopefully reach the plains early or mid-day tomorrow. Then what? How do we find the Baratok?"

"The Tuske," Shujaa said firmly. "If we don't see signs of them right away, we should hike to the Tuske and climb it. We'll be able to see all the plains and look for their trail or smoke or something."

"The Tuske has gyiks on it," Askari reminded her.

"We can handle it," Shujaa said.

"It's not like we haven't dealt with plenty of monsters on this trip," Harcos said, grinning at them.

"We might be able to see the rarohan from up there too," Shujaa added. "It would be better if we could avoid them, assuming Elol and the warriors didn't manage to finish off the whole pack while we were gone."

Harcos pulled out the book, *Monsters of the New World, Book 1.* "I'll look up gyiks and rarohan while we have some time—since we know we might meet them in the next couple of days."

He flipped through the pages of the book, and then began to read aloud:

"Gyiks are the most irritating of gargs. They run in packs like wolves, but are largely self-serving. They attack without warning, will eat anything, and have extremely sharp claws and teeth. They are a little like dog-sized, annoying chickens with claws, standing on their hind legs and using their tail for balance. They are easy enough to kill—knock their heads off with a machete or shoot them through the heart. Their skin can be used for boots or shoes, and their tongues are a strange consistency that can be used as a sponge. If you encounter a large group, simply kill them until there are more of you than there are of them, and the rest will run away."

"Oh, that's great," Shujaa said. "Basically, we have to kill all but three of them."

"We already put a dent in their population when we were up there last week, though," Askari said. "I'm sure it will be fine."

"Rarohan," Harcos said, reading from a different page, "travel in packs with the largest one as their leader. They have an excellent sense of smell and will track prey for weeks or even months once they pick up the scent. They are extremely fast, and a large pack will attack a large group of prey, hoping to divide the group. If you kill the leader of the pack, they will disappear for a short time, but then regroup with a new leader and come back just as hard."

"That's why they ran away after we killed the big one," Askari mused. "Remember?"

Harcos nodded and continued. "The best strategy for defeating rarohan is to use vinegar. Dip your blades in it, as well as the tips of your arrows, or fill spray bottles with it if you have to. It burns their skin and makes them flinch, which in turn makes them vulnerable. And it makes their bones melt if you can get enough of it. Whatever happens, if you meet a group of rarohan, always have vinegar."

"Vinegar?" Shujaa asked. "What a strange strategy. I wonder how Minda figured that out."

"Good to know," Askari said. "We don't have any, but the community should have some, so if they're still being harassed by the rarohan, we can help."

Harcos spent the rest of the night flipping through the book while Shujaa and Askari discussed the various weaknesses of monsters, and strategies to figure out more weaknesses, before they curled up and went to sleep.

The next morning, eager to get to the Plains of Tork, they rose early, packed their bags, and set out. They altered course and headed straight for the Tuske. Only a few miles out, they could see its rocky tip over the tops of the trees. Askari always thought mountains were beautiful, but this particular one was more strange and eerie than beautiful. It reminded her of a tooth that a giant had left behind, the white rocks shining in the sun.

They reached the base of the mountain right before noon and were surprised to see the corpse of the nagy still lying silently at the bottom of the cliff. Its arms were splayed out, draped across trees and rocks, and its mouth open as if it had died mid-scream. It had been partially devoured by other animals, giant holes ripped through its main body, and its tentacles nearly gnawed through in some places. The stench that rose made Askari gag a little, bile rising in her throat.

"Whoa!" Harcos exclaimed. "This is enormous! If we had time, I'd collect some samples to study." He walked slowly in around the nagy, staring at its tentacles and trying to get closer to the head.

"We don't." Shujaa grabbed Harcos' arm and dragged him toward the mountain path.

"Maybe later we can stop—I'd like to grab a tooth," Askari said, hurrying to keep up with Shujaa. Technically, someone else was supposed to present her with a tooth to start her necklace, but none of the elders seemed inclined.

She would just have to start her own collection. "I'm surprised there aren't any hulla here, gobbling up such an appetizing meal. This is their kind of banquet."

"Well, if we meet the hulla again," Harcos said, "we'll send them over this way. Still weird that they can talk, though."

"No kidding," Shujaa muttered.

They began their ascent up the mountain with minimal grumbling. None of them were particularly inclined to make the climb, as sore as they were from the days of fighting and sleeping on the ground, but they all knew it was the best option for figuring out where exactly the Baratok had ended up over the last few days.

"What if we don't see them? The Baratok, I mean," Shujaa asked about a quarter of the way up the Tuske.

"Then we follow their trail," Harcos said.

"And if we don't see their trail?" Askari asked.

Harcos shrugged. "Go back to the old camp, I guess. Maybe they never left, or went another direction."

Askari nodded. She decided not to think about it. They would see the trail; she just had to believe that.

The sun was bright and the sky clear, which would make it easy to see a long distance from the top of the mountain. They saw no sign of gyiks, or any other kind of monster for that matter, a fact which Askari found a little relieving, but also rather worrisome.

"Do you think we'll reach the community today?" Shujaa asked when they were about halfway up the mountain.

"I hope so," Harcos said. "It will make sleeping a lot easier."

Askari didn't respond. She was trying to conserve energy in case they had to fight.

They stopped shortly after that to eat some leftover dewberries, but continued on without too much delay. Polly seemed to be enjoying herself. She frolicked on and around the trail, and as the trees began to get a little shorter, she jumped from the top of one to the top of the next. It was cute, Askari thought, despite her being such an ugly creature. But mostly she was glad Polly was walking, because carrying her up the mountain would have required more energy.

"I think we're high enough now," Shujaa said as the trees became short enough to see over. "We just have to get around to the other side."

"Should be easy enough," Harcos said, making his way across the rocky ground. They continued for about twenty more minutes until a grand, sweeping view of the plains stretched out before them. *The sky is so big*, Askari thought as she gazed at the scene in front of her. The wind danced through the tall, verdant grasses speckled with yellow and white flowers peeking up amid an ocean of green and brown; white fluffy clouds drifted lazily overhead. There was so much space; everything was so big—it might be full of hidden dangers, but at least it was beautiful.

They gazed out at the scene before them for a few minutes before Harcos said slowly, "I... don't see them."

Askari squinted, scanning for signs of broken-down swaths of grass, small moving wagons, people, or anything at all indicating the presence of a large group of humans. It looked untouched. A general sense of foreboding built up in her, a lump in the pit of her stomach—something was wrong.

"Me either," Shujaa said, her expression worried. "They couldn't have moved fast enough to make it all the way through the plains, could they? When we left, they had been sitting still for a day because of the rain, and the next day would have taken a lot more prep time to get going than planned. I wouldn't imagine they've gone that far."

"Unless they went a different direction than they told us," Askari suggested.

"What is... Do you see that?" Harcos pointed in the general northwest direction, frowning.

Askari squinted, scanning the countryside. Then she paused. A thin wisp of smoke rose out of the plains.

"Can you see what it is?" Shujaa asked. "Is it a grass fire?"

"It's too small to be a grass fire," Harcos said, shading his eyes from the bright sun, "and it has rained enough that it should be hard to start one."

"Then what is it?" Shujaa pressed.

"If you look over there," Harcos said, pointing slightly to the left of the smoke, "you can see the trail the Baratok left when going through the plains. They came closer to the mountain than we anticipated—it looks like they're headed toward Arc Hill."

Askari squinted. Sure enough, she saw a wide swath of grass, flattened as if a couple hundred people, their horses, and their wagons had walked across it. Relief washed over her. Arc Hill was several miles ahead, but they could see the top of it like a wart on the plains.

"But if you follow it in the direction it's going," Harcos continued, "it disappears right in the middle of the plains. I can't tell if they made it to Arc Hill or not, and there's no other indication of where they all went."

"We have to go," Askari said abruptly. "We know generally where they went. We know they are somewhere. They might be fine, but they might need our help."

"I agree," Harcos said.

They turned to head back down the mountain, but froze almost immediately. In front of them stood six gyiks, saliva dripping from the sides of their mouths, talons dug into the dirt, their stances ready to pounce. Their greyish-greenish scales almost sparkled in the sunlight, and they seemed a lot fiercer when she could see their razor-like teeth, big ugly eyes, and antennae. She hadn't heard them approach. She mentally kicked herself. If she kept making mistakes like this, she was going to be dead sooner than later.

"Aw, garg's blood," Askari muttered. They were going to have to fight their way down the mountain. The gyiks hadn't disappeared after all. Then she yelled, "Gyiks! Attack!"

She slid her bow over her head, whipped an arrow out of the quiver, and immediately loosed it, hitting the first garg in the stomach. It squealed and fell over, dead. Harcos pulled a blade from his belt, while two knives appeared in Shujaa's hands. The gyiks leaped forward, shrieking and making a noise that sounded like someone scraping a washboard with a metal spoon—a harsh, grating noise that made her hair stand on end. Shujaa threw a knife at an incoming gyik and hit it in the heart, and then she pulled out the spear securely fastened to her back and began to stab as the other gyiks came within range.

"Die!" Harcos yelled, slicing the head off of one gyik and sticking another in the gut.

"I think we're going to have to run!" Shujaa yelled. "There are a lot more of them than last time!"

"I'll clear a path," Askari called out, pulling out her machete and grabbing a knife for her other hand. She slung her bow over her shoulder and began to swipe as fast as she could, slicing off limbs and heads, and maiming or killing garg after garg. "Follow me!"

In quick succession she jabbed three gyiks in their vital regions and then ran past them, pausing only to make sure Harcos and Shujaa didn't need any help. Then she turned her attention back to the gyiks and began to mow them down as fast as she could. She screeched as one got too close and sliced open her leg, but she stomped on its head in retaliation. Another ripped a loose part of her shirt, but she managed to jab it in the eye with her knife, and it fell back far enough for her to take off its head with her machete.

Harcos fell in line behind her, swiping out with his knives and wounding as many gyiks as he could reach. Shujaa came behind them, basically walking backward, stabbing at those that came from behind. Polly was nowhere to be seen. It didn't matter though—Askari's job was to help Shujaa and Harcos survive. Polly was on her own.

Askari killed three more, separating their heads from their bodies. A bluish-black blood poured from their necks and covered the ground with a viscous, glistening liquid. Then she began to jog—the sooner they were on flat land, the better. The gyiks definitely had the advantage on this terrain. Some fell back and disappeared behind the rocks, probably planning an ambush farther down the mountain. But more filled in the space where they had disappeared. Harcos and Shujaa began to jog too, knocking past the gyiks that got close, focusing on getting to the base of the mountain.

It was a difficult run. The rocky, steep ground made footing dangerous, and the gyiks kept launching themselves at the young warriors, trying to knock them down. Askari thought it was a good thing the gyiks were so small compared to other gargs—and incompetent. This many rarohan, for example, and they would have been dinner long ago. The only problem was that there were so many. They kept coming, one garg after another after another. For every one they killed, three more appeared.

Askari dripped with sweat and her hands shook with fatigue. When they finally reached the base of the mountain, she breathed a sigh of relief—but the feeling didn't last for long. The rest of the gyiks were waiting for them at the bottom of the trail, standing in a semi-circle. Askari stumbled to her knees as she tried to come to a halt.

"Why don't you just eat the garg-awful nagy?" she exclaimed in frustration, gesturing toward a long tentacle draped over a nearby tree.

One of the gyiks lunged forward. Askari ducked, slicing through the gyik's belly as it passed over her. Spattered in bluish blood, Askari began to kick and yell as if she was fighting in hand-to-hand combat with the gyiks. Harcos and Shujaa moved quickly, each sticking and stabbing, slicing and killing. But the gyiks kept coming.

Then, Harcos tripped. Shujaa screamed and ran to stand over him, but the gyiks took the opportunity and launched forward. Harcos scrambled, getting to his knees, but now the gyiks were taller than him. He stabbed and jabbed, yelling as they swarmed over him.

"NO!" Askari yelled, fighting her way into the thick of the pack. She aimed her knife at one of the gyiks farther in the back, but it fell over, dead before she had a chance to throw. Askari frowned at it for a second, but didn't have time to think about it—she had to get to Harcos. She cut off another gyik's legs and then stabbed it through the eye. Then she saw yet another gyik at the back of the pack go down, then another. The pack began to chatter as confusion spread through them. Some took off up the mountain, while others made themselves easy targets as they hesitated over whether to pay attention to Askari, Shujaa, and Harcos, or to the mysterious predator behind them.

Askari gritted her teeth. There was something behind the gyiks. It could be people, possibly Baratok—or it could be a bigger, worse threat. The rarohan. Something bigger, meaner. But whatever it was, it was making it easier for her to get to Harcos, and that was step one.

When she reached him, Shujaa was whirling around, stabbing and sticking as fast as she could.

"What's happening?" she gasped, sweat streaming down her face.

Askari bent down and hoisted Harcos to his feet. He had a long bleeding scratch down one of his cheeks and was covered in gyik blood, but otherwise he seemed okay, if scared.

"I don't know," Askari said, leaping forward to slice the head off a gyik coming in fast behind Harcos.

"Hey!" a voice called. "This way!"

"It's people!" Askari exclaimed. It was still possible they were slavers or something, but at this point, she'd take people over gargs, no matter who they were.

"Hurry!" the voice yelled.

"Let's go!" Askari said. "Bigger group, better chance."

Shujaa and Harcos nodded, and the three began to push their way through the remaining gyiks. A moment later, Askari breathed a sigh of relief as a face came into view. It was Elol. They had found the Baratok, or at least some of them.

Elol waved at them and hollered, "Come on! This way!"

Askari, Harcos, and Shujaa took off running, dodging their way through the pack of gyiks, punching, kicking, and slicing as they went. A moment later they were following Elol through the woods; he was quite spry for such an old man. Beside him jogged Sasa, Zaj, and Lyront. Askari took a quick moment to look around, but there was still no sign of Polly.

"We're going to run to the edge of the forest and then split," Elol yelled over his shoulder, "three to the left and three to the right. Hide the first place you can find!"

Askari nodded. They clearly had a plan, and there wasn't enough time for them to share. She would do what she was trained to do: follow instructions. Not that she was very good at it, of course.

She took stock of her injuries as they ran. She had twisted an ankle running down the mountain, and it throbbed with each step. Spatters of tiny burns covered her skin where gyik blood had splashed. One gyik had managed to slice open her arm, though not deep enough to reach an artery. Her upper right arm ached where she had gotten hit by a branch from the tree struck by lightning. Other than that, she was fine, and her wounds would eventually heal.

Up ahead, light filtered through the trees; they were almost to the edge of the plains. The gyiks thundered behind them, making alien hissing noises and sticking out their weird long tongues. Even more had appeared from somewhere, suddenly not afraid anymore, not confused. This was now a hunt.

Elol began to wave and point, first to his right, then to his left.

Askari took the signal; as soon as she stepped out into the Plains of Tork, she made an abrupt turn to the left.

And garg's blood, was she glad she did.

Right on the edge of the forest stood seven enormous rarohan. Their manes blew back in the wind revealing their skeletal faces, and their fangs dripped with blood. Bigger than horses and fiercer than lions, they would have killed Askari the moment she was within reach of their sharp claws. They were clearly waiting, ready, and hungry.

Askari followed closely behind Zaj, who dropped into a crouch behind a large rock. Shujaa slipped over behind a large tree, and Harcos went flat on his face in the grass.

The gyiks burst out of the forest and were met with the loud roar of the rarohan. The gyiks began to hiss and swipe, dodging in and out between the horse-sized, cat-like gargs, who moved with speed and grace, pouncing, biting, and killing gyiks left and right. Askari watched as one rarohan closed its mouth around the head of a gyik, swinging it side to side until the body popped right off and flew back into the woods. A trio of gyiks snuck up on the rarohan closest to Askari and Zaj and attacked all at once, pulling the bones from its skeletal body, breaking them off, and throwing them into the grass. The rarohan howled in pain, and Askari cringed. She had no love for the creatures, but it really did look like it hurt.

Askari was fully engrossed in the fight when she felt Zaj nudge her arm.

"We have to go," he whispered, "or else they'll come after us when they're done with each other. And Elol is already on the move."

Askari nodded and signaled to Shujaa, who kicked Harcos gently; his eyes were locked onto the fight. Zaj ran quietly through the tall grass in a crouch so low he could barely see over the tops.

Shujaa went next, then Harcos, with Askari at the end. She kept her eyes peeled for signs of any other Rarohan or wandering gyiks—or any other gargs, for that matter.

Zaj led them around the outside of the Plains of Tork, and the sounds of the garg fight got quieter as they moved away. It was risky to kill gargs by getting another species involved, yet this was Askari's second time watching the strategy play out in only a few days. It wasn't that the concept was bad, it was just that when you failed, you failed hard because then both groups of monsters would come after you, and they would be even madder than before. You'd be dead. In fact, this was one of the last strategies they learned during training, and Askari's teachers had warned them all thoroughly against the folly and madness—that it should only be used as a desperate attempt, a last-ditch measure.

Askari knew she was the rashest person in the community, which meant... was this a last-ditch measure? What had happened to the rest of the Baratok?

Finally, they ended at a small encampment surrounded by large stones. It was easy to guard, and Askari could see the remains of a small campfire. The area was being carefully watched by Erzci and Agi. Leka sat by the coals, ripping old fabric into rags.

"Askari!" Erzci exclaimed. "Shujaa! Harcos!" He ran forward and pulled them all into giant bear hugs. "I'm so glad to see you!" Then he turned to Elol. "Did you find the gyiks?"

"Yes," Elol replied. "These three helpfully led them down the mountain. They are fighting the rarohan now. But we have no idea how long the battle will last, or how long they will spend taking care of their injured—if they bother to do that at all. We have to move, now!"

Erzci and Agi began to gather up supplies immediately, and Zaj jumped in to help them.

"Let me tie that up," Leka said to Askari, pointing at her arm. "You two injured much?"

Shujaa showed Leka a narrow slice along her neck, and Harcos shook his head. A few minutes later, when everyone was bandaged and the camp had been completely packed up, they set out again, with Zaj in the lead. Everyone followed in single file, and Askari took the last position in line.

They moved as silently as possible through the grass. Elol jogged swiftly, occasionally encouraging the others with soft words. Leka was having the most difficulty, as she was a medic and not trained for long distance running, but she kept up as well as she could. Harcos was also beginning to have trouble, but Askari could see his mouth moving, just barely, reciting the warrior's creed:

"I will not fail
I will always fight
To protect the community
From the monsters that plague our home."

Askari began to mutter it to herself too. She found it strangely comforting, despite the situation they had found themselves thrown into. The thing was, even though she disagreed with a lot of the decisions being made by the elders and the way they ran things in general, this was one thing she did agree with. She would always fight until the death to protect her community from the gargs. No single place or tent or wagon was her home—the Baratok people were her home. They were what she had always known. She never wanted to leave the community; she just wanted make it stronger.

In the center of the Plains of Tork, about ten miles in, Askari could see Arc Hill rising up. It was much smaller than the Tuske, but because the plains around it were so flat, it was extremely visible and appeared larger than it actually was. Zaj aimed them toward the mountain, taking care to vary their course in case anything followed. They finally came close, and Zaj signaled a halt.

A whistle sounded from a few hundred feet away, and Zaj returned the sound. Then he gestured for them to follow, albeit at a slower pace, to Askari's relief. They had run over ten miles after climbing up and down a mountain, and she was ready for some water and hopefully some food.

A moment later, Adelbert came into view, a concerned expression on his face. "You made it back!" he exclaimed. Adelbert was a warrior-in-training, a few months younger than Shujaa, and Askari could see that he was stressed. His eyes were wide and it looked like he hadn't slept in days.

"How many are still missing?" Elol asked.

"Four groups," Adelbert replied, "totaling twenty-three people."

"We found these three," Elol added, gesturing to Askari, Harcos, and Shujaa. "Get them something to eat, and then take them to meet with the elders."

"Yessir," Adelbert replied. "Right away."

Elol and the others made their way in the opposite direction, while Adelbert hustled them through a short maze of tall rocks and led them toward the mountain. They made a left past a particularly large rock, and in front of them opened a large gaping hole in the base of the mountain.

Shujaa came to a dead halt. "I thought we weren't supposed to go in caves."

"This one is safe," Adelbert said. "We checked it thoroughly. I swear."

Shaking her head, Shujaa followed Adelbert into the tunnel, muttering, "Just go breaking their own rules then, why don't they?"

Askari paused at the entrance and took a deep breath. She hated small, enclosed spaces.

Adelbert led them down into the cave. The rock walls wrapped tightly around what Askari thought was a rather small space to be walking through. She could feel herself tensing up, more afraid of this space than she was of the monsters that waited outside it.

"The elders are down here," Adelbert said. "They'll want to see you first—we'll get you food afterwards."

Askari's mind switched abruptly from her fear of the cave to anxiety about what the elders would say to them. She had completed their task, but were the elders still angry? Had they hoped she would die, or at very least, not come back? There was also the added complication of Shujaa and Harcos. What if they got kicked out? Askari would go with them, she knew. They hadn't let her get eaten by gargs, and she would do her best to help them, too.

He led them into a large cavern where Elders Faro, Timo, Sheo, and Kira sat on rocks around a small fire.

"You've returned!" Faro exclaimed, rising from his seat. He reached out to grasp Askari's hand in a symbol of honor and respect, and bowed. "Welcome."

Askari immediately felt a surge of relief. At least Faro wasn't angry.

"Please," he said. "Sit, and have some of our water." He and a couple of the elders offered the three warriors their water skins, which Askari drank gratefully.

"Did you find the book?" Kira asked, eyebrows raised.

"I did," Askari said, "with the help of Harcos and Shujaa." She turned to smile at her friends.

"You two are in trouble," Kira said, turning to Harcos and Shujaa with a disapproving frown. "Disappeared in the middle of the night, without permission..."

"Wait a second!" Askari could feel anger building up in her. Kira hadn't even waited a second to start ridiculing and disciplining. "They haven't done anything wrong!"

"Your task was for you to do, alone," Kira replied. "They put our entire community at risk. What if we had needed them while they were gone?"

Harcos made some strangled noises like he was trying to protest, but Shujaa kept her head down and her mouth shut, ready to take whatever Kira threw at her.

"No!" Askari was not going to let Kira berate her friends for saving her life. She would take all of the blame if necessary. And if they kicked her out permanently for it, well, so be it. She would find her own way. "My task was a death sentence! You sent me through monster-ridden forests to a monster-occupied town to get a book written by an old woman who may or may not know what she's talking about. And Shujaa and Harcos risked their own lives to save me and help me complete the task, without putting anyone else at risk. They didn't invite anyone else, they only took leftover provisions—nothing fresh—and they slipped away when no one would notice. Not to mention—why are we even talking about this? Several of the Baratok are missing and the rest are holed up in this cave, sitting ducks for the rarohan and gyiks and whatever else is waiting out there. And instead of strategizing and figuring out how to get out of this, you're lecturing us!" She took a breath, and Faro jumped in.

"Kira," Faro said, "I'm not saying I agree entirely with Askari, but I do think we should let this issue lie until after we've gotten out of this cave and away from the rarohan."

"I agree," Timo said. She was re-braiding her hair in dozens of thin, neat strands, her fingers moving so fast they were almost invisible. "They've all proven themselves to be strong and capable, and that's the type of warrior we need right now, not angry ones being disciplined."

Sheo nodded and placed her hand gently on Kira's arm. "We'll worry about this later."

Kira glared at Faro, but flipped her braids over her shoulder and sat back down on a rock beside Sheo, arms crossed.

Askari let go of the breath she hadn't realized she'd was holding. She was still angry, but she would put the anger aside and fight for the good of the community. Kira leaned back with her arms crossed, a scowl on her face.

"Sir," Harcos ventured. "What happened to everyone? And the wagons?"

"We were halfway through the Plains of Tork when the rarohan attacked," Faro replied. "We had to scatter—after all, the rarohan couldn't catch all of us at once. One group of warriors burned some of the wagons to scare the rarohan away from the children and the elderly, and another group drove the rest in several different directions to save as many sick and injured as possible. The ones who remain are hidden nearby. Most of the groups met back here—although caves are dangerous, they also offer some protection, and we can fortify them. We are waiting until all of our community has been accounted for."

Harcos nodded.

"Once we have everyone," Sheo added, "then we can prepare to fight our way out."

"What if we don't find everyone?" Askari asked, remembering how she had watched a rarohan drag Harcos off.

Faro shook his head. "We are praying that won't happen."

"Do we have any vinegar?" Harcos asked.

"Vica might have some," Timo said. "Why?"

"The rarohan don't like it, I guess," Harcos replied. "At least, that's what the book said."

"You read the book?" Kira demanded. "That was not for you."

"Oh, go stuff a tentacle in it!" Askari exclaimed, scowling at Kira. "We're having a crisis here! Harcos only read part of the book, and now he knows a lot of helpful things for fighting monsters."

"What did it say about the vinegar?" Timo pressed, ignoring Askari and Kira's argument.

"It burns their skin and melts their bones," Harcos replied, shrugging. "It suggested dipping our blades in it."

"I'll check with the cooks," Timo said, standing up. "I'd be willing to bet they have some—we only have to figure out how much." She disappeared into the darkness of the tunnel.

"Any advice on the gyiks?" Faro asked, turning to Harcos, "now that we've lured them down the mountain?"

"Um…" Harcos thought for a second. "Well, the book said that if there are more of you than there are of them, then they tend to flee. That didn't really help us since there were only three of us, but it might work if a whole community was fighting. It said to keep killing them until you outnumber them, and the rest will go away." He pursed his lips, thinking again. "And that their tongues can be used as a sponge."

"Interesting," Faro replied, nodding. "We can probably make that work, assuming we don't have to fight the rarohan and the gyiks at the same time."

"Perhaps we can arm some of the non-warriors and keep them in the back," Sheo suggested, "to make it look like we have more numbers."

"Yes," Faro replied. "I will speak to Elol." He turned back toward Askari, Shujaa, and Harcos. "Have you three eaten?"

"No," Askari replied, shaking her head.

"Adelbert!" Faro yelled.

He appeared out of the darkness. "Yes, Elder Faro?"

"Get these three some food."

"Of course. Please, come with me."

Adelbert turned to lead them back through the tunnel but halted as Zaj's face suddenly appeared in the flickering light of the fire.

"Elders!" Zaj exclaimed. "I'm sorry to interrupt, but the gyiks have appeared at the mouth of the cave. They are in greater numbers than we've ever seen. We need everyone!"

"I thought they were fighting the rarohan!" Shujaa exclaimed. "I thought they were busy!"

"Must be the rarohan retreated," Harcos said. "Maybe the gyiks killed their leader. Or maybe we got lucky, and the gyiks killed all the rarohan."

"I'd bet you anything we didn't get lucky," Askari muttered. She dropped her travel pack on the ground and repositioned her bow and quiver, then checked her machete. She glanced at Harcos and Shujaa to see that they were doing the same. Then they followed Adelbert and Zaj through the tunnel as quickly as they could. This time, Askari didn't feel the weight of the rock quite so heavily as before, though she swore to herself that she would avoid going in there as much as possible.

They burst out into the light where everyone was fighting around them. The gyiks leaped off rocks onto warriors, ripping wounds with their claws, and wreaking utter mayhem. They were dying in droves, but it didn't matter—they kept coming.

"So many," Shujaa breathed.

"There weren't this many when we left," Harcos replied.

Behind them, up the short mountain, a slew of archers shot gyik after gyik through the eye or heart or neck. They had baskets full of arrows positioned along the ridge, and arrow boys scurried back and forth, gathering arrows as safely as they could from the dead gargs and returning them to the baskets. Below them, a row of sword-wielding warriors fought off any gyik that tried to make its way up to the archers. Everyone else had thrown themselves into the melee. Askari was impressed. They had managed to think out how they were going to protect the cave well in such a short amount of time.

Then she noticed something. "Harcos," she poked him in the ribs with her elbows. "Look!" She pointed up the hill behind the archers.

"Garg's blood," Harcos whispered. A group of gyiks was creeping down from the top of the hill, coming up quietly behind the archers. "There must be another colony that lives here."

"We have to go," Askari said. "We have to get to the archers."

"Save the archers!" Harcos yelled to the other warriors fighting around him. "Gyiks on the hill!" He took off, running toward the path leading upward, swatting gyiks out of his way as he went. Askari whipped out her machete and sliced off the head of a gyik that was trying to sneak up on Zaj, and then she slowly fought her way up the mountain, killing or dismembering one gyik at a time.

In no time, she was breathing heavily, a fresh batch of sweat dripping down her back. A dozen Baratok had been injured already and taken into the cave for treatment. This was a much more difficult battle than the one they had fought on the Tuske, she thought. The gyiks that lived on Arc Hill were bigger, angrier, and attacking with zeal.

Finally, she reached the row of archers, one deep cut across her left upper arm and some other minor scratches. Harcos and Zaj had beat her there and were holding off the gyiks descending the mountain. The archers were trusting Zaj and Harcos to protect them from the gyiks behind them, while they focused on providing support for the warriors below. Askari lopped off the heads of two gyiks and kicked one in the head that tried to take a bite out of her heel. Then Shujaa appeared.

"I got this," Shujaa said, taking Askari's place.

Askari stepped back, sheathed her machete after quickly wiping it in the grass, and then pulled her bow out to take aim at the madness that raged on the plains.

The gyiks moved fast, so she had to move faster. It took her a few missed arrows to get a hang of their style of movement—left to right, right to left, always jumping and dodging. But the more she watched, the better she shot, and the baskets of arrows were always full. She learned that shooting a gyik through the neck didn't kill it, but it did make it easier for someone else to kill. Shooting it through the eye was pretty much the best way to take one down, and shooting one in the stomach did pretty much nothing at all.

Behind her, Harcos kept yelling, "Die!" and "Dead, dead, dead!" and several more warriors had joined Shujaa, Harcos, and Zaj to protect the archers. She focused fully on the scene below. The more they killed, the more the chance they had of the gyiks giving up and retreating.

Then, someone began shouting, "The hulla are coming! The hulla are coming!"

Askari gazed up at the sky. There they were, soaring high over the battle with their human-like faces, eyes scanning the ground. She counted eighteen of them, though there would probably be more coming. They were going to eat well tonight. Askari thought about shooting an arrow their way but decided against it. It was a waste when she knew hulla wouldn't attack. They only ate the dead, and usually only monsters at that.

She turned her attention back to the gyiks, shooting as fast as she could. The hulla made her nervous, so her shooting was a little sloppy, but she refocused her efforts. The gyiks had to die before any more Baratok were injured or killed.

Then her vision was blocked by a large, feathered hulla, gently landing in front of her.

"What do you want?" Askari demanded, scowling at the creature. She remembered the last time a hulla had spoken to her, back outside of the little town—was this the same one?

"Thank youssss," the hulla hissed, "for dinner, Askari."

The archer next to Askari looked at her in terror. "What's going on?" she whispered.

"You're blocking my view!" Askari said harshly, aiming her arrow at the garg.

"She ssssaid you'd be niccccer..." The hulla ruffled its feathers and gave Askari an eerie grin.

"Nice to a hulla?" Askari shook her head. "You're a monster, just like the rest. But if you help us kill those gyiks down there, you'll eat a lot faster."

The hulla laughed, a cawing, grating sound that made Askari's hair stand on end.

"Yousss sssound jusssst like your grandsssssmother..." it hissed, and then leaped into the air, up toward the others.

Askari stared at it, jaw dropped. Her grandmother? The hulla knew her grandmother? She had a grandmother?

"It knows your grandmother?" the archer next to her asked, eyes wide.

"I don't even know my grandmother," Askari replied, watching as it soared over the chaotic struggle on the ground.

That explained how it knew her name, Askari noted, still distracted by the thought that she had any relatives at all, let alone one so close. And still alive? Was it her mother's mother, or her father's mother? She cleared her mind of the hulla and took aim once again, but was shocked to see that the gargs on the ground had suddenly begun to flee. The hulla were flying low over the ground, dropping rocks on the gyiks. Their numbers must have turned the tides.

"I can't believe it," the archer standing next to Askari breathed, lowering her bow. "I've never heard of the hulla getting involved before a battle ended before, let alone because you asked them to." She turned to look at Askari.

All Askari could do was shake her head. It was incredible and disturbing at the same time. Why? Why would they do it? Why would they listen to her? It was good that the fight was over, but she didn't like it. Not one bit.

Askari sat down on the rock, sweat dripping down her forehead and into her eyes. She kept a lookout on the ground below, but other than a few Baratok chasing down a few retreating gyiks, the battle had ended. The arrow boy brought her a bottle of water and she gratefully drank from it. But she knew they weren't done—the rarohan were still out there, somewhere.

CHAPTER 9: THE BARLANG

"YOUR GRANDMOTHER?" Harcos whispered. He and Shujaa were hiding behind a rock near the cave entrance, discussing what the hulla had said. After talking to Askari, the hulla had dropped into the midst of the fray, attacking the gyiks by dropping rocks; Harcos's theory was that their added numbers that made the gyiks run off, as dropping rocks on them hadn't killed a single one as far as he could tell. As soon as the humans saw what was happening, they made a rapid retreat back toward the cave, while the hulla mutilated all the injured gyiks that weren't fast enough to get away, and then settled in to snack on the dead ones.

"That's what it said," Askari replied. "I didn't even know I had a grandmother! And how would she know the hulla? Does she talk to them? Is she friends with them? Why has she been mentioning my name? To the hulla of all things!" She peered out around the rock where the flock of hulla were feasting on the corpses of dead gyiks. Some of the bodies had been dragged into the cave by the Baratok so they could harvest certain body parts for various uses, but the rest were being eviscerated by the ugly human-faced birds. Askari found it nauseating.

"Your mother never mentioned her?" Shujaa asked. "Before she died, I mean?"

Askari shrugged. "I was five. I have no memory of her saying anything. I might have even met my grandmother, but don't remember."

"You should ask the elders," Harcos said. "They might know."

"But then I have to admit that the hulla know who I am, and I have no explanation for that," Askari said. "Seems like that wouldn't go over too well."

"But it was because you told the hulla to help that the gyiks ran off," Harcos pointed out. "We could have lost a lot more good people, but their support ended the fight. The elders can't be too mad about that."

"I imagine the elders probably already know, anyway," Shujaa added. "The other archers heard it say your name. And the hulla have never acted like this. Everyone is talking about it."

"Yeah." Askari sighed and nodded. "You're right."

"Askari!" someone shouted from near the cave mouth.

"Uh oh," Askari said.

"Sounds like you'll be having another chat with the elders," Harcos said, standing up and stretching. "I'm going to get food."

"This is not going to be fun." Askari headed toward the cave, dragging her feet. Adelbert stood at the entrance, a worried expression on his face.

"The elders are looking for you," he said. "You need me to show you the way?"

"No, I remember," Askari said, trying not to let her frustration leak into her voice. After all, Adelbert hadn't done anything.

She ducked low and made her way down the tunnel, trying desperately to stop imagining how it would feel if an entire mountain came crashing down on her, and entered the small cavern where the elders sat around the same small fire. Elol sat hunched over on a rock, eyes drooping with fatigue; he slowly ate dried meat and juneberries, occasionally sipping water from a flagon.

Askari took a seat on a rock near him. She had always respected Elol. To him, it was all about survival—not rules, not structure, not even sticking together. If splitting up was the best chance for everyone to survive, he would have supported it entirely. He had trained her and many other warriors from the ground up. If anyone in this room was on her side, he was.

"Nyilas has brought us some interesting news," Kira said, a frown on her face. Now that Askari thought about it, she wasn't sure she had ever seen Kira without a frown.

"I think I should handle this," Faro said, holding up his hand to stop Kira. He turned his attention to Askari. "Nyilas told us that you spoke with the hulla and told it to help us chase off the gyiks."

Askari shrugged. "Something like that."

"When did you learn to speak with the hulla?" he asked.

"*Learn* to talk to them?" Askari laughed. "I never learned to talk to them—they just started talking to me, back at the village. They seem to like to find me and—" Askari broke off as a loud clicking noise came from the back of the room. "What was that?" she asked.

The noise got louder. Askari squinted into the far corner of the cavern. Someone was standing in the shadows, guarding a large box.

"Make it shut up!" Kira ordered over her shoulder.

"Is that..." Askari jumped to her feet. "Polly?"

The clicking and squeaking got louder, and was now punctuated by someone saying, "Ow!" and "Stop it!" repeatedly. Polly added some hisses into the mix.

Askari strode across the room, dodging the small fire and side-stepping Elder Kira as she tried to block the way.

"Polly!" she exclaimed, holding out her hands, only to be stopped by a tall Baratok stepping in front of her. The minket was in a small cage, rattling the bars and making a huge racket. Her eyes burned red as she slid her talons in and out of her knuckles and glared at them. "Let her out right now, Rudi!" Askari ordered the guard.

"I can't," Rudi replied, shrugging wide shoulders and crossing his arms. "Sorry."

"Fine," Askari said. She ducked around him reached out toward the cage. Rudi leaned down and grabbed her arm tightly, but she flipped the latch on the cage with her other hand before he could pull her away. Polly burst out and scrambled up Askari's leg onto her shoulder, scratching and clawing all the way. Askari grimaced, but bore the pain. She would have done the same in Polly's position.

Rudi let go with an apologetic look. "Sorry," he whispered. He disappeared into the shadows, probably wanting to avoid the fight that was about to happen.

"What have you done?" Elder Kira exclaimed, leaping to her feet. She reached out to take Polly, but Polly hissed and spit in her direction. Askari stepped back so Kira couldn't reach.

"Where did you find her?" Askari asked, scowling at the elders. They had put Polly in a cage! How dare they?

"We found her trying to hide in your bag that you left on the floor," Elder Kira said accusingly. "It's a monster. You know the rules—you have to kill it."

Askari laughed and then scowled at Elder Kira. "No," she said flatly, lying through her teeth. "She's not a monster. She's a rodent. Polly saved my life and I'm not killing her."

Elder Kira faced Askari with a fierce, angry glare of her own.

"What do you mean she's not a monster?" Kira scoffed. "She looks like a minket to me."

"She's a rodent." Askari raised her voice in defiance. "I found her in the forest, and as you've always told us,

225

monsters are trying to kill us. She saved me, so therefore, she's obviously not a monster."

"First we find you're consorting with hulla, now protecting minkets—I always knew you were going to be trouble." Kira's voice was so low, it almost sounded like a growl.

"I wasn't consorting with hulla," Askari shot back. "However, if you'll remember, they are the ones that chased the gyiks off, saving potentially countless Baratok lives. And secondly, yes, I'm protecting this *rodent*, because she saved my life. It sounds to me like you'd rather our people died by the dozen than ever be helped by a monster. Not all monsters are bad, you know." Askari would pretend Polly was a rodent until she died if it meant she was even a little safer from some Baratok (ahem, Kira) executing her when Askari wasn't paying attention.

"Get out!" Elder Kira screamed. Her eyes narrowed and her fists tightened. Askari had never seen her this angry. "Get out right now, and don't come back!"

Askari glared at Elder Kira, her mind and heart racing. If she got kicked out now, she would probably get eaten by rarohan. But she wouldn't let Kira kill an innocent creature, especially not one that had saved Askari's life on numerous occasions. If they wanted her to leave, she would.

"Now, now," Faro cut in sharply, raising a hand as if it would help calm everyone. "I don't think that's necessary. Askari did help us win against the gyiks, and we still have to fight the rarohan. We need every good soldier. But perhaps she can set Polly here loose, and then vow never to interact with monsters again."

"Why?" Askari asked, frowning. At this rate, the elders would condemn the whole community to death by garg. "If monsters can help us, why shouldn't we work with them? You know, the whole 'enemy of my enemy' thing? We're dying here—how many Baratok have died or been injured since encountering the rarohan? And the gyiks? Not to mention, we're still missing over twenty people! This whole situation has got you breaking your own rules—splitting up, hiding in caves, getting gargs to attack each other! We're trapped, and we're going to have to fight our way out. I'd rather use a minket and some hulla to get us out of this than adhere to old-fashioned, straitlaced ideas that are only—"

"Your mother, your father, your grandmother, all had dangerous ideas like this!" Kira interrupted, fury bleeding from every pore. "And even though we brought you up outside of their influence, you are the same! The same!" She turned to face the other elders. "She'll bring us more harm than good, I swear to you!"

"That seems doubtful," Elol spoke up, wiping his mouth with the back of his hand and giving a tired sigh. Everyone quieted and turned toward him—he rarely spoke during elder meetings, and when he did, everyone paid heed. "She has yet to do any harm to the community, despite her tendency to break our rules, and in fact, she's done a lot of good. She saved Shujaa and Harcos, which is their reasoning for going to help her, and her interactions with the hulla ended what

227

could have been a costly battle, as far as lives are concerned. I know you hated Minda, Kira, but let's not lose focus on our real goal here, which is to escape this cave and get back to our normal existence. We need every strong warrior we've got, and Askari is one of the best. You can't deny that."

What did Minda have to do with anything? It must have to do with Minda's distaste of Kira's rules. Askari was distracted for a moment, but then Kira started ranting again.

"I certainly can deny it!" Kira retorted. "She may be skilled with weapons and a fast runner, but she is divisive, disobedient, and unwilling to see reason. If we let her stay, she will destroy our community from the inside out."

"She may change it," Elol said slowly, "but change is not the same as destruction." He put one hand up in the air. "I vote to let Askari stay until after we have gotten out of this predicament. We can reconvene at a later date for further discussion, if necessary."

"Seconded," Faro said, raising his hand.

Slowly, Timo raised her hand as well.

"I vote she be cast out immediately," Elder Kira countered, raising her hand.

Sheo raised her hand, sending Askari an apologetic look. "I'm sorry," she said, "it's just that we are in a tight spot right now and can't afford any more discord."

Everyone turned to Dano, who sat with her head in her hands. Finally, she looked up.

"On the one hand," she said, "I agree with Kira that it is dangerous to have discord among us at a time when we are so vulnerable as a community. However, I think casting Askari out would create a different type of discord, and not actually solve the problem. I vote Askari stay until we're back on our feet. Then we can discuss the matter again."

Askari thought she should feel relieved, but she didn't. She burned with anger from the bottom of her littlest toe to the ends of her braids. She didn't deserve this hatred from Kira. At least now she knew that they knew who her family was and just didn't tell her. She would do some more digging while they were stuck in this cave, so she would know before she got kicked out—after all, it was only a matter of time. She didn't have any intention of following a rule if it was stupid, and even if they let her stay, that wasn't going to change.

She took a deep breath and straightened her shoulders, feeling Polly's fingers dig into her scalp. "I'll be doing something useful with myself if you need me," she said. She strode to the exit, pausing only to pick up her bag as she left.

Harcos and Shujaa were standing in the tunnel when she turned the corner. Askari paused to scratch the minket's head, making soft, reassuring noises.

"Polly!" Harcos exclaimed, reaching out his hands. The minket gladly leaped from Askari's shoulders into Harcos' waiting arms. Apparently, his steady supply of treats had made them best friends. He scratched Polly behind the ears while she purred, and then fed her a tidbit from his pocket.

"What happened?" Harcos asked, happily sharing his snack supply with the creature.

"Well, they didn't kick me out," Askari replied bluntly, "but they did vote on it."

Shujaa's jaw dropped. "They voted on it in the middle of a community-wide crisis?" she gasped.

"Absurd, I know, but we can't talk about it here." Askari gestured toward the narrow light that indicated the entrance to the tunnel. "Shall we get out of this dark hole in the ground?"

"Actually," Harcos said, "we got sent in deeper. They want us to find Vica and see if she needs help with anything. We're also supposed to find a place to bunk."

Askari sighed. She didn't want to be underground any longer than necessary. "Okay."

The path leading deeper into the tunnel was littered with small rocks and pebbles, making for precarious footing. It was also dark; the only light came from two small points—the glow of the fire where the elders now debated their next course of action and the daylight at the entrance to the tunnel. It got darker and darker the further underground they went—then they turned a corner.

Askari gasped, surprised and awed. The enormous cavern opened up around them, the ceiling arching far overhead, with glowing blue lights covering every vertical surface. An underground creek provided fresh water, and the stalactites and stalagmites glistened blue in the darkened room. Several hundred Baratok filled the space, some working, moving around, helping take care of wounded. Others rested on mats or in their bedrolls.

"This explains where everyone went," Harcos said dryly.

"It's beautiful." Shujaa craned her neck around, trying to take in the sight.

"Coming through!" Adelbert shouted from behind them. He was walking backward, carrying one end of a stretcher. A grimacing Baratok lay prostrate, bloody hand clasped over his abdomen.

Askari stepped back out of the way and watched them rush the wounded archer over to one end of the cavern where the medics had set up shop. They were still cleaning up from the gyik fight. The archer had been swiped from behind, and pretty deeply too; blood gushed from the wound. He would be fine, though, once they stitched up the gash.

"Let's go find Vica," Harcos said, stepping forward and leading them deeper into the cavern.

As they moved through the cavern, her initial awe at the glowing plants faded a bit. The cavern might be beautiful, Askari thought, but it didn't make up for the feeling that it might come crashing down on them at any moment—all that rock and dirt and trees, and for all they knew, gargs too.

"Vica!" Harcos called.

"Well it's about time!" she exclaimed, coming over to give each of them a big hug. Her wild hair had been pulled into a messy ponytail that stuck straight out from the back of her head. "I'm so glad you're safe! Now who's this?" She held out her arms to Polly, who leaped from Shujaa to Vica in one clean jump. Vica scratched her behind the ears, smiling. "I had a minket once," she whispered, winking at Askari. "Best friend ever." She turned to look at Askari. "How'd you get Elder Kira to let you keep her?"

Askari shrugged and smiled innocently. "She's not a minket. She's a rodent, and there aren't any rules against those. Are there?"

Vica let out a roaring laugh. "Oh, Askari, you do keep them on their toes, don't you?" She wiped her eyes, chest still heaving in silent laughter.

"Where can we settle in?" Harcos asked, glancing around the already crowded room.

"Well, now," Vica said, letting Polly scurry to Askari. "Why don't you set your bags down in that corner over there? I'll have Luca make up a space for you."

They turned and took their bags over to the corner while Vica spoke in quiet tones to Luca. He waved at them and strode off.

Askari plopped down near the cavern wall, feeling a little bit better about being underground. It was much less stressful to be in this big room than the narrow tunnel, even though logically she knew any part of the cave could fall on her at any time, regardless of how small the space was.

"He'll be back in a jiffy to show you what he's figured out," Vica said pleasantly. "Now, if you will—" She broke off as Rudi appeared in the entrance to the tunnel, waving at her. "One minute."

She walked in his direction as he wove through the crowd of Baratok. Askari watched him for a minute. He was about the same age as she was, tall, and a good warrior. He got message duty a lot though, which meant that all of the elders liked him. Must be nice.

"Vica's waving at us," Shujaa said.

They hurried over to her.

"You three," Vica said, a worried frown on her face, "have a new assignment from the elders."

Askari almost groaned, but caught herself. She didn't want anyone to think she was complaining—she had to do what they asked, no matter how ridiculous, or they would kick her out again.

Vica leaned forward and said in a hushed tone, "They want you to take care of the barlang."

"The what?" Harcos exclaimed loudly.

"Shhhhh!" Vica put her finger over her lips. "Not many people know it's here."

"You knowingly camped in a cave with a barlang!?" Harcos was trying hard not to yell, but he looked as though he was about to have a heart attack.

"Barlang?" Askari whispered, keeping her voice low.

"It's a cave garg," Harcos said, shaking his head with fury. "They're solitary, and as long as we avoid them, it should avoid us. But that's not the point! The point is, *there is a reason we don't go in caves!*"

"We didn't have a lot of options," Vica said calmly. "Now, the elders would like you three to take care of it."

"So... so..." Shujaa broke in, stuttering. "There are rarohan and gyiks outside, and a barlang inside? We're trapped?"

"Not trapped," Rudi said calmly, "if you kill the barlang." Askari noticed that his forehead creases had deepened—he was worried. He had been eavesdropping on the elders, too, so he must know something they didn't.

"What else did they say?" she asked him.

He shook his head. "Their exact instructions were: 'go tell Vica to tell Askari, Harcos, and Shujaa to kill the barlang.' That's it."

"That's what they told you to say," Askari said. "What else did you hear?"

He shook his head rapidly.

"He's bound to confidence," Vica said, "so stop asking. Now, I recommend you take a bow and arrow and some blades, which it looks like you already have, and get going, before night falls. They get more active at night, you know."

Askari stared at Vica for a moment, trying to figure out how to protest, and then gave up. The elders were clearly trying to get her killed. If it wasn't the barlang today, then it would be a rarohan tomorrow, or a harebrained quest the next day. "Where is it?"

Vica pointed across the cavern. "There is a long tunnel, there, where the stream comes through. It's near the end."

"Let's go," Askari said, reaching up to touch Polly, who grabbed her hand reassuringly.

"If I'd known being friends with you would get me into this," Shujaa muttered, "I never would have gone after you."

"Good luck," Vica called.

Askari gritted her teeth and followed Shujaa and Harcos. Of all the jobs she could be doing, this was the last possible one she wanted. Going deeper into a series of caves and tunnels that could collapse on her head at any moment? To find a garg that wanted to eat her and kill it? Her chest tightened, and for a moment she felt a little dizzy, but she took a deep breath. It didn't matter. She had to do as asked. She wasn't afraid to break rules, but this wasn't a good time.

Each of them took a torch from the bin, and then headed toward the first tunnel, which looked like a gaping black hole—a garg's mouth, silent, waiting for prey to wander in. Polly chattered a little when they first entered, but then fell quiet, hanging onto Askari's shoulders.

"You going in?" Marton, the Baratok guarding the entrance, asked. Marton wasn't able to train as a Warrior because he was born with a limp, but he was a natural leader, great at organizing things and solving problems. Everyone knew he would be one of the elders eventually.

"We'll be back soon, hopefully," Harcos said. He led them into the tunnel, his light falling on the damp rock walls around them. "Listen for screaming."

Marton laughed, but Askari could tell he didn't really think the joke was funny.

This tunnel was tall enough that they could easily walk through it standing up, but it still made Askari pretty nervous. A trickle of water flowed underneath their feet, making the pathway slippery, and the shadows from the torches flickered in the darkness, creating pockets of complete and utter blackness. A cold breeze drifted past, making her shiver. She found herself wishing for the days when she was walking alone in the pouring rain, fighting off gambas. After about a hundred feet, the tunnel opened up to a small cavern. A little light from outside shone down from a crack in the rock, but it didn't do much to penetrate the darkness. The ceiling was only a few inches higher than Askari's head, giving her the sensation that she needed to crouch, even though she was technically short enough to fit.

"Nothing in here," Harcos said.

The tunnel kept going on the opposite side of the cavern. Harcos led the way and Askari kept close to his heels, one hand resting on Polly. She found the presence of the minket calming. The next cavern was slightly bigger, but had no gaps to the outside. Askari surveyed the space—the bioluminescent lichen in this one was more of an orangish color. It was pretty, but she liked the blue better.

"This cavern is clear too," Harcos said. "No bats, either, I noticed."

"Probably eaten by the garg," Shujaa suggested, "or hiding from the humans that unceremoniously invaded."

Askari shuddered. That did not sound fun. Bats, hiding somewhere in the caves, waiting to attack them, get in her hair... She reached up and touched Polly for comfort again. Polly would probably love that. She'd eat all the ones she could get her little garg hands on.

The next tunnel sloped downwards into the earth. It got darker and darker, all hints of bioluminescent lichen disappearing. Only the orange glow of their torches lit the way. Askari felt more and more nervous as she imagined the mountain growing up, while the tunnels led them deeper. It meant more dirt to fill her lungs, more rock to crush her skull—the tunnel felt like it was narrowing, tightening around her, and she became aware that her breaths were shallow and she was feeling dizzy.

"Deep breaths," Shujaa murmured from behind her. "Deep breaths."

Askari tried to focus on the flickering light of the torch, tried to put the thoughts of the rock and the dirt and the mountain out of her head. She consciously began to shift her breathing, counting slowly in, then out. In, then out. In, then out. The dizzy feeling faded and her tension lessened, but she still did not want to be down here. Not one bit.

Another cavern opened up around them. Askari took a long, relieved breath as the light spread out before them. This cavern was similar to the one where the Baratok camped—wide open, lots of stalactites and stalagmites, rocks covering the floor. She felt a little better with all the space around her. She wanted nothing more than to be back above ground.

Polly began to chatter and click, jumping down onto the floor and running into the darkness. She came sprinting back, and then turned and disappeared into the dark again, running back and forth between Askari and something Askari couldn't see.

Harcos slid his blade from its sheath slowly and softly.

"Something's there," Askari whispered, hand on the hilt of her machete. "Move forward together?"

Harcos nodded, and Shujaa moved up so they could form a line. Slowly, holding their torches out in front of them, they moved forward, one step at a time. Then Shujaa gasped.

Askari turned; on the floor in front of her lay a dead body. She clapped her hand over her mouth so she wouldn't make any sound. She turned to see Harcos staring at the body with wide eyes.

"That's Raul," he whispered, "one of the missing Baratok." They moved another few steps forward, and a second pair of feet became visible in the light of the torches. Harcos moved toward them. "Phoebe," he whispered.

Then, from deep in the darkness came a low mournful howl, punctuated by a snapping noise. A long arm reached into the light and snatched Shujaa up. She shrieked, shoving her torch toward the creature. For a moment, Askari saw its face, long and bony, with giant teeth and big black eyes, two huge ears, and massive, muscular walking arms that held the head eight feet off the ground. It had four smaller arms, one of which held Shujaa. The others flailed in the air, searching for anything it could grab or touch. Then, it knocked the torch out of her hand; it flew through the air and landed in the corner, sizzling out.

Askari whipped out her bow and sent an arrow flying toward the creature. It bounced off the bone of its face. Harcos scampered forward and drove his blade into the muscular arm, but that bounced off too. Whipping another arrow out of her quiver, Askari looked at its arm, its face, its teeth—and aimed for the eye. The arrow burrowed in; the barlang screeched but didn't let go of Shujaa. Instead, it began to move toward them.

Harcos tried again, this time, lifting up his blade as high as he could and trying to cut off one of the shorter arms. The barlang screeched again, but aimed all three of its flailing arms in Harcos' direction.

"Try the fire!" Askari yelled.

Harcos lifted his torch and held it toward the barlang, trying to burn its flesh. The barlang backed off a little, but still didn't let go of Shujaa.

"You need to run!" Shujaa yelled. "It's too strong!"

"But what about you?" Harcos shouted.

"It's too strong!" she said again. "You know the stories—once you get caught, you never get free."

"No!" Harcos exclaimed.

"Run!" Shujaa repeated.

"She'll have no chance if we get caught too!" Askari yelled at Harcos. "We need different weapons, and we know where it is now!"

She turned and began to run up the tunnel, feet splashing in the rivulets of water that ran across the floor. She stumbled once, slipping on the marble-like pebbles, but leaped to her feet again as she reached the next cavern. If she could get to the main cavern, she could grab something different—an axe, maybe, or a crossbow, and get Marton to start building a wall across the tunnel entrance in case they failed. Then she could come back and help save Shujaa.

Polly leaped off Askari's shoulders and darted back toward the barlang. She chattered and clicked, diving toward the barlang's face. Askari glanced over her shoulder to see Polly run up and over and around, poking it, prodding it, and being generally annoying. The barlang tried to swat her off, first with one arm, then two. Finally, it dropped Shujaa in order to swat at Polly. Shujaa landed on the rock floor with a thud. She pulled herself to her feet and began to sprint toward the tunnel.

Askari glanced back. "Come on, Shujaa!" she yelled.

Harcos reached out a hand to help Shujaa forward, and together they ran, through the tunnel, through the caverns, bursting out into the main cavern where everyone was working and sleeping.

"It's coming!" Askari yelled. "The barlang!"

"And it killed Raul and Phoebe!" Shujaa added, gasping for breath.

"Block the entrance! Block it!" Harcos added.

Marton leaped into action, grabbing a large rock, shoving it with all his might toward the entrance to the tunnel. Several others jumped right in without delay, grabbing rocks from places they had piled them out of the way and throwing them into the tunnel entrance. A moment later, everyone was moving, talking, shouting; the cavern was a hubbub of movement and sound. People scurried around packing bedrolls, food, and supplies, and Vica was shouting orders with a booming voice over the crowd.

Harcos, Shujaa, and Askari dropped their torches began to help shift rocks with the others.

"We need to get it as high as possible!" Harcos yelled over the crowd. "They're slow compared to other gargs, but they can climb walls and hang from ceilings!"

"What are we going to do?" Shujaa asked Askari in a hushed voice, her eyes wide. "We're literally stuck between a barlang and pack of rarohan."

"This is what we get when the leaders of a community break their own rules," Askari muttered. "Yet I'm the only one who ever gets in trouble."

"What rule?" Shujaa asked.

"Never go in caves?" Askari reminded her. "They practically beat it into our heads when we were kids because caves are fun to play in." She wiped the sweat out of her eyes and bent down to move a rock that was a little too heavy.

"Let me help with that." Askari looked up to see Elder Kira standing there. She reached out, and together they heaved the rock onto the pile.

"It's here! It's here!" someone screamed. Askari looked up to see an arm shoot through the opening at the top of the rock pile and swing around, searching for something.

"Someone shoot it!" Marton called from the top of the rock pile. He produced a long hunting knife and began to stab at the barlang's arm.

"We need a crossbow!" Askari yelled. "Regular bows don't work!"

Rudi sprinted up to her, carrying a crossbow. "You're a better shot," he said, handing it to her.

Askari grabbed it. She took aim in the flickering light and squeezed the trigger, letting the arrow fly. It embedded deep into the barlang's arm; the garg howled in pain, yanking its arm back through the gap.

"Quick!" Kira exclaimed, hoisting a smaller rock. "We have to fill the gap!" She ran up the pile and deposited it at the top, gesturing for others to do the same. Everyone leaped into action, creating an assembly line of rocks, each dropped on the top of the pile.

Then, without warning, another arm shot through the hole above the rock pile. Kira screamed as it grabbed her around her waist and tried to drag her through the gap. There were enough rocks that the hole was too small for Kira to fit, so instead, the barlang slammed her against the rocks over and over.

Marton ran up and grabbed Kira's hands, trying to yank her out of the barlang's grip. "Somebody help!"

"No, stay back!" Askari called out.

She took aim again. This was a harder shot—the barlang was moving, and she had to be careful not to hit Kira or Marton. She could hear Rudi breathing beside her, his tension palpable. She squinted and blocked out all the noise and screaming around her. It wouldn't do to think about how much she hated Kira, or about the weight of the mountain over her head, or about the screams of her fellow Baratok, or about how the rarohan were coming and they might all die even if she did make this shot. Instead, she took a deep breath. And then another. The room around her faded like it was a thousand miles away, and all she could see in her mind was the barlang's arm and Kira's body, moving, side to side, up and down, and then even that slowed as she listened to her heart beat. In slow motion, the arm swung left, then right, then right, then left... and Askari let the arrow fly. It thudded into the monster's arm, inches from Kira's own.

Everything jumped back into real time. The barlang screeched again, dropping Kira and pulling its arm back into the tunnel. Kira tumbled down the pile of rocks and lay still at the bottom as several others ran forward to help.

"Nice shot," Rudi muttered beside her.

"But how are we supposed to finish this wall if the garg keeps grabbing us?" Harcos asked, wide-eyed with panic.

Askari shook her head. She had no idea. That's what they were supposed to have leaders for. To figure out problems like this.

"And if we don't finish it," Harcos continued, "then it's only a matter of time before it starts knocking the rocks down—"

He broke off as the barlang began to do just that. It reached out tentatively with one arm and pushed a rock that rolled down the pile and came to a halt at the bottom, before pulling its arm back in. It pushed another, and another, and

Leka rushed in, hurrying to get Kira out of harm's way. Everyone else stepped back.

"What are we supposed to do?" someone yelled.

There was silence.

"Run?" someone else suggested.

"Too late for that," a voice called from the other end of the cave. "The rarohan are coming. They'll be here in less than twenty minutes." Askari frowned. The voice sounded familiar, but she couldn't place it.

A loud roar went up from the crowd as everyone began to process this news. They were stuck between a barlang and a pack of rarohan. Literally. Terminally. A child began to scream, and Askari could hear adults softly crying as well.

"Survival," Askari muttered to herself. Somehow they had to survive.

"That's the spirit." The voice that had announced the return of the rarohan sounded from Askari's elbow. Askari turned.

"Minda?" she exclaimed. "What are you doing here?"

Minda grinned at Askari. She wore loose-fitting grey pants and a black tank top, and carried a large backpack.

"Heard that the Baratok were having a little trouble with some gargs," she replied. "Turns out, gargs are my specialty."

"I don't suppose you have a way to get out of this?" Askari asked.

"Not exactly," Minda said, "but I've got some ideas."

"Like what?" Askari asked.

"First thing we need to do is get these people out of here."

"And how do you expect to do that?"

"Through that tunnel." Minda pointed to the tunnel where the barlang sat, pushing rocks down and slowly making the hole bigger. Marton stood to the side, frantically trying to fill the hole faster than the barlang made it bigger. "There's an exit at the other end. The children and sick can escape out the back while the warriors fight the rarohan."

"I don't suppose you noticed the barlang," Askari said dryly, wondering for a moment what had happened that her life had turned into this ridiculous saga of monster after monster, with no apparent relief, making perverse jokes in the face of certain death.

"I'll take care of it," Minda said. "You got a flashlight? Torch won't work."

"I do," Shujaa said. She jogged to the other side of the room and returned a few minutes later with one of the solar-powered flashlights they had found at the post office. "I don't know how much juice it has."

"I only need it to work for about two minutes," Minda said. She handed the flashlight to Askari. "You're coming with me. And you two—" she turned to face Harcos and Shujaa "—are going to tell everyone in this room to cover their ears. Understand? There is going to be a very loud noise."

Shujaa and Harcos rushed off, shouting to everyone to quiet down and cover their ears while Minda led Askari toward the rock pile.

"Take these and put them in your ears." Minda pulled two rubbery orange things out of her pocket and handed them to Askari, and then she pulled out two more for her own ears. As soon as Askari put them in, she felt like she was standing a little farther away from the chaos, even though she could see everyone running around only inches from her. The world was muted, quieter, calmer—except that it wasn't.

Minda began to scale the pile of rocks with Askari right behind her. She turned and said, "Get your machete out, in case it grabs one of us."

Askari shifted the flashlight to her right hand and slipped her machete out of its sheath with her left, sidestepping to dodge another rock that came rolling down from the top. Behind them, the room began to quiet as people stopped what they were doing and covered their ears.

Crouched low at the top of the rock pile, Minda gestured for Askari to point the flashlight into the tunnel. Askari held it up, aiming for the barlang's eyes. It squealed and stepped back. It made sense, Askari thought, that a cave creature wouldn't like light.

Minda pulled a small metal thing out of her pocket, pointing it into the tunnel toward the barlang, which still cowered and tried to get out of the light. Askari couldn't see it very well, and she didn't recognize what the item was.

"What is that?" she asked.

"A gun," Minda replied, and then she pulled the trigger.

It was the loudest sound Askari had ever heard, louder even than the bell at Minda's house. She felt like her brain was rattling inside her skull, like her eyes had turned to jelly. The sound echoed in the room, and several people screamed.

Then Minda pulled the trigger again—two, three, four times.

The barlang stumbled back and began to scream, a high, piercing sound that made Askari cringe. Then the sound ceased as it tumbled and fell with a thump, lying motionless on the cold cave floor.

Minda didn't waste a second. She crawled through the hole at the top of the rockpile and down the other side to where the massive creature lay stretched out on the floor.

"I feel bad," Minda said softly, looking up at Askari. "Barlangs are peaceful creatures, as long as you don't invade their home." She shook her head and then kicked the barlang as hard as she could. It didn't move, but she leaned over and emptied the gun's remaining bullets into its skull anyway.

Askari stared, frozen. The barlang was dead.

CHAPTER 10: THE ELNOK

THE NEXT HALF HOUR was a blur of activity. Vica and Minda worked together to prepare all of the sick and vulnerable to move, while Elol positioned the warriors to prepare for the arrival of the rarohan. There had been an argument about the gun, which Minda insisted didn't have any bullets left and wouldn't work on a rarohan anyway. They also managed to scrounge up some vinegar, which was now set in strategic places amid the archers and near rocks down on the field.

Askari stood on the ledge overlooking the plains, bow in hand. The sky started as light blue toward the west, then faded to periwinkle. The eastern sky had already begun to show the deepening blue of night. The sun had lowered behind the trees and the stars peeked between the thin, wispy clouds that floated overhead. The moon was still quite bright, though it was now closer to a half moon than a full one.

Then she saw them. The rarohan. But this time there were more—many, many more. The group they had narrowly avoided earlier that day had multiplied from seven into fifty or more. They ran through the plains at a pace that took Askari's breath away, leaving a trail of trampled grasses in their wake. Where had they all come from? It was an army, and to survive, the Baratok had to kill every single one.

The sun dropped a little more, and the moon shone a little brighter as Askari aimed at the incoming gargs.

"Now!" Elol shouted, and thirty arrows flew through the air. One rarohan reared back, screaming, as six arrows hit it right in the eyes and nose. The bones in its face began to steam and melt as it slumped to the ground in a heap of fur.

"I guess the vinegar works," Askari muttered to herself, loosing another arrow. A tiny bubble of hope welled in her abdomen.

A minute or two later, the pack of rarohan reached the row of warriors on the ground, standing shoulder to shoulder to face the monsters. Their job was simple: stall them long enough that the rest of the Baratok could escape. The Baratok warriors roared and surged forward, attacking with swords and spears dipped in vinegar. Askari shot arrow after arrow until her fingers began to bleed.

A boy stopped by with a flask of water; his name was Wil, and he was only about twelve years old. Askari remembered when he was born—he had almost died during childbirth, and now here he was, likely to die in the face of a giant skeletal cat.

"You're supposed to be leaving," she said, gulping the water he offered.

"I'm going to fight!" he exclaimed, and moved on to the next archer.

It got darker and darker with each passing moment as the sun began to disappear. Soon, Askari wouldn't be able to see enough to shoot—the moon certainly wouldn't offer enough light—so she and the other archers would have to descend to the bottom of Arc Hill and fight with blades. She took a breath and stepped back for a moment, surveying the scene below. The rarohan fought with their claws, roaring and attacking, while the Baratok warriors ducked and rolled, trying desperately to land blows while avoiding being sliced open or chomped down on.

At least three Baratok had died, compared to only four rarohan—that was too many. They had to do something. They couldn't keep up this pace. There were too many rarohan, and more of them were arriving every minute.

Then she heard a clicking and chattering behind her. She turned and let out a startled shriek. Polly was—very slowly—dragging a rarohan across the rocks. Askari took a deep breath and looked again—it was dead. It was enormous, and had they not been in the middle of a battle, Askari might have found it rather comical. Polly had the bony tail in her mouth, and was using her entire body to drag the weight of the rarohan up the hill.

"Where did you get that?" Askari exclaimed.

Polly gave a disturbing, red-eyed grin, and slid long, sharp claws out of the back of her hands.

"You killed it?" Askari didn't believe it. If three or four humans with swords and spears couldn't kill a rarohan, how did a tiny little minket do it?

The minket chattered happily, scampering up onto the rarohan's mane and ripping open the back of the head to reveal the skull beneath.

Askari ran over to her, kneeling down beside the dead rarohan. "Wait, wait!" she exclaimed, trying to get the minket's attention. "How, Polly? How did you kill it?" Ignoring her, Polly pulled back a fist, with claws extended, and smashed it through the bone, revealing the tissue inside. She reached in and pulled out a handful of brains. Her attention was now fully on eating.

"Please, Polly?" Askari begged. The garg was the size of a horse, easily twenty times bigger than Polly. Its claws could have easily shredded Polly into spaghetti, but somehow this tiny creature had brought it down. If only they knew how, maybe they could use the same trick to give the warriors some advantage over the rarohan.

Polly gave Askari a side-eyed look while eating a handful of brains. She was clearly not going to be any help. Askari began to examine the rarohan from the back to the front. The head (except for where Polly had crushed the skull) was intact. There wasn't any damage around the eyes or nose. She opened the rarohan's mouth with the tip of an arrow and peered inside. That seemed fine too. Moving down the length of its body, she examined first its front paws—the talons made her a little nervous this close, even though she knew it was dead—then the back paws and tail. Finally, she took a closer look at the skeleton. It was all bone, so no one had ever focused their attention on attacking it—after all, what effect could it have? But as she looked closer, she saw that a large hump connecting the head to the spine was in splinters. It appeared Polly had ripped it open with her claws. Not only that, but bluish blood gushed from inside of the bone. Some kind of artery must have been there, and blood loss had killed it.

"The hump," Askari breathed. "Smash the bone at the back of its neck. Is that right, Polly?"

Polly chattered happily, still chewing on the rarohan's brains.

"Gross," Askari muttered. It didn't matter though—she had the answer. The bubble of hope grew a little bit bigger. Maybe they could still win. She turned to the archer beside her. "I have to go down there," she said. "I'll leave my bow here, in case yours breaks."

"Let the garg's blood rain," the archer said, loosing an arrow into the fray below.

"Garg's blood rain," Askari replied.

She sprinted down the hill as fast as she could go without losing her balance. She had to tell Elol and the warriors. This could turn the battle for them if the warriors could work in pairs. She scrambled into the cave, which was now so dark it would have been impossible to see if not for the torches placed periodically along the tunnel.

"Hammers!" she yelled, sliding into the main cavern. "Do we have any hammers?"

There were only a few dozen people left inside, as everyone else had begun their trek down the barlang's tunnel.

"They're over here, Askari!" Vica called from beside the Baratok arsenal. It looked like most people had opted to take axes, swords, and other types of blades, but there were still several hammers at the bottom, some long handled and some short. Better yet, she saw several mauls, a mace, and a flail.

Askari grabbed as much as she could carry and jogged back up the tunnel to the outdoors, dumping them in a heap just outside of the mouth of the cave. Shujaa stood outside the front door. Her arm was bleeding, and Leka was finishing tying it up.

"We need to spread the word!" Askari exclaimed. "There's a hump! On their back!"

"So?" Shujaa said, looking at Askari intently.

"Smash it! They'll bleed out!"

"How did you learn that?" Shujaa exclaimed, taking the hammer that Askari handed her.

"Polly," was all Askari said before she dove into the fray.

The closest rarohan was fighting Zaj and Sasa. One would attract its attention, dodging its claws, while the other stabbed and sliced at the garg with a blade. Where the vinegar touched the monster, it steamed and the bones seemed to melt. The rarohan would bellow in pain, and then attack again more vigorously.

The rarohan leaped toward Sasa. Askari jumped forward, holding a mace high over her head. The problem was that the rarohan was so tall, it was difficult to get the exact spot. It didn't matter though—she would hit it until either she or it died. Askari brought the mace down, cracking a rib right below the large hump connecting the garg's head to its spine. It roared, and as quickly as she could, Askari brought the mace down again, this time hitting the correct bone. It was the strangest sight to see, as if all at once the rarohan's body didn't work, couldn't function, and it bent in half, trying to claw its way back into a standing position. Blood spurted everywhere.

Sasa leaped forward with her machete outstretched and dragged it across the rarohan's throat. The monster slumped to the ground, dead.

"How did you know to do that?" Zaj yelled.

"Take this!" Askari tossed him a mace. "It's the big lump right behind the head!"

She ran back to the mouth of the cave where she had left the pile of hammers. Half of them were already gone, but there were several new tools there now—sledgehammers, axes, and more mauls. Shujaa must have been spreading the word.

"Askari!" a voice called. She turned to see Elol standing on a rock. "You're with me! Grab a hammer!"

Askari grabbed a sledgehammer with a long handle and ran toward him, ducking as a rarohan claw appeared from nowhere. Then an arrow landed right in the rarohan's eye. It steamed and smoked, and then the face dripped and blurred, melting off. The rarohan collapsed into a heap. Askari waved in the general direction of the archers and kept running. When she came around the rock, she gasped. Elol was facing the biggest rarohan she had ever seen. It wasn't just the size of a horse, it was more like the size of three horses. In order to kill it, she somehow had to get up on its back.

She swallowed and looked around. Rocks. That was what she had; that was what she'd use.

"I'm coming!" she yelled to Elol, and then scrambled up onto the nearest rock. When she reached the top, she looked down. Elol was face-to-face with the rarohan, brandishing his sword.

"Closer!" Askari shouted.

Elol turned tail and ran toward the rock as fast as he could, aiming to pass by it on one side. The rarohan dodged the opposite direction, as if to meet Elol head-on around the other side. Askari crouched down, sledgehammer in one hand, and as the rarohan moved past the rock, she jumped, landing on its bony back.

It was an extremely uncomfortable position, she noted in passing. Like sitting on a tree with lots of nubs of broken branches—a tree that was running around. She straddled the spinal column of the garg, holding on to its ribcage with one hand. She lifted a hand to bring down the hammer, and the rarohan reared, howling. Askari was flung backward and slid down one side of its back, desperately holding on with one hand. But her hand was sweaty, and she began to slip, down,

down one long rib of the rarohan. Gritting her teeth, she flung the hammer over the spinal column, hooking it around a bone and holding on to the handle as tightly as she could.

The rarohan howled again, but this time crouched low. Askari glanced over to see that Elol had tripped and fallen, and now lay on the ground.

"Get up!" Askari yelled.

The rarohan tilted its head, looking around to see what had made noise so close to its head. Hurriedly, Askari pulled herself back up, this time wrapping her arms around the skeleton just before it reared again, its howl piercing the rapidly falling night. The sharp bones dug into her chest and stomach, and she grimaced in pain.

Then the rarohan landed on its two feet again, aiming for Elol. In one smooth motion, Askari sat up, raised the hammer, and brought it down again on the hump behind its head. Then she smashed it again and again, just to be safe. Blood gushed everywhere, covering her shirt. The rarohan screamed in pain, and then its back bent inward, as if it were folding up into a neat pile of bones. Elol leaped up and swiftly pulled his sword across the garg's throat. Blood poured out all over the grass and dirt, as Askari slipped off the monster's back and landed solidly on the ground.

She took a deep breath, but there was no time for more than that. Another rarohan raised a cry as soon as it saw that the largest monster was dead, and they set in again with vigor. Askari stuck by Elol's side as another beast raced forward. It was fight or die.

The sun was completely gone before Askari was able to take a break. She hid behind a rock, drinking water from a flask she had found lying on the ground. All of the archers were now either fighting with swords and hammers, dead, or had fled into the caves. Despite their success with the Polly Method, the rarohan were killing and maiming a good number of their people, and in the twilight, it was hard to tell how many monsters were left.

A moment later, there was a commotion from the center of the pack of rarohan. One by one they began to howl, a grating screech that made Askari cringe. She stood up and peered into the fading light. Two of the largest creatures were up on their hind legs, attacking each other with teeth and claws. One of them was taller and easily knocked the other to the ground. They began tumbling over each other, growling and ripping at each other's faces. The other rarohan had paused their assault to watch.

Then Elol's voice rose above the noise. "Fall back! Into the caves!" Askari hooked the now-empty flask to her belt, and jogged toward the cave. Other warriors swarmed over, some choosing to finish off a rarohan before running, others making a dash for it as fast as they could.

The fastest runners entered the cave first, while the final stragglers had to dodge a couple of distracted rarohan as they made their way toward the hill. Askari found herself stuck in the middle somewhere. She looked around her, noticing that what had started as a group of nearly one hundred warriors was now closer to sixty. If forty people were truly lost or missing so far—that was a huge hit to their community. She wondered if they would be able to recover.

"Askari!" Shujaa exclaimed from behind. Askari turned to see her pushing through the crowd. She wrapped Askari in a hug. "I'm so glad you're okay! Have you seen Harcos?"

"I'm over here!" Harcos called, shouting from the front of the line. Askari felt relieved. In any other situation, Harcos wouldn't have been asked to fight. He was a researcher, a scientist, someone who could read, and he had only received the basic warrior training, enough to defend himself. Shujaa too might not have been asked to fight, though she was much more skilled than Harcos, as she was young, barely of age, and also skilled at plants, potions, and poisons.

"What do you think is happening?" Shujaa asked.

"Some sort of leadership upset," Harcos hypothesized as they drew close to him. "My theory is that there are at least three or four packs of rarohan here—maybe even five. Each pack has their own leader, and as leaders die, the other groups are blending together or picking new leaders. I think that fight is a power struggle."

"That makes this a good opportunity then," Askari replied. "If we get as many warriors as possible into the caves, we can blockade it and escape out the other side, while helping protect the kids and sick."

The line of people slowed as they entered the mouth of the cave. They pushed forward, the people in front running as quickly as they could without falling or stumbling. Finally, they broke out into the main cavern, and everyone began to split off to the sides to make room for the remaining warriors. Askari jogged to the opposite side of the room, where she saw Minda and Faro standing together. Elol ran up to her at the same time.

"What's happening?" Minda asked, her eyes growing concerned.

"There are too many," Elol said. "There was a distraction in the rarohan pack, so I called the rest in. We'll make a barricade at the front and exit through the back with everyone else. There's nothing else we can do."

Faro's face grew pale. "This isn't going to work."

"What do you mean?" Elol asked.

"There's been a complication," Minda said.

"A complication?" A storm brewed on Elol's face. This was no time for complications—it could mean the death of everyone.

"A cave-in," Minda said. "We can't get out the back, not without digging from the other side."

Askari slowly slid to the floor, exhaustion overcoming every ounce of her body. They were trapped. No way out, no way forward. She took deep breaths, suddenly feeling the tightness in her chest, the weight of Arc Hill over her, crushing down, filling her lungs with dirt and soil. They would die here or die fighting, but did any of it really matter?

"Trapped," Askari muttered.

"No!" Faro said. "We can still dig out."

"We don't have that kind of time!" Elol exclaimed.

"Seal the tunnel then," Faro replied. "Perhaps while we are digging out, the rarohan will give up. Maybe we can wait them out."

"Trapped," Askari said again. The world suddenly seemed a whole lot smaller, a whole lot more cramped, a whole lot darker.

"No!" Minda exclaimed. "There is one more thing I can try. I... I just need to go outside. Give me ten minutes."

"We have to seal the cave," Faro argued.

Elol stood silently for a moment, looking back and forth between Minda and Faro.

Minda's eyes quietly begged him to give her a chance.

Elol shook his head. "We have to seal the cave. But yes, I can give you ten minutes. Remember, you are responsible for all the warriors who die during those ten minutes."

"I understand," Minda said. She leaned down and grabbed Askari by the arm. "You're coming with me."

"If there's a chance she can save our community," Zaj chimed in, "I'll go too." Askari looked up, surprised. She hadn't realized everyone was standing around, watching the elders debate. But all the warriors were there, watching.

"And me!" Shujaa called.

"And me." Harcos didn't look happy about it, but there was one thing Askari knew: they were all in it together. Fight or die.

"I will not fail," Zaj said, stating the first line of the Baratok Warrior's Creed.

"I will always fight," Askari said, adding her voice to his.

"To protect the community." Now everyone spoke, their voices united as one.

"From the monsters that plague our home."

Everyone fell silent for a moment.

Then Elol said, "Go. And let the garg's blood rain."

"Garg's blood rain," Minda repeated solemnly.

Together, the group jogged toward the entrance, bursting out into the twilight. The world around them shimmered and glistened, a strange effect of the tiny sliver of light that remained on the horizon. Two rarohan greeted them as they exited the mouth of the cave, though it appeared most of the others had fallen back, waiting for their pack leaders to finish their argument.

Askari opened her mouth and roared as loudly as she could, rushing forward toward the closest garg. Shujaa lifted her hammer high and followed, coming around the side of the garg as Askari jabbed her hammer toward its face. Then, it lifted one massive paw and swiped, slashing through Askari's arm. Askari screamed as Shujaa brought her hammer down on its back. Askari slit its throat for good measure and turned to help the others, only to find that Harcos and Zaj had already brought down the other one.

Minda was standing, watching.

"You better stop that," she said, gesturing to the wound in Askari's arm. It was pouring blood.

Askari nodded, and Shujaa ran up with a rag that she tied around the gash. It was blood-soaked almost immediately, but it would have to do.

Minda continued. "Before I can do anything, I need bodies—human bodies, do you understand?"

"Human bodies?" Harcos asked, a suspicious frown settling on his face.

"What for?" Zaj was also frowning.

"I need four," Minda said. "Get them, and meet me up at the Archer's Stand. Askari, you come with me." She turned and began to jog up the hill, only to be met head-on by a smaller rarohan.

"Got it!" Askari yelled, rushing forward. She picked up a bucket of vinegar that had been set out to dip arrows in, and tossed it at the garg. It squealed, high and piercing, and then melted into a pile of goop and hair.

"Take that!" she yelled. Shujaa and Harcos headed toward the nearest dead Baratok.

Askari shook her head. Whatever Minda had up her sleeve, it had better work, or else all four of them would be dead in minutes. She turned and jogged up the hill, following not too far behind Minda.

Gazing out over the plains, Askari could see very little. The rarohan were hidden in the shadows cast by the moonlight on the grasses, and what little light remained in the sky did nothing to illuminate the ground below them.

Minda stood on the ledge, hands cupped around something small that Askari couldn't see. She began to shake her hand back and forth, and a high, piercing chime rang out over and over, filling the plains with sound.

Askari winced. The sound sent ripples down her back, scraped her eardrums, pierced her skull.

Zaj gently laid the first body on the ledge beside Minda, and then ran to help Shujaa with the second. Askari shifted her focus back to the immediate scene, searching for any rarohan that might be sneaking up on them. Harcos and Shujaa laid a third body on the ledge beside Minda, while Zaj ran for the final one.

The rarohan had paused in their pursuit. Looking back over their shoulders, they crouched low and began to slink down the mountain, back into the plains where they hid among the tall grasses. Minda's chime grew lighter, softer, danced and spun through the night air.

Then, it came. The help.

It floated down gracefully, silhouetted by the periwinkle twilight sky. Its wings spread fifteen or twenty feet tip-to-tip, casting a shadow across the ledge where Minda stood beside the bodies. Its claws were as big as wagon wheels and looked as sharp as a blade, and when it alighted on the ledge, Askari could see its face—and its face was the face of a male human.

Minda bowed. "Welcome, Elnok, Queen of the Hulla," she said. "Thank you for coming."

"Do you offer me flesh?" she roared.

Askari cringed, stepping back slightly, but then stepping forward a little to make up for her moment of weakness. The queen's voice was scratchy and hoarse, uncomfortable like she didn't quite know how to make sound.

"You promised aid!" Minda shouted, standing back up to face the monster as she rested on the rock in front of her. "In return for aid, I offer flesh."

Elnok tilted her head back and began to c-c-c-cawwww, a long and eerie sound that whistled and warbled and pierced the night air. Then, she abruptly cut the sound off, though it still rang in Askari's ears.

For a few moments, nothing happened, and then Askari heard another sound—a rustling noise that was getting louder and louder. The moon and the stars disappeared, and all she could see were eerie human faces glowing in the sky. Then they dove, cackling and cawing to the ground, plucking the rarohan out of the field as if they were no heavier than mice, and dropping them, where they landed in a crushed and mangled heap on the ground.

"Your aid has arrived," the hulla queen said. "Give us until morning."

"This flesh is for you." Minda bowed ever so slightly.

Elnok let out a caw, and four hulla flapped down. Each grabbed one of the dead bodies and lifted it into the air. Harcos sank to the ground, face in his hands. Shujaa grabbed Askari's hand, gripping so tightly she thought it would bruise.

"I don't understand," Askari whispered. Then she thought maybe she did, but the thought was too strange, too horrible to even consider.

Elnok looked at Minda, then at Askari, a grin bleeding out across her strangely human lips and teeth. "I'd like her flesh," she said.

"You can't have her," Minda said. "Get lost!"

"Let her speak for herself." Elnok scooted closer to Askari, sticking her neck out, leering. "What do you say?"

Askari pulled back and then with all the strength she could muster, spit in her face.

The queen pulled back and wiped the spit off with the tip of her wing, shaking her head slowly. "I guess gratefulness doesn't run in the family." She began to laugh, a cawing, scratching sound, and then leaped into the air, soaring overhead.

"Thank you for the flesh!" she screeched into the sky.

"What was that supposed to mean?" Askari muttered, scowling at the diminishing figure of the creature that had saved them. Little black spots began to spot her vision as she struggled to understand what was happening around her.

Harcos let out a muffled sob. Minda bent down to help him stand, but he slapped her hand away.

"I probably should've mentioned it sooner," Minda cut in, her eyes looking old and weary, filled with a deep sadness. "But I'm your grandmother."

"What—" Shujaa tried to ask, grasping for words.

Askari's head swam, and her breaths came in short bursts. Then, everything went black.

CHAPTER 11: THE MINKET

Askari woke, extremely uncomfortable. Something hard and round was poking into her back. She opened her eyes and saw only the flickering of light on the cave walls. All around her, voices murmured, mingling with the occasional snore or a laugh.

"Awake, I see?" Leka stood over her, looking for the world like she was about to fall asleep herself.

"What happened?" Askari murmured.

"Harcos and Shujaa dragged you in."

"Where's—" A chirruping came from somewhere down near her leg. "Polly." Askari smiled. Her head hurt and her thoughts were sluggish, but she was starting to remember everything that happened. "Minda?"

"She's gone," Leka said, checking a bandage on Askari's arm. "You got sliced pretty bad—lost a lot of blood. You need to stay calm and don't pop the stitches."

"She's my grandmother!" Askari exclaimed, suddenly sitting upright. "I have a grandmother!"

"Yes," Leka replied. "Just rest, please?" She turned and headed in the direction of another wounded Baratok.

"You're awake!" Harcos appeared, standing over her. "I'm glad you made it."

"Just a scratch," Askari said.

"You lost a lot of blood." Shujaa was there too.

"What happened?" Askari asked. "All I remember was the hulla coming, and then—I woke up here."

Shujaa and Harcos glanced at each other.

"I also remember that Minda is my grandmother." Askari relished the word. She hadn't ever had family before.

"I'm not sure you want to go telling everyone that," Harcos said, sitting down beside her.

"Why not?" Askari asked. She was excited about it—she had family! For so many years, she had thought all her family was dead. But she had a grandmother! And the elders knew Minda. They knew she existed! And no one had told Askari! They let her grow up believing that she was all on her own, alone, an orphan in the terrible world they all lived in.

But she had a grandmother. One who knew all about the gargs, even talked to hulla, and personally knew Elnok, Queen of the Hulla. One who lived and survived on her own in this wasteland of a world, who could build things and make artificial light. Who studied monsters and how to bring them down. Who had come to rescue the Baratok from the rarohan. Who had saved Askari from her own stupidity. A grandmother.

"Do you remember what she did?" Harcos asked, his voice low.

"Um..." Askari frowned, trying to think.

"She gave Baratok bodies to the hulla," Shujaa said. "She handed them over."

"Yeah," Askari's frown deepened. "I do remember that. What was that about? Were they going to eat them?"

Shujaa and Harcos glanced at each other again.

"No," Harcos said quietly, an angry expression settling across his normally soft features. "That's how they reproduce."

"What do you mean?" Askari's mind scrambled to make sense of what she was hearing.

"They possess the recently dead bodies of other creatures," Harcos said. "They've figured out that possessing a human body gives them access to a brain capable of processing a lot more information than an animal's brain, so they like to steal humans. Dead humans. That's why they have human faces."

Askari's stomach began to roil. "So... so... all the faces of the... the hulla..." She swallowed. "Those were... were..."

"Yup," Harcos said. "They were real people. Dead people. And now they're hulla."

And Minda had given Baratok bodies to them. Willingly. Askari swallowed, and then looked at Harcos. "Did... did you know?"

He covered his face with his hands. "I guessed."

"And you... you let her?"

Tears were falling down his cheeks as he shook his head. "What were we supposed to do?" he sobbed. "They were dying, we were dying, everyone was dying! We were trapped in a cave with gargs at our doorstep and so many people had already died, all of them—" he broke off, pressing his face into his knees. Shujaa reached out and began to rub his back.

"No one blames him," she said, her face sad and worn. "The elders don't, I mean. They blamed Minda and cast her out. But he's right—what were we supposed to do?"

"Fight!" Askari said. They could always fight! Fight or die! That's what they always said.

Shujaa shook her head. "Then more would have died, and the Elnok would have taken us anyway. All of us, not just four. Now we can burn the rest, give them a proper sending."

"But... but..." It was too horrible to think about. Now there would be four gruesome hulla, with faces that they knew, that they recognized.

"I picked people I knew," Harcos said, tears still streaming down his face. His eyes were red and puffy; he had probably been crying for hours. "People who I knew would volunteer if they thought it would save the Baratok. And so I could recognize them if I ever saw them again, give them a proper burial."

"I..." Askari swallowed and lay back down. "I think I need to sleep."

"You should," Shujaa said. "We're packing up to leave in the morning."

Askari gazed around the room as Shujaa led Harcos away. To her left, the Meszaros family sat on boxes, Ri, Cal, and toddler Jay. Jay cried softly and Cal rocked him, while Ri sharpened her knives. Near them, Agota and Adelbert flirted as Adelbert dressed a nasty-looking scratch on Agota's leg. Askari was glad both of them had survived. Beyond them, a small group of young warriors in training played dice: Gyala, Pali, Dome, Duci, Sari, and Barta. The Pek family was now up to three kids, and they played a game of stones next to a large stalagmite. Fia sat toward the back, rocking her newborn and singing softly. Vica was talking to Ferko, offering him some soup, and over near Askari, Leka and her team of medics moved about, working to bandage up wounds and ease pain wherever they could.

All of these people, and hundreds more, were saved because of her grandmother. And yet, her grandmother had done a most unspeakable thing. Askari began to cry, tears sliding down her cheeks and onto the pillow of her bedroll. She didn't know what to think or how to feel. She didn't know what to do.

Polly stood up, stretched, and climbed over Askari's prone body. She began to lick the tears from Askari's face, then turned around three times and curled up in Askari's arms. Askari fell asleep scratching the minket's head.

The next morning was a buzz of activity as the Baratok prepared to leave the cave. The elders let everyone get barely enough rest, and pressed them to prepare for travel. They wanted to leave the Plains of Tork as soon as possible, to avoid encountering any rarohan that the hulla hadn't killed.

Askari's arm throbbed, but Leka had cleaned it out and wrapped it tightly; plus, many had been injured far worse than Askari had, so she chose not to complain. Instead, she headed out into the daylight to see where she could help.

The sun shone brightly in a cerulean blue sky, and there wasn't a cloud in sight. It was a gorgeous day, which made a strange and uncomfortable contrast to those who were weeping over the eviscerated corpses of their children, siblings, and spouses. All over the field, Baratok were finding the people they loved, wrapping them in blankets, and laying them in large pyre a short distance from the cave. Few talked; besides the wind, all Askari could hear was weeping.

She took a few deep breaths to calm herself as her eyes moved across the scene in front of her. Some warriors helped families move the bodies, and some were building a pyre of dead wood under and around them.

In the opposite direction, Faro directed the efforts to pull the remaining wagons out of hiding. They had also somehow managed to save most of the horses, probably because the rarohan were more interested in eating the humans than the animals. Still others entered and exited the caves, carrying boxes and baskets of food to load onto the wagons, or stretchers with wounded who were bundled into the wagons among the food and supplies.

Askari was assigned carrying duty by Vica, who was not one to let someone sit idle for long. For hours, Askari carried box after box, bag after bag, basket after basket out of the caves, and handed them off to one of the Baratok who was packing the wagon. They had lost three horses and six wagons, and so were short on space—which meant the children would walk alongside the healthy and the warriors.

By noon, the first five wagons, accompanied by a contingent of warriors, pulled out, headed for the edge of the plains only three miles away. They would forge their way through the wilderness once more if they had to, as long as they weren't sitting ducks for the rarohan again. A few minutes later, the next wagon pulled out, following the first a short distance behind. The last wagon was still being loaded, rapidly crammed with the few remaining items.

Less than twenty minutes later, all the wagons had moved out, surrounded by warriors, children, families, and anyone who could safely walk. Askari stood in the back, waiting to take her position as the warriors responsible for protecting the back of the line began to move forward.

"You, you, you, and you." Elol appeared, pointing first at Zaj, then Askari, Shujaa, and Harcos. "Come with me."

"Zaj, you know what to do with this." He handed Zaj a bag of something and a torch, then handed a second torch to Askari. "Teams of two," he said. "Go back down into the caves, make sure everything we need is out, make sure we didn't leave anyone sleeping behind. If you find any bodies, carry them out. Then extinguish any torches and meet me here." He pointed to the cave entrance, and then turned and strode off toward the pile of carefully wrapped bodies.

The four warriors fell into line, striding into the cave. Zaj and Harcos turned off at the first cavern, and Askari and Shujaa continued down into the larger one. It was a mess. Trash had been left everywhere, remnants of food and ripped clothing, broken boxes and baskets, bloody bandages. She saw a couple of bedrolls, probably belonging to the deceased, and a heap of broken weapons.

"A lot of stuff got left," Shujaa said, holding up a pair of shoes.

"But how critical is it?" Askari asked. "I think they mean mostly arrows and boxes of food, right?"

Shujaa nodded. "These have holes in the bottom, too."

"They had to cut back so they could fit wounded in the remaining wagons," Askari said, making her way around the edges of the cavern. They had inspected about half when Harcos and Zaj reappeared.

"We'll take the first tunnel," Zaj said, pausing to push something into the cracks of the rock in several places. Then the two disappeared into the darkness, only the flickering light of their torch visible from around the bend.

Askari and Shujaa finished searching the cavern and determined nothing was necessary to save except for a photograph that Askari slid quietly into her pocket in case someone had forgotten it.

"I guess we'll take the second tunnel next," Askari said, sighing. A small heap of rocks still remained from where they had tried to blockade the main cavern from the barlang, but the garg had been dragged further down the tunnel and more out of the way. They moved slowly down the tunnel, keeping their eyes peeled. There wasn't much in the tunnel—a few scraps of this and that, but nothing more.

The barlang had been dumped in a cavern to one side. Flies buzzed around it; otherwise, it looked pretty much the same as it had when it was alive, but not moving.

"I almost feel sorry for it," Askari said.

"That is a very dangerous line of thought," Shujaa said. "You need to remember that monsters are just that— monsters. You can't start to feel sorry for them, otherwise you'll let your guard down, and then you'll be dead."

"But what about monsters like Polly?" Askari asked. "If you think about it, the barlang was living quietly in a cave, eating plants and bats, minding its own business." Askari shrugged, gazing at the strange, bony face of the dead garg in the flickering light. "Then we showed up, barged into its home, and expected it not to fight back."

"It was harvesting us," Shujaa said.

"It was eating meat that wandered into its house," Askari argued. She knew it was dangerous to start to think of monsters as friends, but they weren't all evil either. They weren't as smart as humans, only bigger and stronger and more powerful. And not all of them were bad! Like the fulek. It ate plants, for goodness' sake, and all it wanted was to have its babies in peace. Askari was starting to truly believe that assuming all monsters were bad and needed to be killed was just as dangerous as assuming they were all harmless.

"In the grand scheme of things, it doesn't really matter," Shujaa said. "The elders will never change their minds about it. Our best bet is to stay quiet. Don't go spreading those ideas around camp, okay? Keep your head down, or you'll find yourself on another dangerous journey to garg knows where. And there's no guarantee Harcos and I are going to track you down next time."

"I know," Askari said, sighing.

They continued moving down the tunnel. As they reached the next cavern and the tunnel began to open up around them, Shujaa gasped.

"What is it?" Askari asked, taking a few steps forward.

Shujaa pointed to the ground. "They never took them out," she whispered. "Only moved them."

On the ground lay a heap of mutilated bodies, the missing Baratok that the barlang had killed. Askari felt a surge of anger, and her compassion for the barlang all but disappeared. The bodies smelled awful, as they had begun to decompose, and the flickering light of the torch cast an eerie glow that made their faces look like they were moving.

"Let's walk to the end of the tunnel," Askari said, turning her head away, "and then come back to carry them out."

Shujaa nodded. They carefully stepped past the bodies. Askari gritted her teeth and turned her eyes forward, hoping the awful image wouldn't remain burned into the back of her eyelids forever.

The rest of the tunnel was largely empty, except for a broken stretcher that had been tossed against the wall and some bloody bandages that had been discarded on the floor.

"Think we could fix up this stretcher enough to carry some bodies out?" Shujaa asked, picking up one end and examining the broken part.

Askari bent down and frowned at it. "It looks bent, not fully broken. And it doesn't matter if we drop the bodies—I mean, we don't want to, but they can't get hurt any more—"

"I know what you mean," Shujaa replied. "Let's try it."

They carried the stretcher back up to the pile of bodies and carefully rolled one onto it.

"His name was Jozsa," Shujaa said. "I didn't know him, but he was a gatherer."

Askari swallowed, trying to keep from gagging. She nodded and bent down to lift one half of the stretcher, trying not to drop the torch. Shujaa lifted the other side, and they began to walk slowly up the tunnel toward the main cavern.

"What took you so—" Zaj said as they entered the cavern. "Oh."

"There are six more bodies," Askari said. "We need to team up, with someone holding a torch."

"We can use torch stands," Zaj said. He went over to one side of the room and picked up three simple wooden stands, designed to hold a torch upright. He gestured to Harcos to grab some unlit torches. "We'll set this up. You guys take—" he leaned over and glanced at the face, "—Jozsa up to Elol."

Askari and Shujaa carried the body up the tunnel and out into the plains, blinking in the bright sunlight.

"Set him over here," Elol said, waving at them from near the pile of bodies. "We don't have any more shrouds, unfortunately." He helped them place the body with the others, and then put a small cloth over Jozsa's face. "How many more?"

"Six," Askari said. She turned and headed back into the caves with Shujaa on her heels.

They were surprised to see that Zaj and Harcos had set up torches all the way down to the pile of bodies. There was only the one stretcher, so they met Harcos and Zaj coming up, carrying another body by its legs and feet.

"Marcsa," Shujaa whispered as they went by.

Each body they carried up, Shujaa named: Jozsa, Marcsa, Bolidsar, Borika, Rikard, Sebestyen, and Tres. Each time they went back down, Zaj pushed more white stuff into the nooks and crannies of the cave.

"What are you doing?" Askari asked once. Zaj shook his head and kept moving.

Finally, they finished.

"Anyone else?" Elol asked as Askari and Shujaa laid out Tres next to the other six, the last on the heap of bodies.

"Nope," Zaj said.

"No one," Askari said.

Elol nodded to Zaj, who turned and headed back toward the cave. Then he gestured for the other three to follow him to a large rock, a piece of granite the size of a small house, a good distance from the cave.

"Crouch down here," he said, "and cover your ears."

Askari frowned, but did as instructed. What could they possibly be doing? A moment later, Zaj scurried around the edge of the rock and threw himself flat on the ground, hands over his head. Askari stared at him in confusion. Then she turned and peered around the edge of the rock—

A ball of vibrant orange fire and smoke billowed from the mouth of the cave. A thundering sound rattled the trees, rumbled the ground, and rolled over them like a wave followed by a rush of heat washing over and around the rock. Askari ducked back around the edge of the rock and squeezed her eyes shut as bits of grass, rocks, and dirt blew through the air. She held her hands against her ears, waiting for it to end.

She couldn't believe it—they had blown up the cave. They had destroyed everything—and sure enough, next she heard a rumble and a roar as the cave itself collapsed. She turned to look again. The fire was gone, and there was nothing but smoke and charred grasses. Grey dust billowed up around the edges of Arc Hill, which originally had only one peak, but now had two and a shallow valley over where the cave had been.

"Why?" Askari asked. "Why?" It didn't make any sense. "That was a potential safe place, where we hid from the rarohan, and that someone else could use."

"Caves," Elol replied sternly, "aren't safe. We have always said that. We will stand by that, especially given our mistake this week. You saw what was in there—who knows what else lurks that we had yet to discover? We've done the world a favor by destroying a potential home for monsters, and destroying any monsters that might have still been there. I stand by the decision."

Askari stared at the blackened entrance to the cave, and then squinted as something small and furry came scurrying across the ground toward them.

"Polly!" she exclaimed as the little creature scrambled up onto her back.

Elol frowned at her thoughtfully, but then turned his attention back to the row of more than fifty dead Baratok, wrapped in shrouds.

"Now," he said, "we need more wood, and then we can send them home."

The group split off in different directions, each going to search for dried wood that would help create a hot fire. Askari headed back toward Arc Hill, while Shujaa and Harcos went toward a small copse of trees a short distance past. When Askari got to one of the big rocks that sat at the base of the hill, she slid down, head in her hands.

"Hey," a voice said.

Askari looked up, startled to see Minda standing over her. The old woman sank down into the grass beside Askari and sighed.

"I'm sorry I didn't tell you that I'm your grandmother before," she said. "But I thought I was never going to see you again. Then the hulla came and told me you were in trouble, and I couldn't stay away."

"Why did you leave?" Askari asked.

"It's the biggest regret of my life." Minda plucked a piece of grass and began to wind it between her fingers. "I thought you would be safer without me. Better without me."

"Am I?"

Minda shook her head. "I don't know. But you're stronger than I ever was. You're incredible, Askari. You have your father's eyes and your mother's spirit. If only your mother could see you now."

"Were you there when... when she died?"

"I was. I hunted down the pok that killed her, and I killed it." Minda had twisted the grass so tightly around her finger that the tip was turning pale. "When she died, I almost killed myself too. But then I decided instead maybe I could do something useful, like make this world a better place for you. Haven't done much good, I suppose. Wrote a couple books on monsters. Saved your father from himself a few times."

Askari frowned. "I thought he was dead—I mean, that's what they told me."

Minda let out a derisive snort. "Lesson number one: never believe anything they tell you unless you saw it with your own eyes." She shook her head. "No, your father got kicked out for being too hotheaded. It was right around the time you were born. He was always running off on his own to battle monsters or test them for weaknesses. Then one day, he brought a gamba home and put it in a cage. He poked and prodded it until finally he discovered that if you poked them in the right place, they would explode."

Askari smiled a little. It was a funny image.

"Unfortunately, it exploded all over Kira, and even though it caused her no harm whatsoever, that was the last straw. We didn't know your mum was pregnant until a few weeks later, and the only reason she stayed with the Baratok was because I asked her to. I thought it would be safer for you." Minda shook her head again. "I should have taken both of us when I left."

"So, you weren't there when I was born?" Askari asked.

"I was," Minda replied. "I traveled with your father for a while, and then we got word that your mother was pregnant. We both went back, but Kira and the elders told your father he had to get out or they would kill him. He begged me to stay, so I did for a while. But I couldn't take it and your mother encouraged me to go. I moved to the village where you found me, so she and your father would always know where to look if they needed me. I went back and forth between the village and the community for a while, but ended up liking it better on my own. I don't know where your father is now, if he's still alive."

"Why—" Askari paused, unsure of how to ask the question. She didn't want to offend her grandmother, but she couldn't not know.

"Anything," Minda said quietly. "Ask anything."

Askari swallowed. "Why did you give the bodies to the elnok?"

Tears began to well in Minda's eyes. "I didn't know what else to do. Elol was right. We could have sealed the doors and waited it out, dug our way through the back. But there was no guarantee. We might have all died—it was a risk. But for the price of four of our dead, there was a guarantee that we would be saved. So many people—" her voice broke, "—so many people I knew personally, have known for my entire life, worked with, experienced the end of the world—" She began to cry in earnest now. "They have... have already died. I couldn't stand by and let more go for the sake of a few bodies whose souls had already left. And I couldn't let anything happen to you."

She put a hand over her eyes and took a few deep breaths, then wiped away the tears.

"I've watched so many people die, Askari." Minda shook her head. "I couldn't let it happen to you."

Askari leaned forward and pulled her grandmother into a tight hug, tears falling down her own cheeks. They lived in a world of impossible decisions. Every day was an impossible decision. And Minda had lived through so many days already.

She leaned back against the rock and sat quietly for a few minutes, thinking about the people in her life she had never known, how many of them had left or died, and marveling that she had one back with her. But they would have to part ways again soon. Too soon. She had a thousand questions, but didn't know which ones to ask.

Finally, she said, "It's my fault, you know. That my mother is dead."

"No, no it's not." Minda shook her head vehemently.

"It's my fault," Askari repeated. "I went to play in a house that I knew I wasn't supposed to go into, and it had a pok living in it. Mum got between it and me, and she was poisoned. I've always known it was my fault."

"No," Minda repeated emphatically. "It was never your fault. It was Kira's fault and the monster's fault. You remember that, okay?"

"What do you mean, Kira's fault?" Askari asked, frowning.

"That village was known to be inhabited by close to thirty poks, but it was also said that there was a treasure trove of batteries there that no one could get to. Kira—" Minda turned and spat on the ground beside her— "decided it would be a good idea to camp near the village so we could sneak in and grab the batteries. As if no one had tried that before, ha! We even found dead bodies and skeletons around the area, so it was obvious it was a bad plan. This incident is what made them set up all of their ridiculous rules regarding towns."

"I tried to take you with me when I left," Minda said, shrugging, "after your mother died. I thought maybe we could find your dad and make our own family. But Faro talked me out of it. He said you'd be safer with them, and I thought he was probably right." She paused for a moment and smiled. "You used to call me Mini."

Askari had a flash of memory.

She was five years old and screaming. *"Mini, Mini! Take me to Mommy!" she screamed. "Take me to Mommy!"*

"I can't take you, sweetheart," a much younger Minda whispered. "Please, please be still."

Askari shook her head to clear her mind of the memory. "I do think I remember a little," she said.

They sat quietly for a few more minutes, but Askari knew she had to go soon. She couldn't sit here with her grandmother all day. "How did the hulla know my name?" she asked.

"I told them that if they ever found you, they should let me know," Minda said. "And they did."

Nodding, Askari stared at her grandmother's profile for a moment.

"I never gave Kira your message," Askari said.

Minda laughed. "That's probably for the best."

They sat for a little longer, until Askari said, "I have to go find wood for the fire. Or they'll come looking for me."

"I know," Minda replied. "I just want you to know—if you ever need me, find a hulla, okay? I'll come running."

Askari stood and gave her grandmother another long hug.

"Before you go," Minda said, "I have something for you." She pulled an object out of her pocket and handed it to Askari. It was a leather thong with a rarohan's tooth threaded through it. "I noticed you didn't have one." It was the first tooth for her own necklace.

"Thank you," Askari said, overwhelmed. It wasn't just that someone had finally given her her first garg's tooth, or even that it was her grandmother who did it. It was that she suddenly understood—the teeth that the elders and warriors wore meant so much more than just conquest, so much more than monsters killed. They meant battles, struggles, lives lost.

"Each tooth you collect," Minda said, "represents those that died. Never forget them." She reached out and tied it around Askari's neck.

"I won't," Askari replied. "Ever."

Minda leaned forward and gave Askari another hug.

"And remember," Minda said, pulling back to look into Askari's eyes. "Watch your back—some humans are more dangerous than monsters."

Askari watched her walk away through the tall grasses, sidestepping dead rarohan and disappearing around the back of the hill. She turned to go find wood and was surprised to see Polly moving slowly toward her, dragging half of a tree, completely dead and completely dried out. Polly dropped it at Askari's feet.

Askari smiled at the minket. "Thank you," she said, turning to drag the branch the rest of the way toward the pyre. The others were there, adding their own branches and leaves. No one spoke; they remained quiet as they moved about their work.

It was a strange feeling, Askari thought. So many of these people she had known, or kind of known. They had been her family, her tormenters, her trainers, her leaders, her

285

friends. She could feel a pressure building up behind her eyes, but no, she would not dishonor them by crying. They were gone. They would want her to focus on the future. She would honor them by sending their ashes into the sky.

Five. She had been five when she had experienced her first sending, at least that she could remember. It was her own mother. They had built a large, tall pyre, and gently laid her mother's body on the top, wrapped in a dark red cloth someone had found. Elder Dano had called it a tablecloth. And then someone had lit a match, and there was fire and smoke, and Askari could remember crying and screaming until someone took her away and sang her to sleep. And when she had woken the next morning, her mom was still gone, and she had cried again, and every day for a while, until one day, she had stopped crying.

"Askari!" Shujaa said gently. "You've been standing there for five minutes. Keep moving." Her voice was firm, but also understanding.

They dragged branch after branch into the pile, dead cottonwoods and some pine, a few branches of dry walnut. They traipsed up the now rearranged hillside and pulled out as much dead wood as they could find—branch after branch, tree after tree. Polly disappeared again, showing up again nearly half an hour later, dragging an entire pine tree with dead, dry needles, the wood too as dead and as dry as they could hope for. Askari had no idea where Polly had found it, but together, the humans dragged it up onto the pile and stepped back. The branches rose almost twice as high as Shujaa and covered the entire row of bodies.

Elol took a deep breath and pulled out his fire kit.

"Stand back," he said. He leaned down and carefully set a small branch on fire. Then, he reached out and tossed it onto the pile. The flame began to lick over the wood and dried leaves until a large log burst into flame. After that, the fire began to burn hotter and hotter, a column of red-orange flames leaping up from the bodies and into the branches above them.

Askari moved back away from the fire. It burned hot, much hotter than she had expected so soon. Black smoke billowed into the sky. The flames were mesmerizing, gold and white, yellow and red, all mixed with billows of black smoke and crackling, spitting wood.

They all stood, staring at the blaze, watching as flames rose higher and higher, until a massive roaring fire towered over them. Askari stepped back several times, as the heat from the flames grew more and more intense.

Then she glanced to one side and saw Polly slowly bow, face to the flames, hands open in honor of those who were being sent. Elol saw the motion too and let out a strangled cry. Tears streamed down his face. Askari looked on in awe. She had never seen an elder cry—it was their pact, to rejoice at those who had found the ultimate freedom, not to mourn that they were lost. Yet Elol wept, fully, in the open. And beside him, Polly lay on the ground, bowing, face to the dirt, honoring those who had died.

Askari didn't know what else to do, so she too knelt, face to the dirt, and wept.

She didn't know how much time had passed when she felt a hand on her shoulder. She looked up to see Elol standing over her, eyes red. He helped her to her feet and then gathered her in a tight hug.

"Thank you," he whispered, "and know that I am honored to fight alongside your minket, and I will defend her with my life."

"Thank you," Askari whispered, suddenly feeling relieved, as if a weight she didn't even know she had been carrying had lifted.

He released her and then spoke to and hugged the other three gently.

"Now," he said softly, "the time for mourning is done. We must go and leave this to its fate. But I want to say to each of you, thank you." He met their eyes, one at a time. "I will never forget what you each did here today."

Elol turned his back to the fire and strode through the grass, never once looking back. Zaj followed him, single file, then Shujaa, Harcos, and Askari. She glanced back over her shoulder as they moved away. The fire glowed a burning red. The sun had sunk below the edge of the trees, so now stripes of blood orange and vibrant yellows streaked across the sky, making it seem as though it too were on fire.

Askari faced forward and walked, one foot at a time, toward home.

WANT MORE MONSTERS?

There are plenty more to come! Join Ariele's Patreon page for monthly chapter releases (get the next chapter before anyone else!), desktop wallpaper drawings of the monsters, posters, postcards, the audio version, sneak peeks, and more! Join up for as little as $1/month.

Visit   www.patreon.com/arielesieling   for   more information.

And may the garg's blood rain!

ACKNOWLEDGEMENTS

No book is written in a vacuum, although, literally speaking that could make for some interesting challenges.

I would like to thank Zoe, first off, for her invaluable help with editing and suggesting improvements to the manuscript. As always, I don't know what I would do without her.

Next, I'd like to thank my mom, Nancy, for reading the manuscript in a variety of different forms, and again providing invaluable assistance.

I would also like to thank Evan, for listening to me talk endlessly about this project, and helping me with the audio version and several of my marketing tactics.

I'd also like to mention Wanted Mountains Publishing, for doing a quick and last minute proofread.

Finally, to Josh, who read every version of the manuscript (from the miserable first draft, to the moderately better second, to the hugely improved third, all the way to the final version), and whose suggestions were critical to the put-togetherness of this book.

ABOUT THE AUTHOR

Lifetime writer and lover of cats, Ariele Sieling delves into the exciting possibilities of science fiction from her home in Baltimore, MD, where she lives with her husband and their menagerie: a dog, three cats, and a fish. She is the author of *The Sagittan Chronicles* series, the *Rutherford the Unicorn Sheep* series, and *Land of Szornyek*.

You can connect with Ariele by signing up for her newsletter. Get updates on what's happening not only with *Land of Szornyek*, but other her other series, and life in general. You can visit www.arielesieling.com for more information.

You can also find her on Facebook, Instagram, Twitter, or Patreon (@arielesieling).

OTHER BOOKS BY ARIELE

Want more? Check out the books in Ariele's other series by visiting www.arielesieling.com.

Her titles include:

LAND OF SZORNYEK

- *Tentacles and Teeth*
- *City of Dod (Coming Soon!)*

THE SAGITTAN CHRONICLES

- *All In: A Prequel (FREE ON AMAZON!)*
- *The Wounded World*
- *The Clock Winked*
- *The Lonely Whelk*
- *The Polylocus Problem*

RUTHERFORD THE UNICORN SHEEP

- *Rutherford the Unicorn Sheep Goes to the Beach*
- *Rutherford the Unicorn Sheep Visits the Apiary*
- *Rutherford the Unicorn Sheep and the Walnut Skunk Thanksgiving*
- *Rutherford the Unicorn Sheep and the Christmas Surprise*
- *Rutherford the Unicorn Sheep Makes Pancakes*
- *Rutherford the Unicorn Sheep Goes for a Hike*
- *Rutherford the Unicorn Sheep Walks the Dog*

Made in the USA
Middletown, DE
16 March 2019